Hayley was a believer

Her friends said Hayley was so choosy that no man could meet her expectations. Hayley said she knew her own mind.

All her life Hayley had been running second. And just once, with one special man, she wanted to come first.

Hayley believed in a love she hadn't tasted, believed that someday she'd find the man who would see the magic in her.

So when Hayley was given the golden apple, she closed her eyes and wished with all her heart that she could know how it felt to be cherished.

ACKNOWLEDGMENTS

My thanks to Kathy Clark and Christine Pacheco, who originally conceived of a series set at The Stanley Hotel and were kind enough to think of me.

Much love and appreciation to Emma and Kathy, enthusiastic partners and wonderful friends; to Karan, the fifth sister; to Evan, an agent and a gentleman; and to Jan—our hearts are with you.

Thanks also to Frank Normali, owner of The Stanley Hotel, for giving us the grand tour and allowing us to let our imaginations run wild in and around his hotel. The hotel in my story represents my attempt to capture the beauty and charm of the real Stanley, but the characters and scenes set therein are one-hundred-percent fiction. They are not intended to reflect on the real staff or guests of The Stanley Hotel in any way, shape or form. Although I do believe there's magic at The Stanley, there is not and has never been a golden apple akin to the one I describe in these pages. Atalanta's Apple, a.k.a. MacPherson's Folly, is a pure flight of fancy.

And last, but never least, many thanks to Scott, the apple of my eye.

Julie Kistler
May, 1989

BEST WISHES

JULIE KISTLER

Harlequin Books

TORONTO • NEW YORK • LONDON
AMSTERDAM • PARIS • SYDNEY • HAMBURG
STOCKHOLM • ATHENS • TOKYO • MILAN

Published February 1990

First printing December 1989

ISBN 0-373-16329-0

Prologue

The time was drawing near.

Harry smiled. Soon, very soon, he would have to part with the apple. But not quite yet. He weighed the smooth lump of gold in the palm of his hand, turning it this way and that, fascinated as always by the play of light over its gleaming, radiant surface.

The golden apple was indescribable. Beautiful, yes, but magical, too, and strangely alive. Collectors and museums the world over had offered to pay almost anything to possess it. They didn't realize that no one ever really *owned* this apple of gold.

He held it, letting it warm his hand with its soft glow. He could almost feel the life, the pulse, of each of the thousands of years of its existence. If he concentrated, he could see again the parade of faces in its history, each lovely in her own way...from Atalanta, the Athenian maiden who'd run more swiftly than any man, to Scottie MacPherson, the Colorado gold miner whose striking beauty had been disguised by layers of dust and bad temper.

Who would be next?

Harry's smile was bittersweet. Each recipient was touched by the golden apple, but not everyone benefited. Some of the apple's ladies had been clever—some foolish—some kind—some greedy. And in the end, only a few had seen through the obvious temptations of the apple to find the magic hiding inside.

This time Harry planned to choose wisely.

This time the apple would bring wonderful wishes, great magic, incredible happiness. This time . . .

Harry smiled to himself.

The time had come.

Chapter One

It was going to be *her day*. From the moment she got up, Hayley Austin had the weird feeling that this was it—the day of a lifetime. Of course, she'd thought that quite a few times in the past, too, and nothing terribly exciting had happened. Nevertheless, today was different and Hayley's whole body tingled with the anticipation that something special was hovering on her horizon.

The March air was nippy as she shut the door of her pretty little house, took the two steps off the slightly crooked porch, and started the hike down to the main road. Belying the chill, the sun shone brightly, casting tiny sparkles upon the light snow cover, and behind her, the Rocky Mountains rose white and misty into the morning sky. It was beautiful, but she shivered a little as she turned up her collar and burrowed her hands into the pockets of her heavy wool coat.

Over the past four years, Hayley had made this particular trek hundreds of times, either on foot or by bike. It was, after all, the most direct route to her job as front-desk manager at The Stanley Hotel. It took her down the hill, across the highway, up and around another, steeper hill, past the bosses' condo, and into The Stanley Hotel through a funny old tunnel in the basement. It might just be her usual route, but she enjoyed every second of it. She'd been born and raised here in Estes Park, high in the Colorado Rockies, yet there was always a new season, a different flower, a gorgeous sky to admire.

Today her good mood was aided by the fact that she wasn't going to work. Oh, she liked her job as front-desk manager well enough, and she really enjoyed being in charge, running a tight ship, keeping things just so, but it was still a relief to turn over control every once in a while. So today she was on her way to her monthly Sunday brunch at The Stanley Hotel with two of her oldest and dearest friends. With these women she'd survived everything from first loves to final exams. Since then they'd gone their separate ways, but first and foremost they were still friends.

Now Nicki was back in Estes Park, running her own horse and carriage business, and Kate—sweet, brilliant, romantic Kate—was trying to put her husband's death behind her as she reforged her career as a history professor.

The realization that she'd be seeing her pals again, hearing familiar jokes and sharing reminiscences, quickened Hayley's steps as she neared her destination. Within a few moments she was abreast of the elegant old hotel. Breathing deeply, inhaling the cold, clean mountain air, she angled past the side entrance and went to the front of the hotel. Normally, when she was in a hurry, she entered through the tunnel at the side, but not today. No, in her present mood, she wanted to absorb the whole front view of her favorite place.

The Stanley Hotel stood starkly white against a stunning backdrop of snow-covered Rocky Mountains and pale blue sky. Hayley's smile widened. She adored this place. And today, with its pristine white columns and red-tiled roof shining in the sunlight, it seemed more magical than ever.

Of course, it wasn't smart or practical to believe that there was magic at The Stanley. In her head, Hayley understood that. She knew quite well that it was only a hotel—prettier than most, with a bit of a past—but when it came right down to it, just two-by-fours and plaster.

In her heart, however, she held on desperately to the hope that there was still room in the world for dreams, fairy tales and magic spells. She might not admit it, she might not even truly believe it, but it was there, nonetheless.

She smiled wistfully at the big old hotel. Maybe today would be the day....

Her whimsical train of thought was interrupted by a flicker of movement near the hotel. It was the strangest feeling, but she knew at once that she wasn't alone.

She peered into the shadows, certain that someone was standing behind one of the classic white columns that flanked the front of the hotel. Whoever it was seemed to be spying on her. She'd assumed that she was all alone, and it annoyed her to discover she wasn't. So who was behind the pillar, and why was he or she intruding upon a private moment?

It was a he—most definitely a he. As he moved out of his hiding place, she saw that he was tall. Her eyes widened. Very tall. And broad-shouldered, with a graceful, loose-limbed sort of stride.

Because of the battered fedora he wore pulled down over his eyes, she couldn't see his face, and she had no reason to believe that he was in the least interested in her. Yet she was still sure he'd been spying on her, and quite irritated with him because of it.

She squinted at him. The dazzlingly bright light bouncing off the white hotel and white snow was almost blinding, but that didn't deter her. Now that she'd seen him, she wanted to know what he was doing, skulking around *her* hotel.

His head was turned away and his hat dipped even lower as he ambled down the stairs toward the pool area. If he'd been watching her before, he wasn't now. In fact, he was ignoring her.

So what the heck was he doing?

Of course, there was no reason for her to be so curious. The hotel had all kinds of guests coming and going at all times—of varying degrees of weirdness—and she didn't spend her time worrying about them. But curious she was.

She supposed it was the fact that his face was hidden. Or maybe it was the romantic fedora he was wearing, with its accompanying images of Humphrey Bogart and Indiana Jones. Ever since she'd seen *Casablanca* at the age of ten, she'd had a secret fondness for men in hats. But whatever the reason, he *was* mysterious.

She frowned. No matter how mysterious he was, she was running a few minutes late, and standing around staring at The Stanley and its odd guests wasn't helping matters. After one last, reluctant look at the tall man in the terrific hat, she turned and raced up the wide front steps toward the lobby.

HE SET HIS LIPS in a grim smile and purposely kept a low profile as the slim young woman slipped inside the hotel. Damn. It suddenly occurred to him that his disguise might be a bit too conspicuous. The reaction of the pretty lady with the frank stare was not a good sign.

Glancing at the doors she'd disappeared through, he narrowed his eyes thoughtfully. Although women didn't gawk at him on a regular basis, he couldn't say he minded. His lips curved into a rakish smile that would, he knew, have astonished his colleagues back at the museum in Omaha.

"In for a penny, in for a pound," he said softly. Now that he'd thrown away the last vestiges of a rational life in what might prove to be a vain search for ancient treasure, he might as well go all the way.

Besides, he was getting sort of attached to his second-hand hat. He resettled it firmly on his head and put thoughts of the lady with the curious eyes on the back burner. Time to get back to business.

"Time to find the damn thing," he muttered. He retraced his path around the empty, winterized swimming pool, taking the first steps in his methodical plan to locate the elusive object of his search.

Sooner of later he'd find it. He had no doubt of that.

HAYLEY HATED being late. And by the clock that was happily chiming above the front desk, she could clearly see that she was a good ten minutes overdue to meet her friends. Waving at the front-desk clerks, Hayley shrugged out of her coat and headed for the restaurant, hoping to get in to brunch before her friends began without her.

But when a hopeful "Hayley? Is that you?" came from the direction of the front desk, she knew she couldn't ignore it. She recognized the mixture of panic and relief in the desk clerk's tone, and understood immediately what it signified. Trouble. The clerk on duty obviously had a problem she was hoping Hayley could solve.

It was a familiar situation. As front-desk manager, she was required to untangle anything and everything that arose, from lost reservations to heart attacks in the lobby, and even the occasional ghost sighting. But that was during the week, when she was on duty. This was Sunday, and she was technically in the clear. Nevertheless, she knew before she was even asked that she'd do her best to fix whatever the problem was. She couldn't turn something as fundamental as her connection to the hotel off and on according to the calendar.

Casting one last, longing look at the entrance to the MacGregor Room, where Nicki and Kate were undoubtedly waiting, Hayley turned back to the dark wood expanse of the front desk.

Quickly assuming her professional role as the person in charge, she calmly asked, "What's up?"

"Carmelita Carmichael," fumed Meg, a tiny blonde with angelic curls and a notoriously short fuse. "That old bat's back again."

"Shouting, swearing, throwing threats around—even worse than the last time," chimed in Mike, the other clerk, who was hiding behind a partition.

"Why here? Why us?" Hayley mumbled. As she pondered, a gentle tap on her shoulder startled her. She spun around, but there was no one there.

Hayley's hazel eyes were wide when she gazed back at Meg. "Did you see anyone behind me? I could've sworn somebody tapped my shoulder."

"I didn't see anything." Meg shrugged. "Maybe ghosts again, huh?"

It was a recurring theme at The Stanley. Guests swore they heard the piano in the Music Room, when there was clearly no one playing it. They felt cold drafts sweep across the lobby late at night, or heard a child's laughter waft down the hallway on the fourth floor. Hayley had never encountered anything the least bit extraordinary, and, as she often remarked, it was a little disappointing. She'd worked there for years and years, in one capacity or another. From hotel baby-sitter to part-time waitress to bellboy, she'd done it all. Was one little nudge from a ghost too much to ask for in all that time?

Apparently following the path of her thoughts, Mike laughed. "You wanted a visit from the ghost, didn't you?"

"Not at this exact moment," Hayley murmured. As she scrutinized the empty space behind her, she wondered if she really had felt anything. She was on the point of deciding that she'd imagined it when she heard a noise.

"Psst," someone hissed from across the lobby.

She peered in the direction of the sound. "Who's there?"

"Psssst," the voice said again, longer and more sibilant this time. "Over here."

It was coming from behind the Stanley Steamer, the classic car that sat in the front part of the lobby in honor of F. O. Stanley, who'd founded the hotel in 1909. His Stanley Steamers—automobiles that had enjoyed great popularity in the early years of the century—were F.O.'s pride and joy. He had even used them to ferry hotel guests from Denver in the early years of the hotel's existence. This particular model, a dark green runabout, was a magnet for Stanley guests on the lookout for photo opportunities. Generally, however, people did not hide behind it and hiss at the front-desk personnel.

"Excuse me?" she ventured.

"Over here," the voice repeated, a bit testily. "Will you come over here, please?"

As Hayley hesitated, Meg cleared her throat meaningfully. "And what are we supposed to do about Carmelita Carmichael? If you leave us here to deal with her by ourselves, we're both quitting."

"This will just take a second."

Curious guests were beginning to stare and point at the car in the lobby; Hayley saw that she had no choice but to handle the mystery of the hissing Stanley Steamer before anything else.

"Don't get upset," she told the clerks firmly. "I'll be within earshot if she comes back."

"As long as Mrs. Carmichael stays away from me," Meg replied ominously, tossing her curls.

Hayley cautiously approached the lovely old car that dominated the other side of the lobby. As she neared it, a round little man with a full white beard popped up from behind the back wheels. He was beaming at her.

"Did you need something?" Hayley asked kindly.

"Yes," he replied with a twinkle. "You."

"Me?"

"You."

"What about me?"

"I need to speak with you." The little man hesitated, glancing around at the curious onlookers. "It's quite important, but somewhat of a delicate matter. Not at all appropriate for eavesdroppers, if you know what I mean."

"A delicate matter," she echoed. "I see."

Oh, dear. A nut case. Undoubtedly he thought he was James Bond, and the KGB was watching him from behind the mirror in his hotel room. That one had been tried before. The Stanley's elegant surroundings drew all kinds.

Trying to appear sympathetic, Hayley led him past the crowd toward a more private setting—one of the lobby's groupings of dark green damask chairs. But he was bouncing slightly from one foot to the other, rubbing his hands together in excitement, and didn't appear to want to sit down. Hayley regarded him with interest. If he were a few bricks short of a load, which still seemed within the realm of possibility, he certainly didn't look it. He was neatly dressed in forest-green corduroy pants and a dapper little jacket with leather patches on the sleeves, and his white hair and beard were carefully trimmed.

In fact, now that she thought about it, she decided he was a very cute little man. With his rosy cheeks and ready smile, he reminded her a great deal of the man who'd played Santa

Claus in *Miracle on Thirty-fourth Street*. Just what she needed. Santa Claus in March.

"Is there some way I can help you, Mr....?"

He ignored the hint. "You are Hayley Austin, aren't you?"

"Yes, that's right. And you are...?"

"Harry," he returned after a moment. "Please call me Harry." He beamed again, wreathing his round face in a sunny smile. "Oh, Miss Austin, this is all so exciting. I'm quite sure this time, you see. Oh, yes, *quite sure* I have the proper person."

"Excuse me?"

As Hayley regarded him with both confusion and caution, he reached into his pocket. He didn't have a chance to get whatever it was he was poking around for, however, because the voice of an irate guest blasted through the lobby, startling everyone within earshot.

Carmelita Carmichael had returned.

"Oh, my word," the Santa Claus man mumbled. "Perhaps this ought to be postponed."

Hayley patted his hand. He was awfully sweet for a nut case. "Maybe that is the best idea. Why don't you come back by the desk later?"

Taking a deep breath, she wheeled, steeling herself to enter the fray at the front desk.

"Psst—Miss Austin?" She turned back in time to catch the little man's conspiratorial whisper. "Beware the Ides of March."

She assumed a smile and assured him she'd do just that. And then she was off to settle the argument and figure out what the problem was *this* time. The extremely cranky Mrs. Carmichael had been waltzing in and out of the hotel every few days for the past month. Each time she arrived, she brought storms and disasters in her wake. She was a very formidable lady, and nothing pleased her. Especially not the front-desk staff.

"Hello again, Mrs. Carmichael," Hayley said quickly, attempting to take the older woman's elbow and steer her away from Meg's sputtering, angry face.

"Well, well. Don't tell me there *is* some supervision around here?" the woman said sarcastically, snatching her arm away. She pointed a large, square fingernail at Meg. "I hope you're planning to fire that incompetent young fool. She hasn't the vaguest idea of how to treat a valued customer."

"I already quit," Meg retorted.

"You aren't quitting," Hayley put in sternly, "but maybe this would be a good time to take a break." As Meg stomped into the back room, Hayley faced Cranky Carmelita. "Now then, I'm sure we can handle whatever the difficulty is. Why don't you tell me about it?"

"I would like to check in."

Hayley nodded politely and waited for the rest of it.

"I've been here since seven this morning!" In one peremptory motion, the woman thrust aside a wool shawl, yanked up the sleeve of her sturdy tweed jacket and transferred her umbrella from one hand to the other, making a point of checking her watch. "I don't think it's too much to ask to be checked in after waiting patiently for three hours and forty-seven minutes."

There had to be more to this story than a simple check-in. Of course, it was rarely possible to check people in at 7:00 a.m., and the clerks had undoubtedly pointed out that fact several hours ago, but they should have been able to get her in before this. So what was the real problem?

"She wants the Caitlin suite," Mike whispered from his hiding place behind the partition. "It's occupied."

The picture became clearer. Mrs. Carmichael was demanding the hotel's most popular suite, and somebody was already in it.

"Who's got it?" Hayley asked quickly, weighing her options for getting out of this with a minimum of bloodshed.

"Honeymooners. Till Tuesday."

Hayley allowed herself a small sigh. She could hardly kick out honeymooners, even if Mrs. Carmichael threatened a fistfight in the lobby. "How about the Ben Stern? Is it occupied?"

"Open."

She sent up a small prayer of thanksgiving. "I'm very sorry, Mrs. Carmichael, but the Caitlin McDonald Suite is not available. However, the Ben Stern Suite *is* available, and I'm sure you'll like it just as well."

"I want the Caitlin McDonald." The woman clenched her prominent jaw. "No substitutes."

Hayley remained perfectly calm, but her jaw was set just as stubbornly. "That is simply impossible. Would you like the Ben Stern? Or should I make a reservation for you at another hotel?"

"What? Are you actually suggesting I take my business elsewhere?"

"If we don't have accommodations to your liking, I'm afraid that's your only choice." She gave her nemesis a level look. "It's up to you."

Fire spit out of Mrs. Carmichael's puffy little eyes. "I'll take the Ben Stern."

"Lovely. Mike, why don't you check Mrs. Carmichael in?"

"For now," the woman added in a menacing tone.

Hayley shook her head, giving Mike an encouraging smile and edging away from the desk before she blew up and decked Mrs. Carmichael herself.

Now maybe she could get to her much-delayed brunch. Even though she had technically won the battle with the irate guest, Hayley raced into the dining room feeling upset. It was hard to pull herself out of her embattled mode and revert to a calmer, Sunday brunch feeling. But when her friends rose from their table to greet her with hugs and smiles, her good humor returned.

"Sorry I'm late."

"Don't give it a moment's thought," Kate said calmly. "Nicki just arrived as well."

Nicki's large, dark eyes were alight with humor. "Yes, but twenty minutes late is *early* for me."

They exchanged glances and burst into laughter. Nicki was notoriously late, and it drove the others crazy, especially when they met at The Stanley, since she only lived next door. Speculating on how late she'd be *this* time had become a running joke between Hayley and Kate.

"We have another problem also," Kate added in her usually precise tones. "Stand up, Nicki."

Nicki reluctantly rose from her chair. She was wearing the same soft, full, raspberry-colored knit dress Hayley had on.

Charming.

It was hardly surprising, since they both lived in Estes Park and shopped at the same stores. But it *was* annoying.

"Oh, well." Hayley shrugged. "It looks better on you, anyway."

That was a foregone conclusion. Of course it looked better on Nicki, with her long, lean body and dramatic fall of dark hair.

It was nothing new. She and Nicki had practically grown up together—they'd even shared a locker in high school—and Hayley had learned a long time ago to deal with her friend's good looks. Admittedly, at first she'd been intimidated. As a medium-tall girl, with no claim to anything extraordinary in the looks department, it hadn't been easy having a best friend with impossibly long legs and a siren's lure for the boys.

Hayley smiled to herself. As things had turned out, Nicki got stuck with one boyfriend all through high school, and Hayley was the one who played the field. She'd found out that guys actually seemed to prefer the ordinary type.

Ordinary she was. Average height, average weight, brown hair, hazel eyes—she could've been a poster girl for Ms. Average America. But she was friendly, enthusiastic, and a very good listener, and that seemed to stand her in good stead with the male half of the world's population. No, she couldn't honestly say she'd ever had difficulty attracting men. The real problem was what to do with them once they insinuated themselves into her life and her living room.

Men. Hayley shook her head, pulling herself away from her familiar, depressing reflections upon her love life. She'd long ago decided that she preferred the company of her friends, where she could relax and enjoy herself. With them she didn't have to expend so much energy, whipping up enthusiasm for anything from the National Hockey League to designer coffee, if that was what the man in her life was into.

No, her friends accepted her the way she was—plain old ordinary Hayley, who liked bad jokes and fast food, who spent too much on lingerie and put too little into savings, who was a demanding boss behind the front desk, but let her house and puppy run wild when she was on her own time.

Now that she had the company of her friends, she told herself sternly, she should at least pay attention and appreciate them.

As they went through the buffet line, Hayley concentrated on what Nicki was saying about her stables and the lean times over the winter, when carriage rides weren't in great demand. She told a funny story about a customer with a balky horse, then turned to her old friend. "You look a million miles away, Hayley. What's happening to you?"

"Well, actually, I've had an eventful morning." She shook her head doubtfully as she hit the highlights of the Carmelita Carmichael story. "Maybe I ought to get into a different business."

"Hayley," Kate said reprovingly, "I've told you for years you don't belong working at a hotel. You were the best history student I ever had. I've never seen such intellectual curiosity."

"Curiosity, period," Nicki added. "You're the only woman I know who reads the ends of mysteries first. Not to mention the fact that you peek through keyholes."

Hayley gave her a shocked glance. "I do not peek through keyholes!"

"What about the time there was a hole in the wall of the boys' locker room?"

"That wasn't a keyhole."

"Close enough."

"It wasn't a keyhole!"

"Okay, okay. But you looked, didn't you? And you can't deny that you open your Christmas presents weeks before Christmas and then rewrap them, so no one will know you already opened them."

"I did that *once*."

"Ha!"

"Nicki!"

"Curiosity killed the cat, kiddo. And one of these days, yours is going to rebound on you, too."

"It's good to be curious," Hayley maintained stubbornly.

Nicki opened her mouth to start another round, when Kate interrupted. "Ladies, ladies," she said sternly, calling them back to order. Almost ten years older than the other two, she was often inclined to offer advice and instruction. "The important point is that you ought to forget hotels and go back to history, and you know it. We *all* know it."

Hayley and Nicki traded smiles; they recognized the return of Kate's soapbox.

"It's important to go after your dreams, to do what's important to you." Kate shook her head, ruffling a few of the copper-colored tendrils that were not caught up in her pretty French knot. Kate was precise in dress and speech, punctual to a fault, but a few strands of hair always escaped her sleek hairdos, as if to remind her that no one was perfect. "I know you like your job," she continued, "but you need more, Hayley. You need to push yourself to your limits. You need a challenge."

"Well, actually," Hayley admitted, "I've been thinking along those same lines. No, I'm not talking about going back into history," she cautioned, raising a warning hand as she saw enthusiasm color Kate's delicate features. "But I did take a step forward, here at The Stanley. They've created a new position, and I put my name in for it."

Nicki leaned forward immediately. "Okay, spill it. What kind of position?"

"Hold on, hold on." She held up a hand and laughed. "I don't even know if they'll think I'm qualified."

"For *what*?" Nicki asked impatiently.

"Assistant manager. This would be of the whole hotel, not just the front desk."

Before she had a chance to elaborate, Hayley heard Kate cough softly and raise an eyebrow. She sent Kate a quick glance. "What is it?"

"Only me, Miss Austin."

The Santa Claus man was perched behind Hayley's elbow, twinkling again as he leaned closer. Her eyes widened in surprise. He hadn't been there a minute ago. Where had he come from? "Oh, hello," she said. "I didn't see you. Harry, wasn't it?"

"That's right." Behind his hand he whispered, "I thought perhaps we might discuss that matter I mentioned earlier."

"Oh, yes." She edged her chair to one side so that she could look at him directly. "The delicate matter, right?"

"Exactly." He inclined his head, indicating that she should follow him. Feeling like Alice through the Looking Glass, she went along.

As he darted behind a potted palm, she asked, "What is this all about?"

Furrowing his forehead and glancing around quickly to make sure no one was watching, he reached into his inside coat pocket and drew out a small, shiny object. He held it out to her with all the trepidation of an artist showing off his newest work.

"For you, my dear," he murmured in a reverent tone. As the round golden orb glimmered in the subdued restaurant lighting, he tilted his head and stared at it. Then his focus shifted to Hayley. "Absolutely and positively for you."

Almost without thinking, she whispered, "It's beautiful."

Glowing and flickering there in the palm of the man's hand, it looked both warm and cold at the same time, although that didn't seem possible.

It was an apple—a small, golden apple—and it was simply beautiful.

"Take it," he offered gently. With the apple shining and beckoning in his palm, his hand slid a little closer. "Take it."

She tried to back away, but couldn't. She felt like Eve in the Garden of Eden. The apple beckoned, and she only had to reach out and take it. *Take it*. The apple of knowledge...the apple of desire...all she had to do was take it....

"I—I couldn't," she stammered, but her gaze was caught and held by the small, alluring golden toy.

"You must."

"But it's gold. And I don't even know you. How could I take a gift like that?"

"You must," he said simply. "It's meant for you."

Licking her lips, she couldn't resist reaching out just far enough to touch the tip of one finger to the shimmering apple. She had this overwhelming curiosity to feel for herself what it was made of. Its luminous gold surface felt slightly cool, not at all scary, but very interesting.

"It *is* beautiful." Her eyes found his. "Are you sure about this?"

He nodded, his eyes sparkling. Then he took her hand and gently set the apple upon her palm. Her fingers closed around it of their own accord, and the tingling feeling she'd had all day went right through the roof. It was as though the apple was electrified. She opened her hand and stared at it.

"What is this thing?"

The Santa Claus man ignored her question. "Remember, only three," he said slowly. "You must remember that, my dear. Only three. There can be no exceptions."

"Three what?" Hayley murmured, staring at the apple. It felt warm in her hand, almost hot in the center, radiating a gentler warmth to her fingertips. Why would it give off heat? It looked like gold; it felt like gold. Gold wasn't supposed to be hot to the touch! "What *is* this thing?" she asked again.

There was no answer. One moment the little man had been standing there behind the potted palm, warning her about threes; the next moment he'd vanished into thin air.

Chapter Two

"Did you see where that man went?" she demanded, marching back to her table.

"What's going on?" Nicki interjected. "Who was he?"

"I have no idea."

"He didn't say who he was?"

"Harry—that's all he told me."

"What did he want?"

Slowly she pulled her hand from behind her back, revealing the apple. "He gave me this."

"Good heavens!" Kate sat up abruptly and very nearly knocked over her water glass.

"He just gave you this and flew the coop?" Nicki asked.

"Oh, he mumbled something like, 'Only three,' whatever that means." She dropped her voice to a low, spooky tone. *"Only three, my dear. Only three!"*

"How very odd," Kate said softly.

"Three *what*?" Nicki inquired.

"I haven't the vaguest idea." Hastily she set the apple on the white tablecloth, uneasy about holding it any longer. It seemed to have a magnetic attraction to her hand that made her uncomfortable. "I wouldn't take anything that man says too seriously. The last time I saw him, he told me to beware the Ides of March."

Nicki laughed. "Maybe he told you to beware of March, because he knew he was going to give you this goofy present right in the middle of it."

"I would hardly call it 'goofy,'" Kate said thoughtfully. "It looks very much like real gold, and that alone makes it worth a lot of money. But it also reminds me of something...."

Nicki slid the apple into her own hand and examined it more closely. "What could it possibly remind you of?"

"I can't get a handle on it." Kate frowned. "It's right on the tip of my tongue, but ..." She shook her head. "No, whatever it was, it's gone."

"Kate!" Nicki's brown eyes flashed with mischief. "You can't stop now. Hayley's dying to know what this thing means. Aren't you?" she prompted.

Hayley shrugged. "It's not that big a deal."

"Oh, I see." Nicki held the apple aloft. "Strange little men give you solid gold apples every day. You can afford to be blasé." She paused a moment, then frowned at the apple. "What do you suppose he meant by 'only three'?"

"That is indeed the question of the hour," Kate agreed.

A wide smile curved Nicki's lips. "Three wishes is my guess."

"Hold on just a minute here." Hayley ran a hand through the tousled chestnut waves of her hair as she tried to clear her head. "What kind of crazy idea is that? Three *wishes*? Like in the fairy tales?"

"Aladdin's Lamp," Nicki offered promptly. "The Goose that Laid the Golden Egg."

"What about King Midas?" Kate asked. "How many wishes did he have?"

Nicki laughed, getting into the spirit of the thing. "And isn't there one about an old man who ends up with a sausage on the end of his nose, and then he has to use his last wish to get it off?''

"And a talking fish," Kate added. "Do you remember a fairy tale about a talking fish?"

Information about fairy tales with three wishes—accurate or not—was coming fast and furious now.

"So there's historical precedent for wishes coming in threes!" Nicki announced.

Hayley resisted. "Since when are fairy tales the same as history?"

"What difference does it make?" Nicki asked gaily. "You've just received a solid gold apple from an odd little man who told you, 'Only three.' Now granted, he may be crazy—" She broke off, then added, "Or all three of us may be crazy. But the bottom line is that you've got three wishes coming, Hayley, my dear." She held the apple under Hayley's nose. "What will it be?"

Hayley's eyes swept from one to the other. "You can't be serious!"

"Of course we're serious," Kate said lightly, her calm voice contradicting the spark of humor that lighted her soft gray eyes. She picked up the apple and twirled it by its tiny gold stem. "What do you say, Nicki? Counting Hayley, who obviously doesn't believe in magic, there are three of us. In other words, one wish per customer. Therefore I think it's only fair that Hayley give us the extra two wishes. Don't you agree?"

"Sounds good to me." Nicki tried to hide her smile. "A magic apple," she mused. "Maybe you need to activate it somehow to get your wishes. Go on, Hayley, rub it." As she dropped the apple onto the center of Hayley's plate, her smile widened. "Maybe 'I Dream of Jeannie' will appear in a puff of smoke—right here on our table!"

Hayley relaxed. Obviously, they weren't taking this thing any more seriously than she was. It was simply a case of a sweet little man who'd taken a liking to her and presented her with a gift. Maybe Harry was an incredibly wealthy old geezer who got his kicks out of giving expensive apples to front-desk managers at hotels he liked.

"No, wait—I've got it!" Nicki exclaimed. "Forget the wishes for a minute. Let's try Adam and Eve for a while—you know, like the apple of temptation and the serpent and all that?"

"I believe it was the apple of knowledge, not temptation," Kate said dryly.

"But maybe Harry's really an emissary from a snake," Nicki continued triumphantly.

"What would a snake want with me?"

"Okay, so it's not a real snake, but somebody with the personality of a snake. I've got it—he's a diabolical Eastern potentate who gives golden apples to the women he picks out as concubines!"

"Concubines?" Hayley groaned and closed her eyes.

"This has possibilities," Kate said with a small smile. "But what about, 'Only three'? How does that fit in?"

"She only has three days left, before the pasha or whoever he is comes to collect her and makes her his love slave. What do you think?"

Kate hid a laugh behind her napkin. "Nicki, you never cease to amaze me."

"I think she's gone over the edge," Hayley ventured. "This is worse than the first idea. Besides, everyone knows that diabolical Eastern potentates go for blondes. If he was choosing love slaves, he'd have gone for Cybill Shepherd or Princess Diana."

There was little time to consider the question. Their conversation was rudely interrupted by raised voices with ugly implications.

Trying to be inconspicuous, Hayley shifted her chair. Across the room, her least favorite battle-ax, Carmelita Carmichael, was chewing out one of the waiters. He was a nice kid who hadn't been with the hotel long, and from the looks of things, he wouldn't be staying much longer. Self-respecting employees turned in their resignations the moment "that woman" entered the picture.

"The Stanley has a calming effect on most people," she said softly, "but it isn't doing a thing for Carmelita Carmichael."

Much as she'd have liked to wring Mrs. Carmichael's neck, Hayley knew that the restaurant wasn't her bailiwick; in this case, discretion was the better part of valor. If she tried to interfere, it would probably only make things worse, since she wasn't exactly Mrs. Carmichael's favorite person at the moment. Maybe if she let her rant and rave for a while, it would all blow over.

Feeling like a coward, Hayley purposely inched back her chair the other way, so that she wouldn't have to look at the poor waiter getting the riot act read to him—just as a fresh burst of sound boomed out from behind her.

Hayley cringed. "You want to know what I'd really wish for if this apple worked?" She held up her pretty little trophy, so that the others could see the shimmering reflection of the overhead chandelier in its golden surface. Once again it established an immediate, magnetic connection with her hand, drawing her in, blocking out the rest of the world.

"Well?"

Hayley looked up, confused. She had no idea what it was she'd been planning to say.

"Are you going to tell us what you'd wish for or not?" Nicki demanded.

A new round of insults directed at the unlucky waiter brought Hayley back to reality. She squeezed her hand around the apple. "I'd wish for Mrs. Carmichael to fall under a bus. That would solve about half my problems at the moment."

Nicki twisted a long strand of dark hair between her fingers. "Really, Hayley, I'm disappointed in you. Is that the best wish you can come up with, wishing for some old lady to fall under a bus? Surely you can think of something better than *that*."

"*Really,*" Kate agreed. "How very mean-spirited, Hayley."

"Okay, okay." She smiled, trying to get into the spirit of the thing. Contemplating the apple, she let its spell take over.

In the surface of the apple she saw patterns of swirling gold, forming and reforming themselves into fluid whorls and spirals. It was magical, beautiful, and it seemed as if her most dearly held wishes would surely come true, if she could only distinguish what she saw. But it was indistinct, elusive. There were no specific wishes there, just a general feeling of warmth and light in the entrancing pools of gold. She felt dazed and scattered, not at all herself. It was like staring at the face of the sun.

It was also sort of spooky. She shook herself and pulled her eyes away. But she didn't relinquish her hold on the apple.

"Well? What will it be? A cushy job? Tons of money? Or a date with Tom Cruise?" Nicki suggested. "The entire world is at your disposal, Hayley. Be creative here."

"All right." She sat up straighter, accepting the challenge. As she held firmly to the golden orb, one thought kept pressing itself upon her consciousness. She smiled warmly. "I wish the man of my dreams would walk through that door and sweep me off my feet. How's that for a wish?"

"Ah—the classic," Kate murmured. "I have to admit that 'tall, dark, and handsome' is one of my personal favorites, too. Yes, that's right," she added dryly when she saw disbelief on her friends' faces. "Even stuffy old Kate. But don't tell my students. It would ruin my reputation."

Nicki said nothing. As the others concentrated on their food, she played awkwardly with her silverware.

Issues involving men were difficult for Nicki; they all knew that. She was in limbo these days, neither really married nor divorced, but certainly not living with her husband. When she'd returned to Estes Park, her husband had stayed in Los Angeles, and Nicki wasn't saying why. Under different circumstances the three friends might have shared this troubled time—brought it into the open and lessened its power to hurt. For all Hayley knew, Nicki and Kate talked about it frequently when she wasn't around. But she was acutely aware that her own presence made any discussion of Nicki's marriage impossible. Why? Because Nicki's husband was also Hayley's brother.

Nicki and Dan had been together ever since high school, when Dan was the star quarterback on the football team, nicknamed Danny Touchdown for his ability to sneak the ball into the end zone. Everybody loved Danny Austin, so it had been no surprise when Hayley's best friend Nicki joined the club. And Hayley, being a good pal, had talked her brother into taking Nicki out on a date.

The rest was history—childhood sweethearts with a happily-ever-after ending. Until Nicki came back to Estes Park alone.

For the time being, their conflicting loyalties and emotions were too strong to sort out. Although they'd been friends forever, they couldn't seem to manage the current situation. Why had Nicki come running back to Estes Park? Why didn't one or the other of them get a divorce, if the marriage was over? Hayley wanted to know, but she couldn't pry, wouldn't push. So it remained an uncomfortably empty space in an otherwise terrific friendship.

Kate intervened to lighten the tense silence. "Heavens, Hayley, what are you doing wishing for the man of your dreams? I swear, you wouldn't recognize him if he did magically appear and sweep you off your feet. You're too picky."

"I'm not that bad." She grinned, glad of the diversion and pleased not to have to worry once again about Nicki and Dan. "I'm just holding out for Harrison Ford," she insisted. "One of these days he'll forget about his wife and find me."

Nicki shook her head. "Face it—you wouldn't even go for Harrison Ford."

"Try me."

"Since when was mortal man good enough for you?" Kate inquired. "I've forgotten the exact parameters of your requirements, but I do know that no man has yet lived up to them."

"I have one requirement, and one requirement only."

Kate chuckled. "One requirement? Let me wager a guess here. Your one requirement is that any man you date has to be perfect in all respects. Is that it?"

"Of course not," Hayley said loftily. "And dating isn't the problem, anyway. I'll date practically anyone who can speak in complete sentences without drooling. But getting seriously involved, now that's another matter entirely."

"Oh, I see," Kate said sagely. "And what's the one big hurdle for serious contenders?"

"I have to come first in his life." Although she knew her friends were teasing her about her impossible standards, Hayley was adamant on this score. "That's my only rule, and I really don't think it's so much to ask." She leaned forward and spoke with determination. "It's very simple. He has to be willing to put me before everything and anything else in his life. If I could meet a guy who'd care more about me than about his car or his job or his racquetball game, I'd snap him up in a minute."

"Good luck." Nicki pushed away her plate. "That's about as likely as getting Harrison Ford to drop his wife for you."

"Not necessarily," Kate put in. "I was married to a man who definitely put me first. He treated me like a queen."

Hayley glanced at her, surprised. Kate rarely brought up the subject of her late husband. He'd been quite a bit older than her, and had died almost two years ago, but Kate couldn't seem to forget him. Hayley had noticed the sadness in Kate's eyes whenever Martin's name was brought up.

"You were lucky," Nicki returned quietly. "And Martin was a rare bird. You can't judge the rest of the species by him."

"All I know is that I was very happily married, and I had no complaints about Martin's priorities."

"No one's arguing with that. But I still say that most men are selfish down to their toes. They want the women in their lives to sit back and tell them how great they are."

"And when did you become an expert?"

"One marriage apiece, Kate—I'm as much of an expert as you are."

"Don't fight, okay?" Hayley sighed. "I think you've gotten off the track, anyway. I'm not concerned about all men. I just want *my* men—or man—to pay attention to me. Is that so much to ask?"

"Hayley," Nicki responded. She leaned over and laid her hand upon her friend's arm. "You really sound upset about this. Are you okay?" Her tone was brimming with concern.

Come on she felt like saying. *I'm Hayley, remember?* She was supposed to be the positive, assertive one, the one who had no problems, the one who listened to other people's sob stories and then made jokes until it didn't seem so bad. She was the one who faced lemons with a smile and a few wisecracks and ended up with lemonade. It was her stock-in-trade.

She'd spent a lifetime perfecting her act as the kind of person who put on a happy face. She was a good listener, but not a good sharer of her own woes, not even with her best friends.

"You can tell us, Hayley," Nicki said gently. "All you want is for someone to pay attention to you, right?"

The way Nicki put it, it sounded so pitiful, so childish, but to Hayley it didn't feel like that at all. It felt strong and right, like demanding her due after a period of deprivation. It was something that had been building for a long time. She'd tried hard not to resent it, but the truth was, she'd always been low man on the totem pole. Good old Hayley— so accepting, so adaptable. No one ever wasted a moment worrying about Little Miss Sunshine.

At home it had been her brother, the golden boy star athlete, who came first. Growing up, her brother Dan had been the center of attention. His schedule was catered to, his meals were prepared specially, his knees bandaged, his hand held and nerves soothed before a big game. In a family that valued athletic prowess above all else, Hayley barely amounted to a second-stringer.

Actually, she loved her brother very much, and certainly didn't blame him for being the star of the family. But after she'd left home, she'd come to the realization that it didn't have to be that way. She didn't want to play second fiddle anymore, not with her family, not with her friends, and definitely not with the men in her life.

"Do you remember Jim, the guy I met my senior year in college?" Her lips curved into a rueful smile. "He was in the best fraternity on campus—he dressed beautifully—he was even a jock, so my parents liked him. We went out for almost two years. Two years of my life I spent, telling myself how lucky I was to have this great guy. So what if he treated his car better than he treated me?"

Nicki shrugged. "I kind of liked Jim. He seemed okay to me."

"Oh, right," she said sarcastically. Now she was back on track as flippant, funny Hayley, cracking jokes. "I finally dumped him after I broke my ankle hiking. I was writhing in pain, and he insisted on stopping on the way to the hospital to check on the score of the Broncos' game!"

"That's life, kid," Nicki said with a sigh.

"Not my life." Hayley kept her tone light and frivolous, trying to belie the importance of what she said. "If somebody wants me, he's going to have to make me the absolute center of his universe. That's my rule."

"And she says she's not picky." Nicki raised her hands in defeat.

"I don't know," Kate said thoughtfully. "I have a feeling our friend Hayley is pretty much of a marshmallow, when it comes right down to it. If an interesting man came along—one with a little drama, a little mystery to appeal to that curious soul of hers—I think our Hayley would be swept away in the twinkling of an eye."

"I don't know if I want a mystery man," Hayley countered. She had a fleeting thought of the man she'd seen outside the hotel earlier that morning, but dismissed it. The mystery about him was all in her head; almost certainly he was a regular hotel guest with a penchant for interesting hats. "There's one big problem with mystery men. Who knows where they've been? And where is this one in particular supposed to come from?"

"You wished for him, didn't you?" Nicki waved a careless hand. "He ought to be walking through the door any minute now."

They laughed, enjoying the picture of Hayley's dream man being picked up and dumped at The Stanley against his will. Then their voices were once again lost in a rising tide of shouts and threats, as familiar strident tones soared higher and higher behind them.

"What is that woman's problem?" Nicki demanded. "I don't think I'm naive, but I've never heard some of those words before." She focused her attention on the scene that was developing behind Hayley's shoulder.

Hayley squeezed her eyes shut. She didn't want to look. But her hearing was still in perfect working order, and her ears recorded the sound of Mrs. Carmichael screeching, while the rest of the room sat in stunned silence. *Talk about losing your appetite,* Hayley thought. One last, nasty comment blasted out, something about minimum standards of human decency, which made very little sense under the circumstances. The words were followed directly by the stomping of feet and then an unholy crash, bash and uproar. For a few moments the terrible din sounded as if a ten-piece brass band had thrown itself onto the floor. As the noise subsided, everyone in the dining room began talking at once.

"Good grief," Hayley whispered, opening her eyes. "What's happened now?"

No one answered. Her friends' attention had been captured by whatever had made that horrific noise. Nicki and

Kate were staring past her, as if aliens had landed in the dining room of The Stanley Hotel. Well, that would account for the noise, wouldn't it?

At this point she could hardly avoid looking to see what the commotion was all about. As she turned, she noted that every eye in the place was directed at the scene. Mrs. Carmichael was in the center of it, of course.

Apparently departing the dining room in a huff, the disagreeable dowager had somehow collided with a busboy. From the looks of things, she'd fallen beneath him, knocking a huge tray of dirty dishes out of the hapless boy's grasp and scattering plates in every direction. The only reason the woman's mouth was shut was that the busboy was still sitting on her. There was definitely going to be hell to pay when Mrs. Carmichael recovered the use of her ample lungs.

"And I thought this day was going to be special," Hayley muttered. "This wasn't exactly what I had in mind."

"Is that woman hurt, do you think?"

"No, I don't think so. Just stunned at the moment." She rose from her chair and placed her napkin neatly upon the seat. Unfortunately, she knew her duty in the current situation. "I imagine Mrs. Carmichael will begin bellowing anytime now, as soon as she catches her breath and gets out from under the busboy."

"Did you say Mrs. Carmichael?" Kate asked suddenly. "The one who—?"

"Did you say busboy?" Nicki chorused. "Didn't you wish for her to fall under a—?"

"Well, yes, but . . ." No. It couldn't be. But how much of a coincidence was it that she'd wished not five minutes ago for the woman to fall under a bus? And what had she done? Fallen under a busboy. Hayley didn't know whether to laugh or cry.

"Outrageous!" someone roared, and everyone within the state of Colorado now knew that Mrs. Carmichael had found her voice.

"I have to try to settle her down," she told her friends. "She's apt to go on for hours."

"Good luck," Nicki offered.

"Be careful," was Kate's word of warning. "She's back on her feet, and she's wielding an umbrella of some sort. It looks as though she's attempting to attack someone over there. I think it may be the man who helped her up and brushed her off. Biting the hand that fed her, as it were."

Things were going from bad to worse. Hayley had visions of hotel liability for umbrella-inflicted injuries to half the guests. Almost unconsciously scooping up the apple and sliding it into her pocket, she dashed to the other side of the dining room, paying no attention to the whispers or comments she heard on the way. Getting the uninvolved people back to their brunch would have to wait; right now, the formidable old woman had backed someone into the corner, and rescue was the first order of business.

"Excuse me," Hayley called. "Don't you think you ought to put down the umbrella?"

"You again," the woman snarled. Steam was practically coming from her ears as she whirled toward Hayley, waving her umbrella in the air like a sword. "I suppose you've staged this whole charade to try to get rid of me!"

"Now, let's not get too excited." The woman had clearly jumped over the line from mere unpleasantness into a state of uncontrollable fury. Still facing her, Hayley carefully circled to her other side, where the hostage was trapped. "Let's all calm down, shall we?" As the woman wavered, momentarily forgetting the person she'd been trying to impale with her umbrella, Hayley maneuvered herself between them, whispering, "Get out of here," over her shoulder at Mrs. Carmichael's target.

"What do you think you're doing?" he shot back. "Carmelita," he said gently, trying to wedge himself in front of Hayley, "This isn't what you want to—"

"Shut up, you, you interloper!" Mrs. Carmichael began to advance on both of them, her umbrella pointing menacingly at about midriff level. "How dare you follow me? It's unforgivable! It's unethical!"

"Carmelita," he tried again, but the moment he opened his mouth, her face only became further mottled with rage.

"Be quiet, will you?" Hayley demanded.

"I don't need your protection." Again he attempted to get out from behind her, so that he could face Mrs. Carmichael directly.

"Be quiet!"

As the words came out of Hayley's mouth, the older woman took an unexpected lunge. Hayley had no choice but to jump back, in the process flattening the man behind her against the wall and leaving neither of them a viable escape route. Her own body was plastered rather intimately against his, and she could feel the imprint of his large, strong chest and firmly muscled arms, which kept trying to wind themselves around her to pull her out of the way.

It was odd, very odd. Even in this abominable situation, with a crazed woman bearing down upon them with a rapierlike umbrella, somehow Hayley knew that he was wearing a buttery-soft suede jacket that felt marvelous under her fingers. She knew without thinking that he was tall, that he was lean and rangy, that he smelled like wild raspberries, that his body felt wonderful pressed against hers. It made no sense to notice these things when she was frightened and staring down the point of an umbrella. Nonetheless, she felt the puffs of his warm breath on the top of her head, and she inhaled the delightful odor of raspberries.

It was probably just a side effect of the adrenaline rushing through her, but Hayley was acutely aware of every movement made by the man behind her, a man she still hadn't seen. Her heightened awareness of his presence sent her pulse racing faster, making it difficult to assess the direction of Mrs. Carmichael's onslaught or to forecast her next move. Thankfully, the woman chose that moment to retreat a step. With the umbrella starting to wobble, the termagant paused to regain her bearings.

There was a frown on the woman's large, square face as she forcefully pulled down her sturdy tweed jacket, wiped her brow, and tidied a strand of frizzy gray hair that had threatened to stray.

Hayley assumed this was all leading up to a complete retreat, and sighed with relief. If she didn't get herself at least a few inches away from this man very soon, she was going to break into a cold sweat. Collecting her wits, she turned to face the man whose body she'd become so familiar with in such a short time.

"I'm sorr—" she began—just as Mrs. Carmichael took a vicious poke with her umbrella in the vicinity of Hayley's bottom.

Without a word, the man swept her into his arms and strode swiftly across the dining room, bearing her safely out of the combat zone.

Hayley got a good look at his face for the first time.

"Oh, my God," she whispered to no one in particular. "It's Indiana Jones."

Chapter Three

He heard her say something about Indiana Jones, and he knew from the expression in her wide, hazel eyes that he was in trouble.

Damn Carmelita, anyway, for putting him in this position. All he'd wanted to do was lie low and find one small, elusive item. So what was he doing? Creating a disturbance, making himself the center of attention, and rescuing a silly, interfering woman who was staring up at him as if she were starving and he were a Christmas goose.

Didn't she realize he wouldn't be hauling her around if there were any other way to prevent bodily injury?

Yeah, sure, he mentally chastised himself. So why was he holding on to her so tightly? Maybe because the little fool had leaped in front of him, trying to save *him,* when he had a good foot in height and seventy pounds on her. Maybe because she felt pliant and vulnerable in his arms. His arms tightened around her as if of their own volition. Damn, but she felt good. If only the curve of her hip under his fingers weren't quite so soft, or the feel of her slim arm wound around his neck quite so warm . . .

He gritted his teeth and looked around for a good place to put her down before this got further out of hand. Since when did he have chivalric impulses?

And why was she gazing at him like that, all dreamy and sweet? It had to be the outfit. Once again he cursed himself for wearing the hat. It probably conjured up all kinds of romantic fantasies for impressionable females. Of course, it was supposed to be a disguise so that he could follow Carmelita without her spotting him, but that hadn't worked too well, had it? She'd known it was him right off and taken after him with her umbrella.

And now he had the added burden of this young lady with the innocent eyes and the enraptured expression. What was he going to do with her? And more to the point, what was he going to tell her about why he was dressed like Indiana Jones?

He tried desperately to think up a reasonable explanation for this morning's bizarre events, but his mind was blank. All he could come up with was the truth, and that wasn't going to do anybody any good.

Safe and secure in his strong, warm arms, Hayley was in a daze. He might not be Indiana Jones—not really—but he wasn't far off, with the same kind of rugged jaw, high cheekbones, and the most incredible blue eyes she'd ever seen. Framed by long, thick lashes, they were a crystal-clear aquamarine, the color of a swimming pool on a sunny day.

He was carrying her easily, striding across the dining room toward the door with a minimum of fuss, acting as if he made a habit of this sort of thing. Behind him, Hayley could hear Mrs. Carmichael shouting in frustration. She peeked over her protector's shoulder, just in time to see the old woman surrounded by half a dozen waiters, who were doing a good job of blocking her path. It was obvious that her plan to skewer this man was thwarted for the time being.

Surreptitiously, Hayley reached out to touch the front of his bomber jacket, fingering the soft, sand-colored suede. It was an automatic gesture, like petting a kitten or strok-

ing the collar of a fur coat, done simply because his jacket
felt so soft under her hand. Besides the jacket, he was
wearing a khaki cotton shirt, open at the neck, and khaki
pants with little pleats at the waist. *All he needs is a whip,*
she thought crazily, wondering if this were all a hallucina-
tion. It wasn't every day a person got a chance to languish
in the arms of Indiana Jones.

He slowed and then stopped outside the restaurant door.
Carefully he set her back on her feet. His hands lingered on
her shoulders, as if he were reassuring himself that she was
all in one piece. Then they fell away abruptly, his jaw
clenched grimly, and he stared at the floor. He seemed ill at
ease and tongue-tied.

All she could think of was how gorgeous his eyes were,
how broad his shoulders were, and how handy his rescue
had come in. It was like a dream.

Or a wish, she thought suddenly. *My wish.*

Hayley came back to earth with a thud. Blinking, she took
her fingers away from the front of his jacket. She needed to
think about this, but her mind was whirling. Apples—
wishes—dream men—it was absolutely bizarre! She forced
herself back to the hard, cold facts. Okay, so first she'd
wished that Mrs. Carmichael would fall under a bus, and the
old bat had fallen under a busboy. Then she'd wished that
the man of her dreams would sweep her off her feet. Now
she'd been swept off her feet—literally—and if this wasn't
the man of her dreams, he was doing a very good imita-
tion.

Not even her best friends knew that she'd rented the
Raiders of the Lost Ark video fourteen times, just to drool
over Harrison Ford. In her heart of hearts, she had a thing
for men with steely eyes and battered fedoras. Like this one.

Shaking her head, she decided she was behaving like a
lunatic. Who'd ever heard of magic apples showing up in

the middle of Sunday brunch? People said that The Stanley Hotel was magical in its own right, but this was taking things a bit too far. A magic apple with three wishes? It simply couldn't be....

"Is something wrong?" he asked, in a low, cautious tone.

"Ah, no." She ran a hand through her hair, making a worse mess of the tousled brown waves, and gave him a limp smile. How could she imagine for one second that the apple had made all of this happen? It was ridiculous.

With a jolt of recognition, she realized he was the man she'd seen earlier outside the hotel. The hat would've given it away immediately, if only she hadn't been so caught up in dreamland. He also had the mysterious air and the long, lean body she'd noticed from the start. So therefore, she admonished herself, it was all perfectly reasonable; he was a hotel guest who'd been there before the apple ever appeared, and he had nothing to do with dreams or wishes.

People had begun to gather in the lobby. Many of them were chattering loudly about the events that had transpired in the dining room, casting inquisitive glances at Hayley and the man in the hat.

"Aw, hell," he said with feeling. "Now look what you've done."

Her head snapped up. "What *I've* done? What's that supposed to mean?"

"Everyone's staring," he said tersely.

His blue eyes were rather chilly, and not too captivating at the moment. In fact, she was beginning to reconsider her first notion that he in any way resembled the man of her dreams. Dream men weren't supposed to grow unreasonably sullen and freeze you with their aquamarine eyes.

"So?" she challenged, braving the onslaught of his gaze. "It seems to me that you're the one who lugged me out of the dining room like a sack of potatoes."

"If you hadn't thrown yourself in between Carmelita and me, I wouldn't have had to rescue you, and it wouldn't have caused all this fuss."

"The fuss was going on long before I got involved."

"I could've calmed her down if you hadn't gotten in the middle," he countered.

"I saved you from being skewered."

"You almost got yourself skewered."

"Some people would thank me for interceding."

"*Some* people would thank *me* for the rescue."

"Thank you," she said primly. "Never let it be said that Hayley Austin doesn't do her duty."

His only response was a muffled "Hrmph" as he searched his pockets. It reminded her of the way little Harry had rifled *his* pockets prior to pulling out the apple. If Blue Eyes pulled out an apple, Hayley thought wildly, she was going to scream. He didn't pull out anything. He just kept poking.

"Did you lose something?" she asked finally.

"My glasses," he told her reluctantly. "I guess they fell off in the altercation with Carmelita."

"Your glasses?" She tried to laugh. He wore glasses! Didn't he know that dream men came with twenty-twenty vision?

He shrugged. "I guess I'll have to go back in there and get them." Mrs. Carmichael's voice boomed from the dining room, and he flinched visibly. "Maybe later. But I will have to find them. I can't see without them."

"Before you leave..." Hayley ventured. Could she help it if curiosity was getting the best of her? "What did you do to make Mrs. Carmichael so angry?"

One of his eyebrows rose sardonically. "I'm here. That's enough to set her off."

"Well, I can relate to that. She doesn't like me much, either." She glanced up at him thoughtfully. "But she's never tried to run me through with her umbrella."

He changed the subject as deftly as he could manage. "I really wish you hadn't thrown yourself in between the two of us. You could've been hurt."

"The whole dining room could've been hurt. I think she's seriously deranged, but of course, you know her better than I do."

She waited a moment, but he offered no more information. In fact, he seemed to be ignoring her as he focused all his attention on his watch. They'd just been through a truly strange experience together, she'd languished in his arms, and now he'd forgotten all about her. *Men.*

"You do know her, don't you?" she asked. "And therefore you'd know if she were really dangerous, or if this was a momentary aberration, right?"

After a moment he looked up at her. "Sorry?"

Yeah, that's what I thought. He wasn't paying attention. *Man of my dreams, phooey.*

"I said that you and Mrs. Carmichael must know each other quite well for her to go after you like that."

"Don't be absurd." He was tall, very tall, up somewhere in the six foot four, six foot five range, and he was looking down at her sternly. She began to feel very small.

"She's just...a competitor," he continued vaguely. "We're both on the trail of something important, and I suppose she's upset that I showed up here, too. We all get a little crazy in this business."

Now she was definitely curious. Nicki's warning that curiosity killed the cat reverberated in her mind, but she firmly silenced it. She had been launched into the middle of this situation whether she liked it or not, and she had the right to know what it was all about. "What's 'this business'? What are the two of you 'on the trail of'?"

He clammed up immediately. "It's nothing important."

"You'll excuse me if I don't believe you."

He offered no further explanation, and she tried to remember if she knew anything about Mrs. Carmichael that might offer a hint as to his business with her. The older woman wasn't the sort one shared casual chitchat with, and there was no space on the registration form for the guest's occupation, even if anyone had cared to get nosy when she checked in. All Hayley could recall was that Mrs. Carmichael had been very closemouthed when they'd inquired into why she kept coming to the hotel. The staff had ventured a few theories—that she was carrying a torch for the owner— that she was staging a hostile takeover of the place—that she simply liked to harass all of them—but had thus far come up with nothing concrete.

Well, whatever she was doing here, Mr. Blue Eyes was doing it, too. Hayley was still unsuccessfully attempting to sift through all of her conjectures, when he tipped his hat to her and backed away.

"Excuse me," she persisted. "I didn't think we were finished."

"I don't like standing here, being the center of attention," he allowed, narrowing his eyes at her for a second. "Did you tell me what your name was?"

She crossed her arms over her chest and glared at him. She had definitely mentioned her name, and clearly, any man of her dreams would've noted it. Meanwhile, this bargain-basement version slipped down even further in her estimation. "Hayley," she muttered.

"Goodbye, Hayley." He nodded, tipped his hat again, then turned and hiked up the stairs to the guest rooms.

Damn, she thought. He and Mrs. Carmichael were knee-deep in something to do with the hotel, and she wanted to know what it was.

"Well, you're not going to find out at this rate," she chided herself out loud. "You didn't even get his name."

There was, however, the cheerful thought that he appeared to be a hotel guest, since he'd just headed upstairs. If she was on her guard and did a little digging, she might be able to find out who he was and what the heck was going on.

With that in mind, she couldn't help humming to herself as she once more returned to the dining room to continue brunch with her friends. She'd envisioned today as special, and it was certainly turning out to be that. Odd, different, spooky and downright weird. But *special.*

"Who was that man?" her friends demanded the second she hit the table.

"I don't know."

"What a rescue!" Nicki exclaimed. "I can't believe he carried you off like that."

Kate cleared her throat meaningfully and set her chin on the bridge of her hands. "You do realize she was swept off her feet, and by a man who looked exceptionally interesting from here. Has anyone else noticed the significance of these events occurring at this particular time?"

"I noticed," Nicki said cheerfully, her deep brown eyes warm with laughter. "Hayley, your wishes are coming true."

"Don't be ridiculous," Hayley scoffed, but she slipped her hand into the pocket of her loose skirt and slid the tip of one finger against the apple, to reassure herself that it was still there. As she purposefully steered the conversation to a discussion of Mrs. Carmichael and her disgraceful behavior, she cupped the apple in her hand and ran her fingers over its smooth surface. Once again it was warm, and it gave off curious vibrations, as if it had a pulse, as if it were alive.

Could it be . . . ?

No. Absolutely not.

It was crazy to believe for one minute that magic or some other supernatural force had pushed Mrs. Carmichael into a busboy or brought that man into her life in such an absurd fashion. Besides, who cared? As soon as she found out what he was up to, she'd get him *and* Carmelita Carmichael out of The Stanley Hotel for good. And that would be just fine, as far as she was concerned.

Even if he did smell like wild raspberries.

"MONDAYS ARE BAD ENOUGH without getting the Spanish Inquisition to boot," Meg groused.

Ignoring the comment, Hayley persevered. For several hours, she'd been trying to quiz Meg while appearing disinterested in her answers.

"He would've checked in yesterday morning," she repeated. "Very tall, wearing a hat like Indiana Jones. Blue eyes—knockout blue eyes. I really think you'd remember him if you saw him."

"I don't think I checked him in," Meg returned. "But I was pretty upset about Mrs. Carmichael, and I wasn't paying all that much attention."

"What about you, Mike? You were on duty yesterday, too."

But Mike shrugged his shoulders and turned back to the reservations list he was scanning, and Hayley sighed with frustration. Mike was usually on another planet, and today was no exception. He probably wouldn't have noticed if Dolly Parton and her backup band had waltzed through the lobby.

Finding out anything salient about her mystery man was turning out to be more difficult than she'd anticipated.

When she first came in this morning, she'd asked the morning staff if they knew anything about the blue-eyed man, but they didn't. Now she'd turned to the people on the three-to-eleven shift, who had both worked yesterday morning, but they weren't providing any answers, either. She'd tried to be casual about it, but she knew she wasn't fooling anyone. Why had this become so important to her, all out of proportion to its significance in her life?

But she already knew that answer. No matter how hard she denied it, it was because she was afraid she'd wished the man with the beautiful blue eyes into her life. Only by locating him and going over him with a fine-tooth comb could she hope to prove to herself that he was a standard issue mortal man, and not the stuff of dreams.

"I could always use my third wish to find him," she mumbled under her breath.

Unfortunately, she didn't have the apple with her. After yesterday's bizarre events, she'd stuffed it into the back of her overflowing lingerie drawer and tried not to think about it. But it kept popping up in her thoughts, all pretty and shiny like a new penny. It might've been nice to take it out every once in a while, to look at or maybe to touch—to feel its warm, golden...

She shook her head at her own foolishness. Between the apple and the mystery man, she was in serious danger of losing her grip on reality.

"You know, Hayley," Meg said with a smug little grin, "when you originally brought this up, I thought the guy was a deadbeat or something, and you wanted to find out who he was to check his credit." Her grin widened. "But now, the way you're describing him, I'm beginning to think it isn't his credit you're worried about."

"Get serious." Hayley made a good show of straightening a stack of papers on the desk behind the check-in counter. She sent Meg an unamused glance. "He happens to be involved with Mrs. Carmichael in something that seems a little weird to me, and I'm pretty sure it has something to do with the hotel."

Meg looked puzzled. "The hotel? What could they want with the hotel?"

"I don't know yet," Hayley replied grimly. "But I do know that Mrs. Carmichael has been in and out of here every few days for the last month. That's suspicious in and of itself, like she's casing the joint."

"Casing the joint?" Mike asked. "What does that mean?"

"You know—nosing around, like burglars do before they rob a place."

Mike sighed. "You watch too much TV."

Hayley ignored him. "Yesterday Mrs. Carmichael accused this other guy of following her here. Then he told me they had business together. Now to me, Mrs. Carmichael's trips, plus this suspicious guy, plus his admission that they're here for the same reason—all add up to funny business with The Stanley right smack in the middle of it. And if The Stanley is involved in anything shady, I want to know about it." She shrugged. "I have to protect the guests, don't I?"

"Oh, come on," Meg said impatiently. "I mean, Mrs. Carmichael is hardly the type to commit burglary. Can't you see her hoisting that bulldozer of a body up three flights and over somebody's windowsill?" Her eyes grew round as she considered the possibilities. "But wait a sec—a partner could. Wow... That's what you think, isn't it? Mrs. Carmichael and this guy are masterminding some plot to rob the hotel. Or the guests!"

"Maybe." Hayley leaned closer. "I saw an episode of *Remington Steele* once, where a whole bunch of rival thieves descended on one hotel, because they all wanted to steal a priceless painting that was due to show up there."

"Oh, I get it! Like some guest has something valuable, and this guy and Mrs. Carmichael are going to rip it off. Wow..."

"Exactly." It occurred to her that her theory was about as reasonable as the existence of a magic apple, but she refused to be deterred. Whatever those two were up to, she wanted to know. If her fears were groundless, well, then she'd be relieved, wouldn't she? "If you do remember seeing anyone who fits that description, let me know, will you?" she reminded Meg. "I'm going into the back to go over next week's schedule."

"Hayley," Meg reminded her, "this is only Monday. Why are you doing the schedule so far ahead?"

"Because I want to," she said ominously. *Because I need to do something to get my mind off all this craziness.*

"Give me Friday off, will you?"

"I'll think about it." Hayley sat down at her desk and poked at her papers with a pencil. Normally, doing the schedule was one of her favorite things; she liked the balancing act it represented. But today she couldn't concentrate. She kept staring into space, musing on apples and men and other bizarre tricks of nature. When had life become so strange?

She had been sitting at the desk, wasting time for over an hour, when Meg suddenly appeared in front of her.

"Uh, Hayley?" she said uncertainly. "I think I just saw the guy you were talking about."

"Oh, him," Mike interjected, tossing the words over his shoulder. "Yeah, I did check him in. Was it yesterday? Maybe Saturday. Name began with a *W*. Or maybe an *M*. Something like that. Aw, I can't remember. I think he's from Kansas. Or was it Nebraska? Maybe Iowa."

Trust Mike to be so sure of his information, Hayley thought, frustrated. Quickly she dumped the papers onto the desk and peered into the lobby from her post behind Mike and Meg. "Where?" she whispered.

"He just came out of the restaurant and he's headed for the elevator. No hat, but he's really tall. You did say he was tall, didn't you?" Meg leaned over the counter so she could get a better view. "Light brown hair, wire-rimmed glasses. Is that him?"

"Could be. I'll just take a look."

In a flash, she'd hustled into the lobby. She spotted him immediately. After waiting all day, trying to eke out information from desk clerks who'd had no idea what she was talking about, Hayley was filled with a profound sense of relief. She wasn't losing her mind; he really did exist.

But now what? Should she stride right up to him and ask, "Are you plotting something dire against my hotel? Oh, and, by the way, did you happen to be dropped here in answer to a wish I only made as a joke?"

As she pondered the question, she was spared having to imagine an answer. He turned abruptly and headed straight toward her. All she had to do was open her mouth and say, "Hello."

She lifted her chin and gave him one of her best smiles. Men always responded well when she was being friendly. Now all she had to do was get him talking. "How are you today?" she asked brightly.

"Oh, hello," he said quietly. "I'm fine. And you?"

He looked her up and down, wishing he didn't find her so appealing. But she was very pretty, in a natural, unpretentious way. Just the way he liked. Yes, there was definitely a spark of something different about her that made him very uneasy.

She was wearing gray trousers and a loose black blouse with a little bar pin at the collar. Medium brown hair fell to her shoulders in careless waves, and she had hazel-brown eyes that sparkled with intelligence and curiosity. Her features were standard issue, except for her mouth. She had a great smile—wide, friendly, open—the kind that made you want to smile, too. Something about the way the corners turned up carried a hint of mischief, a suggestion of naughtiness lurking behind that girl-next-door appearance.

He'd never cared much for beauty queens or long-stemmed fashion plates. No, he'd always been a sucker for smart girls, the fun, outgoing type, the ones who had enough spunk to boo at baseball games and throw popcorn at the screen if they didn't like the movie. The kind who blasted you if you acted like a jerk. Suddenly uncomfortable, he remembered yesterday, when he'd gotten grouchy about being the center of attention, and she'd told him it was his own stupid fault.

In other words, under other circumstances, this lady would've been just his type. His heart sank. He didn't need and couldn't afford that kind of distraction.

Damn. Looking at that devil-may-care mouth, he liked her already. Which was impossible. He had no business tripping over a perky little brunette, no matter how terrific her smile was, when he had set his sights on one goal and one goal only. A mere woman could never compare with the prize at the end of this game. And for all he knew, she represented another competitor for the brass ring, cozying up to him to get information.

Common sense told him to steer clear, but he couldn't seem to resist that friendly smile. He opened his mouth, and words came out before he knew what was happening. "Are you a guest here, too?"

Her smile widened. "I work here," she said sweetly. "I manage the front desk."

"Oh. I see." Full-blown, her smile was sensational. Sunny. Sparkling. Warming him right down to his toes. He knew he was in deep, deep trouble.

Good grief, he was tall. He should've been intimidating, and he was, in a way. He certainly wasn't overly friendly. But somehow she got the impression that he wasn't trying to be rude or unsociable, and that he even liked her. So why was he staring at her mouth that way?

She forced herself back to business. He was hiding something, she was sure of it, and that was the key.

"I see you found your glasses." Not witty or charming, but it was the best opening gambit she could manage on short notice.

He touched the top of his wire rims. "I think Carmelita kicked them under a table. One of the lenses popped out, but otherwise they're no worse for wear."

The glasses dulled the impact of his stunning eyes, but they didn't affect his appearance. Without the hat, she could see that his light brown hair was straight and longish, flicking the edge of his collar in the back. He was wearing the suede bomber jacket again, this time over a dark crewneck sweater and jeans. The narrow steel rims of his glasses made him seem more intelligent, but no less...large. Maybe she was becoming intimidated after all.

Silence hung between them for a few seconds, and Hayley jumped in to bridge the gap. "Are you here on business?"

"In a way."

Well, that didn't get her too far. "What kind of business?"

"Well, I'd...uh...I'd prefer not to say."

"Why not?"

No answer. Hayley considered, and decided she was tired of pussyfooting around. Taking his elbow, she leaned closer. His arm was warm and alive under her fingers, not at all ghostly or dream-induced. She dropped his arm—and her voice—at the same time. "I know something funny is going on. And I think you'd better tell me what it is."

"Something funny?" he echoed. "What's that supposed to mean?"

Even under duress, she couldn't admit that she was worried he was a phantom of her dreams. So she resorted to her other line of inquiry. "You and Mrs. Carmichael," she said. "You're doing something shady at my hotel, and I'm not going to put up with it." She gave him what she hoped was a quelling stare. "We have standards here at The Stanley."

He almost smiled. "I see. Well, I can allay your fears on that score, anyway. Carmelita and I are both reputable professionals, and we have no intention of doing anything to hurt the hotel."

"Fine." Except, of course, that he and Mrs. Carmichael had already done several things to hurt the hotel. Like fighting in the dining room, for one. "What profession would that be, exactly?" At his confused look, she added, "That you and Mrs. Carmichael are both so reputable at."

Damn. This was going too far. But Holly—no, that wasn't it. What was her name? Well, whoever she was, she didn't look as though she was willing to back down. Sizing her up, he decided he could certainly handle one little slip of a girl. He was no ladies' man, but he had a brain, didn't he? Her he could figure out. But if he wasn't careful, she'd sic hotel security or someone else onto him. Professionals he wasn't so sure about. Better to satisfy Holly's curiosity as best he could, without really giving anything away, and then get the hell away from her.

After considering for a moment, he told her, "I'm an assistant curator at a museum in Omaha."

"An art museum?" she demanded, still clutching to her cockamamie theory about a priceless painting at the hotel.

"No. It's a historical museum." She waited for more, and he sighed, giving in to the inevitable. "I'm here on the trail of a particular antiquity I want for my collection. And that's all I'm saying. It's completely aboveboard, and it has nothing to do with the hotel." He narrowed his eyes. "And it's really none of your business."

"It became my business when Mrs. Carmichael aimed her umbrella at me." She stared at him as she mused. "What did you call this thing you're looking for—an antiquity?"

She had a sudden vision of pagan slaves decked out in jewel-studded ankle bracelets and cuffs. King Tut's tomb. The Holy Grail. Or—good grief—the Lost Ark. As in Indiana Jones.

But no, she realized, that was nonsense. His antiquity was much more likely to be something ordinary, like an ugly brown pot with two-dimensional people shooting arrows, or a big white statue of Venus with no arms. Yes, she could definitely picture this guy nuzzling up to a life-size statue of a nude woman. Something in marble as cold as his ice-blue eyes.

He shook his head. "Look—all I want to do is get the item I came for. As soon as I get my hands on it, I'm hot-footing it back to Omaha before anyone can steal it. I'm no threat to your hotel, I promise."

"It must be quite an, uh . . ." What had he called it? "An item."

"Oh, it is." His eyes suddenly gleamed with excitement. "It is."

"And what exactly does Mrs. Carmichael have to do with all this?"

He clenched his jaw. "She's looking for it, too."

"You're kidding." The stodgy wardrobe of tweeds and walking shoes fit the picture, but Hayley couldn't imagine Mrs. Carmichael sitting in a pit of mud, looking for old shards of pottery or bits of bone. "I can't believe Mrs. Carmichael is an archaeologist."

"She isn't." He looked disgusted. "She represents only one client, a very wealthy collector, who couldn't care less what she finds him, as long as it's expensive and everybody else wants it, too. All he does is stockpile treasures, just to say he owns them."

Both Mrs. Carmichael and Blue Eyes were searching for some elusive antiquity, and now they were both at The Stanley Hotel. "You think this thing is here at The Stanley, don't you?"

"I don't know where it is. But the sooner I find it, the sooner I leave. And the sooner you see the last of Carmelita."

A definite incentive.

She made up her mind at that moment to do whatever was necessary to help him find his "item." But where could it be? Statues of Venus or any related paraphernalia would stand out like a sore thumb in the genteel but twentieth-century surroundings of The Stanley.

Except, of course, for the gallery right on the premises that specialized in rare antiquities. She kicked herself for overlooking the obvious. Stanley co-owner Judith Normali operated a gallery called Ancient Art International right inside the hotel. It included all kinds of extraordinary pieces, from an Egyptian sarcophagus to a massive funeral vase, exactly the kind of thing he supposedly wanted.

"Your antiquity wouldn't by any chance be in the Ancient Art International gallery, would it?" she asked slowly.

His eyes flashed with excitement. "Maybe that's it. Maybe that's what Carmelita knows that I don't know. Has she been there?"

"If she had, I'm sure we would have seen bits of pottery thrown around the lobby," Hayley told him grimly. "She goes through life on the slash-and-burn plan."

A smile broke across his spare features. "If Carmelita hasn't been there, it sounds perfect."

"Don't get too excited. I'm going with you to make sure this is on the level."

"As long as you're not in collusion with one of the other collectors, I don't care if you watch me sign the check."

But as Hayley steered him toward the gallery door, she heard a familiar bellowing coming from the front desk. She was getting very tired of hearing that sound.

"It's her again," she said with a sigh.

Quickly he dragged her behind him and edged them both around the far side of a convenient pillar.

"What's she doing?" Hayley whispered.

"Chewing out the girl at the front desk."

Poor Meg. Twice in two days was too much for anyone to take. Hayley was torn between marching across the lobby to lend a hand and staying right where she was, out of umbrella range. "What's her problem this time?"

"She said something about suing the hotel for falling down in the restaurant yesterday."

"Oh, no." Fun and games, magic wishes, ancient treasures—it was all fine for a little while, but Hayley knew better than to ignore reality and her job responsibilities. She knew she had to step in and resolve the problem at the front desk. "Look, I've decided that you can probably be trusted in the gallery by yourself. Duty calls."

He set his jaw. "Wait a second."

"I'm sorry, but if she's talking about suing the hotel, I have to get over there."

"No—I mean, yes, I agree completely. That's just what you should do." He knew it wasn't smart to start picking up partners, but he needed a diversion. Holly—or whatever her name was—was the only one handy. "Listen, as long as you're talking to her anyway, you can keep her occupied for ten minutes or so, can't you?" He grabbed her shoulders and stared right into her eyes. "Just talk to her long enough for me to check out the gallery without her spotting me, okay?"

She couldn't help noticing that now that he was on the trail of his armless Venus, he was a real dynamo. His beautiful eyes glowed with blue fire, his face was flushed, and he looked as if he were running a fever. His large hands felt warm and hard against her shoulders, and she had to remind herself to breathe.

"You will do it, won't you?" he asked urgently.

"Well...okay...I guess...sure." She swallowed. With an effort, she broke away from the intensity of his gaze. "I mean—I was planning on trying to talk to her, so I suppose I can hold her off for a few minutes." Feeling more in control, she added, "But don't leave me hanging, do you hear me? Case the gallery and get right back here. I want to know if you find your...item."

"Case the gallery?"

"Look it over," she explained impatiently. "Doesn't anyone see the right movies?"

"Excuse me?"

"Forget it. Just get back here on the double, okay?"

"Right."

He held out a long, slim, tanned hand, and Hayley took it. He shook her hand gravely. "Thanks, kid," he said softly, and then bent to kiss her lightly on the cheek. "See ya."

She stood stock-still for a moment, still feeling the brush of his lips against her cheek, whirling in time to see him disappear inside the Ancient Art International gallery in search of the elusive item he wanted so badly.

If he was planning to hotfoot it back to Omaha as soon as his armless Venus showed up, she had the irrational and completely selfish hope that Venus would stay away for a long, long time.

Chapter Four

"Now, Mrs. Carmichael, you're feeling much better, aren't you?" Hayley said lamely. She'd settled the curmudgeon in the lobby's cushiest chair, brought her several stiff belts of Scotch from the bar, listened to a series of tirades, and murmured sweet, soothing words until her cheeks ached. Amazingly enough, it actually seemed to have done some good.

At first Mrs. Carmichael had been less than pleased to see Hayley. She seemed to blame her for much of the altercation in the restaurant, and was clearly frustrated that Hayley had escaped without puncture wounds. But now, due no doubt to the ample flow of liquor, her voice had trailed off to a dull roar and her insults were growing a good deal milder.

"If only *he* weren't here," she mumbled. Her chin had dropped onto her chest, and her words were muffled by layers of tweed. "He's too smart by half."

"He?" Hayley asked very casually. "Who's he?"

Mrs. Carmichael looked up shrewdly. "Your boyfriend. You think I don't remember the two of you playing Perseus and Andromeda yesterday, but I do. I know you're in cahoots with that blackguard."

"Pardon?"

"If you heed my advice, young lady, you'll have no more to do with that one! The costume does not make the man. Remember that. He's no more Indiana Jones than I am." Mrs. Carmichael hiccuped but forged ahead. "Actually, I'm much more the adventurer type. He sits in a museum all day and dusts the shelves, whereas *I* travel the world over."

"Yes, I'm sure you do," she managed, as the woman launched into a lengthy recital of her travels. As Mrs. Carmichael's story stumbled along, Hayley gazed into space and let her mind wander back to the man with the blue eyes. How was he doing in his search of the gallery? *What* was he doing? She felt a flutter of exhilaration at the very idea of his mysterious mission.

Taking advantage of a momentary silence from her companion, she asked nonchalantly, "By the way, what's his name?"

Mrs. Carmichael blinked slowly. "Whose name?"

"The man you don't like—the one you called a black-guard."

"Ha! As if you didn't know."

"But I don't—honestly."

"He's an interloper, do you hear me?" Mrs. Carmichael moved closer, breathing Scotch fumes over Hayley. "Tell him to go away. Tell him I'll never let him get his hands on it, anyway, because I got here first. Tell him—"

Sensing danger, Hayley patted the other woman's sturdy knee. "Don't get yourself all upset about it. If you could just tell me his name..."

But Mrs. Carmichael wasn't listening. The disagreeable woman appeared to have lapsed into an impromptu, inebriated nap. Well, there'd be no more information forthcoming from her for a while. Hayley sighed.

"Psst," she heard behind her. "Holly!"

She closed her eyes and counted to twenty. Here she was, helping him out, and he couldn't even bother to remember her name! She slipped away from Mrs. Carmichael and charged behind the pillar where she'd last seen him.

As if one slim pillar could hope to hide almost six and a half feet of broad-shouldered man.

Her hands twisted themselves into fists as she glared up into those splendid blue eyes. "My name is *Hayley*," she told him indignantly. "Hayley Austin. If you call me Holly again, you will regret it."

"I'm sorry." He backed up a step, obviously astonished. "I—I've been a bit distracted—I didn't realize . . ."

"Forget it." Now she felt like a jerk for making a big deal out of it, but it made her crazy that he couldn't or wouldn't recall her name. Far from being first on his priority list— which was a requirement for her dream man—she wasn't even important enough for her name to stick in his memory for five minutes at a time. "It's Hayley," she repeated.

"Okay, okay. I get the idea."

"Which reminds me—what is your name?"

"Look, we have more important things to worry about at the moment. I came up empty in the gallery." He looked wistful. "Great place, though. There's a Judean flask in there I'd give my right arm for. Too bad it doesn't fit my museum in the least."

"Forget the Judeans. So you didn't find your armless Venus?"

"What?" His eyes narrowed behind his glasses as he scanned her face for clues. "What armless Venus?"

The picture of a crumbling statue of a nude woman without benefit of arms had become so firmly engraved in her brain that she'd completely forgotten she didn't really know what he was searching for. "Your *thing*, your item—you didn't find it?"

"Nothing even close."

"So what do we do next?"

"We?" He took one look at the sunny smile, at the sparkle in her eyes, and immediately sent his gaze skimming in the opposite direction, so he wouldn't have to notice how damned attractive she was. Unless he stopped this right now, she'd be as irreparably caught up in the search as the rest of them. And as for him, well, he'd be overboard without a life preserver, lost in the depths of her smile. "Thanks for your help," he said quietly. "I can handle it myself from here on in."

It was as if all the air had been let out of her tires. Even as she told herself this was the best idea, that she had work to do and a life to get on with, she knew she didn't really want to give in and go away.

If only he weren't so darned interesting! If only his mission weren't so mysterious, so intriguing. As she gazed at him, she saw that he was wearing that distracted, consumed look again, as if the object of his search was so spectacular that even thinking about it transformed him. How could a normally curious person—okay, an exceptionally curious person—walk away from someone whose face looked like that?

Straight out she told him, "I'm not letting this go until I know more about what you're doing. I want to know who you are—exactly—and what you and Mrs. Carmichael are hunting."

"I can't tell you."

"Oh yes, you can." She regarded him with a level gaze. "I know enough at this point to be a real thorn in your side if I want to. And maybe I want to." A new idea formed in her fertile brain. "Maybe I want to be your partner."

"Partner? Not in a million years," he muttered.

"We'll see."

He removed his glasses and cleaned them over and over, trying to think of a way out of this mess. His worst fears were being realized. A front-desk clerk with visions of the Venus de Milo dancing in her head...a front-desk clerk with golden-hazel eyes and tousled hair and a smile that knocked him for a loop...and she wanted in on his quest.

It was an impossible idea, but a voice in a tiny corner of his brain had begun to ask, *Why? Why not bring her along for the ride?*

Because it's too important, he told himself severely. *Because she'd get in the way. Because I can't afford to make mistakes when I'm finally this close to what may very well be Atalanta's Golden Apple.*

Ah, yes. Atalanta's Apple. It was the stuff of mythology come to life. The original story involved a Greek youth who tossed a beautiful golden apple into the path of an Athenian maiden during a footrace, so that she'd stop to look at the apple and lose the race, thereby losing her hand in marriage to the crafty youth. The maiden's name was Atalanta.

Through the centuries, a golden apple had popped up here and there, supposedly carrying magical powers with it, and it had been dubbed Atalanta's Apple in honor of the Athenian maiden. Now he was convinced that the obscure object of Greek mythology could be traced to an appearance in Colorado in 1898, and might reappear at any moment. The person who found it and the museum that showed it would be catapulted to international fame.

It should be me, he thought for the hundredth time. *It will be me.*

He wanted it. He wanted to be the one who judged whether it was real or fake.

He coveted it. He coveted it with every fiber of his being.

And he needed it. He needed it to prove to the world and to himself what he was made of.

So how could he sit back and let a stranger horn in on something like that? Even if she was an awfully appealing stranger.

He gave Hayley a speculative gaze. He couldn't afford her snooping around and being more of a nuisance than she already was. She knew about him, and she knew about Carmelita, and it wouldn't take much digging to find out where they came from and what they wanted. If she decided that a search for lost treasures at the hotel was great publicity and announced it to the world, he'd be buried under amateur treasure hunters and reporters from the *National Enquirer*. He'd never find the apple. So it was clear that he was going to have to tell her something. But what?

Stall, his brain told him. Stall, until you can think up a decent story to allay her suspicions. "Can we talk about this later?"

Hayley raised an eyebrow. "Are you trying to get rid of me?"

He glanced over at the lump in the lobby that represented Carmelita's supine, snoring form. "I'd rather not have to contend with Sleeping Beauty, if it's all the same to you."

"All right," she said coolly. "Where and when would you like to take this up again?" She considered for a moment, and a very interesting idea occurred to her. Why not? She wasn't a particularly reckless person, but if there was ever a time to be reckless, this was it. "How about tonight?" she asked. "Dinner?"

The mischievous curve to her lips was more pronounced than before. What was she up to? Although it flew in the face of common sense, he heard himself say, "Sure. Why not?"

She beamed at him, giving him the full benefit of her twenty-four-carat smile, weakening his knees. "Terrific."

"Terrific," he repeated soberly. Was she crazy? Or was he? Could he possibly hope to have dinner with her and not give away all his secrets? "I'll meet you in the MacGregor Room at eight."

He turned as if to go, and Hayley set a firm hand upon his arm to hold him. "You know, I still don't know your name."

"Mas—" he began.

But "Mason, darling!" trilled across the lobby from the front door before he could finish.

As Hayley and the man she now knew as Mason both whirled to see who'd spoken, a heavily perfumed, lavishly bosomed woman launched herself in their direction.

"Charming," Hayley managed to mutter between clenched teeth, as the new arrival began to bill and coo at Mason. She wondered if there was a woman alive fond of other women with large breasts and lousy taste in perfume. Hayley coughed as flowery, cloying fumes wafted up her nose. She tapped her foot in annoyance, waiting for her supposed dinner date to escape and speak to her.

After a moment he managed to extricate himself from the clinging vine's clutches and awkwardly faced Hayley.

"Mason," she said with a less-than-thrilled smile. "It seems we've been introduced, after all."

"It's Mason Wilder," he said darkly. "And this is Oliv—"

"Olivia MacPherson," the curvy woman interrupted in a breathy little whisper of a voice.

Hayley noted that it was not Olivia *Wilder*, which meant that at least he wasn't married to the bimbo. Thank the Lord for small favors.

The "bimbo" had jet-black hair done in a Miss America pouf, enough eye makeup to suit Cleopatra, and palest ivory skin. "I'm here to help sweet, darling little Mason in his search," she cooed. "Aren't I, doll?"

His embarrassment might have been amusing under other circumstances, but Hayley wasn't feeling all that charitable. How dare he be partners with a piece of brainless fluff, when an intelligent, competent person had tried to help and he'd told her he could handle it all by himself? *Partner? Not in a million years,* he'd said. Just like a man to be thinking with his pants instead of his brain.

He detached Olivia's arm from his own, muttering, "Olivia, please."

"But, darling," she cajoled. "Of course I'll help you."

"This isn't a party. It's a serious expedition. I understand your interest, but don't worry. Once I find it, you'll be the first to know. Until then, you might as well relax. Maybe even go home," he tried hopefully.

"Don't be silly, darling," Olivia breathed, batting her heavy eyelashes. "I wouldn't think of going anywhere with all this *excitement*"—she crinkled her nose and almost squealed the word—"going on."

"Charming," Hayley repeated ominously.

With a wave of her hand, Olivia floated off on a cloud of perfume to check herself in at the desk. As a parting shot, she called, "See you at dinner, darling."

Hayley waited for Mason to tell the silly woman that he already had a dinner engagement. But he didn't. "So much for my dinner invitation," she murmured under her breath. Picking up volume, she announced, "If that was your girlfriend, I think you have lousy taste."

"Don't be ridiculous."

"About your taste in women?"

"About Olivia being my girlfriend." He grimaced. "Absolutely not."

"*She* thinks she is."

"No, she doesn't," he mumbled. "She just . . . oh, hell, I don't know. She acts like that because she thinks it's endearing."

"That much I figured out for myself," Hayley said sensibly. "So why didn't you tell her to leave you alone?"

His expression was pained. "I can't."

"Why not?"

"You're very nosy, you know that?"

She was taken aback for a moment. Then she said calmly, "And you're very arrogant. Evens out rather well, don't you think?"

"No, I don't think."

"I've noticed."

He glared at her, and she smiled back at him with satisfaction. She couldn't explain her reaction to all of this, except for the fact that she was excited, enervated, and ready to go looking for armless statues at the drop of a hat. It was fabulous—the adventure of a lifetime!

Even without knowing what the ultimate goal was, she already felt as if she had a vested interest in this hunt for ancient treasure. At first she'd told herself she was protecting the welfare of the hotel, but she knew there was more to it than that. Whether it was the romantic idea of searching for lost antiquities, the satisfaction of foiling Mrs. Carmichael, or even the petty, but perfectly natural, fun of lampooning a woman like Olivia, she *was* involved—involved with Mason Wilder, whether he liked it or not. And she didn't plan to let any clinging vines get in the way. Taking his arm casually, ignoring its strong, warm feel under her fingers, she ventured, "Now tell me, why do we have to put up with Olivia?"

He caught the use of "we" again, and it made him very uneasy. "It's the search. She's another competitor," he allowed. "I've been trying to convince her that I'm better suited to finding it than she is, but she isn't buying. And don't be fooled by the way she looks. Olivia's no dummy. She's as much of a threat as Carmelita, maybe more.'' Seeing that Hayley was about to interrupt, he held up a long hand to stop her before she started. ''And that's all I'm going to tell you, so don't bother trying to badger me.''

She didn't know whether to be insulted or pleased that she was getting to him. ''I've never badgered anyone in my entire life.''

''You're one for the books.''

Hayley felt curiously happy. ''Thanks. I think.''

Shaking his tawny head, Mason edged toward the staircase. ''I'll see you later.'' As an afterthought, he turned back and saluted. Giving her a small, crooked smile, he added, ''See you later, *Hayley*.'' Then he ambled up the stairs.

''I'll see you at dinner, Mason,'' she called out after him, then added to herself, ''You can count on it.''

MASON WAS SPRAWLED on the bed in Room #401, with piles of papers and photographs carefully spread out around him. He peered at figures in sepia-tone photographs from turn-of-the-century Colorado, an illustration from a newspaper article of about the same time, the tiny markings on a Greek vase in an eight-by-ten glossy, and every other scrap of evidence he had on Atalanta's Apple and the similar object known in Colorado lore as MacPherson's Folly.

He kept coming back to the same conclusion—they were the same apple.

To prove the apple's pedigree, all he had to do was get his hands on it, without Olivia dithering around, without Carmelita butting in. And without Hayley Austin.

Hayley. Remembering her reaction to the fact that he'd finally gotten her name right, he couldn't hold back a small smile. He had her pegged, all right. She was smart enough to pick up the clues he'd unintentionally dropped, assertive enough to call him on the carpet if she felt he deserved it, and foolhardy enough to jump in between Carmelita's umbrella and himself.

Cute kid.

His smile widened as he realized how much she'd hate that particular label and how much he'd enjoy teasing her with it. Under other circumstances, he'd have plied her with popcorn and Three Stooges videotapes. He'd make her laugh, so that he could see her smile again. She was just that kind of girl. Woman, he corrected himself. It took a full-grown woman to push herself between Carmelita and himself, to invite *him* out to dinner, to capture his imagination so easily when he already had plenty to think about.

But this was the wrong time, and he was the wrong man to be captured. He had one chance to get his apple, and there was no room for mistakes. Hayley Austin was a mistake.

Exerting care and self-control, he picked up the photo of the Greek vase. He forced himself to gaze at it steadily, without blinking, getting himself back on track by imagining all that he would have within his grasp, if he could only locate the elusive apple.

In his mind's eye, he saw the Omaha Museum of Western History, now a small, undistinguished collection, transformed into a showplace. He saw himself delivering lectures to the most august bodies, saw his name in the most prestigious journals, his face on talk shows from coast to coast. He saw himself bringing the dusty pages of history alive to spellbound audiences. At long last, Mason Samuel Wilder IV would live up to his illustrious name.

But it wasn't going to be easy. He stared into space, methodically cataloging the obstacles in his path. First, he'd have to keep an eye on Carmelita, so she didn't get ahead of him. And he'd better keep an eye on Olivia, too, to make sure she was placated and wouldn't cause trouble later. Last, but not least, he'd have to keep an eye on the delightful Ms. Austin, damping down his impossible attraction long enough to get her out of business that didn't—couldn't—concern her.

The only problem was, this scheme required three eyes.

He kicked a load of papers onto the floor, bracketed his arms under his head, stretched out his long frame on the bed, and stared at the ceiling.

It promised to be a long evening.

BUSINESS OR PLEASURE, that was the question.

Hayley perused the contents of her closet one more time. Living on her salary, she had to pick and choose carefully when it came to her wardrobe. And unfortunately, she suffered from an addiction to expensive lingerie. She might look like Ms. Average America on the outside, but under her clothes lay whisper-thin teddies and delicate bikinis decorated with tiny bits of ribbon and lace.

Right now she was standing in a sleek, cream silk camisole and tap pants, and what she needed to do was find something equally sensational to wear on top of them. What would be an appropriate outfit for a front-desk manager who wanted to feel like an adventurer for once?

"Maybe I should just wear what I've got on," she mused. "*That* would get his attention."

Fluffy, her shaggy gray and white mutt of a dog, barked happily, as if he'd read her mind and seconded the motion.

"No, Fluff, I'm not going in my underwear." She leaned over and ruffled his coat, letting him give her a sloppy kiss on the chin.

As he snuffled around her knees, she turned her attention back to her closet. She needed something that looked dressy without going overboard, and nothing she owned thrilled her. She had a slip of a black dress that she was dying to wear, one she had gotten on sale at the end of last summer, but she had to reject it. Her 34B couldn't hope to compete with Olivia's cleavage if it became a battle of décolletage. Reluctantly she decided she'd better go for class and forget about trying to be slinky.

It was silly to be so concerned, anyway. Surely Mason, who couldn't even remember her name for more than five minutes at a stretch, wouldn't notice what she wore. With a sigh, she settled for the sapphire silk blouse and pants she always wore in a pinch, pulling out the matching jacket with a flourish. It was a morale booster of an outfit, because she liked herself in blue, and the shoulder pads in the jacket made her feel like Joan Crawford.

"Go out and do battle!" she exhorted herself, although she wasn't sure why. Maybe the golden apple's influence was making her feel feisty.

When she'd picked out her lingerie earlier that evening, she'd transferred her prize from the back of her drawer to the bedside table, so that she could look at it as she dressed. It was odd how often her eyes were drawn to it, and how reassuring it was to see it there, glowing softly in the subdued light. Every time she glanced its way, well-being and confidence enveloped her.

Shrugging into her blouse, she turned toward the apple again. But it wasn't there. Except for a box of tissues and her alarm clock, the scrubbed pine nightstand was empty. Where was the apple?

Quickly buttoning her blouse, she bent to check under the bed and around the floor, just in case a gale-force breeze had knocked it over and rolled it somewhere. No such luck. The apple was gone.

Don't panic, she told herself. It had to be there somewhere; solid gold fruit did not get up and walk away. She ducked under the bed to inspect the area once more.

"Woof," rumbled Fluffy, tapping her leg with a large paw.

"Not now, puppy," she murmured, batting him away, but he wouldn't go. He put his head down and nudged her in the side until she finally emerged to chastise him. "Fluffy, what's go—?"

She broke off abruptly, grabbing for the apple that was hanging from her dog's mouth. "Well, that answers that. You stole it, didn't you? It was bright and shiny, and you thought it was a new toy."

Clutching the apple to her chest, she stood up and let relief sink in. It had not disappeared in a puff of smoke, it had not been stolen, and she had it back in her hot little hands where it belonged. Thank goodness.

"Don't you ever do that again," she ordered, shaking a finger at the cowering dog. "And don't whine at me, either. You scared me to death."

Fluffy romped around in circles, clearly seeking forgiveness, while Hayley took the apple down to the kitchen and carefully rinsed it off. Dog slobber and golden apples had no business mixing.

Then she toted it into the living room and stuck it securely behind a three-volume set of James Fenimore Cooper on the top section of her bookshelves. She still couldn't believe that the dog had shanghaied it like that. "You better not have wished for doggie treats while you had it, Fluffy, old boy. I can just imagine you stealing my third wish and wasting it on chew bones."

The puppy whimpered, as if to assure her that he hadn't wished for anything, and Hayley laughed as she reached down and patted the fuzzy head. "I was only kidding, silly. It doesn't really give wishes." But she wondered if she believed her own words.

She dashed back upstairs and finished dressing in a flash, refusing to think about the apple, and practically flew to the hotel. She'd wanted to be early, to get to Mason before Olivia had a chance.

But when she raced into the lobby, she saw that she was already too late. Olivia, almost falling out of a red velvet gown, flanked one side of the entrance to the restaurant, while Carmelita Carmichael, dumpy in olive tweeds, held up the other. Mason, meanwhile, was slumped in a chair nearer to Hayley, hiding behind a newspaper and beneath the brim of a cowboy hat.

Setting aside the newspaper, he looked up at her with an expression of relief, and Hayley was inexplicably glad to see him, too. But she didn't fool herself that he was actually growing fond of her. She supposed that anything looked good next to a battle-ax and a clinging vine.

"Hi," he called.

Up to that point, he hadn't thought of anything to say that might sidetrack her. But she was welcome company after he'd stewed in his room all afternoon, wondering if Carmelita or Olivia were on to something he wasn't. He hated inactivity, and he hated not knowing what his next step should be. All he could do was watch and wait until he found a clue, or one of the others made a move. It was torture.

"I'm glad you're here, Hayley. I've been waiting."

She smiled brilliantly. He'd gotten her name right, the little dear. "What's with the cowboy hat? Where's your fedora?"

"Carmelita knew it was me immediately, even under that hat." He shrugged as he rose and took her arm. "So this is my new disguise."

Hayley regarded him with pity. "How could you think a different hat would fool her? One glimpse of those shoulders and you're a goner."

"My shoulders?" he asked in confusion. "What's wrong with my shoulders?"

She felt her face grow warm. "Nothing's wrong with them. They're very...broad. Very nice."

"Oh, I see." He supposed that that was the equivalent of a man telling a woman she had nice gams. He wasn't quite sure how to react; however, he was fairly sure that his current lack of response was not the best choice. *Snap out of it, Wilder.* "Thank you. I guess."

Standing near to him, she caught a whiff of wild raspberries again. She'd never met a man who smelled like that, and the question came out before she had a chance to control herself. "Have you been picking raspberries lately?"

"Raspberries?" First his shoulders, and now the way he smelled. He wasn't sure how much more of this he could take. "It's soap. My sister gave it to me for Christmas. I, uh, kind of like it."

"So do I, Mason," Hayley murmured. She smiled to herself, secretly enjoying the faint blush on the cheeks of such a tall, rugged-looking man. "So do I."

Tossing the cowboy hat onto a nearby chair, he led her toward the entrance to the restaurant.

"You know," she whispered, "it might have been better to eat somewhere else. I love the MacGregor Room, but it doesn't exactly hold fond memories for you and me and Mrs. Carmichael."

"We'll get through it."

"I suppose. But the heart-to-heart chat you promised me isn't going to be easy with those two hovering around."

"Who said they're joining us?"

Hayley sighed. "I don't think we have a choice."

Exactly as she feared, Olivia and Mrs. Carmichael both showed every intention of hanging around.

"We've been having a little chat," Mrs. Carmichael said, bearing down upon them. Her eyes were a little bloodshot, but otherwise she looked none the worse for having belted down so much Scotch earlier in the day. "Olivia and I have compared notes. It seems you followed me, Dr. Wilder, and then Olivia decided to check up on you. How many more of your imbecilic colleagues are going to show up here to plague me?"

"*Dr.* Wilder?" Hayley inquired.

He shrugged. "History."

"Oh." Her eyes lit up with interest. "I was a history major in college, and I have a friend who teaches at the university in Boulder."

"How thrilling for you, I'm sure," Mrs. Carmichael trumpeted; sarcasm dripped from every word. "My own fields of study are mythology and anthropology."

"And I don't study anything." Olivia giggled.

The disagreeable dowager pressed her lips together. "Spare me, please."

"I'd love to." Mason sidestepped her neatly and drew Hayley with him into the dining room. "Table for two," he said pointedly.

"That's going to be so crowded," Olivia fussed, crinkling her nose. "Why not get a nice, big table where we can all be cozy?" She signaled to the maître d'. "Garçon, garçon," she called breathlessly. "Table for five, please. And bring us champagne—oodles of it!"

"Five?" the others chorused. There were only four people standing there.

"Why, haven't you seen Angus yet? He arrived shortly after I did. I thought it would be just jolly for the whole group to sit together." Olivia smiled with saccharine sweetness. "We can talk over old times."

Although she was only having dinner with Mason to find out more about his quest, Hayley had been harboring a secret desire to have him alone for a few minutes. Okay, so she'd decided he wasn't the man of her dreams, but he was still pretty cute. And those eyes . . . She breathed in, hoping for a whiff of wild raspberries to fortify her for a crowded, noisy dinner. Instead, she almost choked on heavy perfume. Rudely brought back to reality, she mumbled, "What did she say? Angus?"

"Another rival," Mason muttered. "It appears the gang's all here."

They followed helplessly behind the two ladies Hayley had mentally dubbed the battle-ax and the clinging vine. Given this crowd, she didn't hold out much hope for Angus.

He was huge. Not quite as tall as Mason, Angus Potts was a good deal wider and some thirty pounds heavier, with great tufts of reddish-blond hair and a droopy mustache. Introducing himself, he held out a gigantic paw, squeezed the life out of Hayley's hand, and draped himself over a seat between Olivia and her.

For the first five minutes he spoke to no one. He just sat, gulped champagne and glared at Olivia.

"How are you, Angus?" the curvy beauty murmured after a long pause, batting her jet-black eyelashes. "Long time no see."

"Not long enough," Mrs. Carmichael blustered. "I imagine you followed Olivia. Tell me, is there anyone we can expect to be following *you*?"

"This is it, Carmelita, and you know it." Mason sat back and surveyed the rest of them. "We're the only ones who believe in it."

"Yes, but I didn't know about *her* before now." Mrs. Carmichael pointed a large, square finger in Hayley's direction. "Imagine, pretending to be a lowly desk clerk and plying me with liquor."

"I wasn't pretending to be anything," Hayley said coolly. "I *am* the front-desk manager at this hotel, and I'm only involved in this affair because you keep creating disturbances."

"Hmph," the older woman grumbled, then spun around to glare at Mason. "How many more of your paramours can we expect to pop up?"

"Paramour? Really!" Hayley sniffed. Mason put a hand upon her arm as if to reassure her, or perhaps to restrain her. His touch was soft and gentle and it felt exactly right, resting there on the silk of her sleeve. As she met his gaze, she realized that she was enjoying this small, shared moment in the midst of the storm around them; her lips curved into a quiet smile.

"Well?" Angus said loudly, his voice rumbling as though it were coming from a great distance. "Now that we're all here, now what?"

"Now nothing," Mrs. Carmichael sputtered. "Now you all go away and let me collect my apple."

"Your what?" Hayley almost choked as champagne went up her nose. She sat up straight, knocked away Mason's hand, and stared at Mrs. Carmichael. "What did you say?"

"My apple," the older woman repeated. "As if you didn't know."

With a sinking feeling in her heart, Hayley inquired blankly, "What kind of apple?"

"Gold," they all said at once.

"Gold," she echoed. "What a surprise."

Chapter Five

"A golden apple from Greece," Olivia added. Hayley noted that she'd suddenly lost her cutesy voice and now sounded like a real person instead of a cartoon vamp. "It's called Atalanta's Apple."

"After the island that supposedly sank?"

She didn't know why she cared what they called it, but asking questions was a way of avoiding the fact that she was in shock. She felt like an idiot for not having figured it out. Yet how could she have known?

Her apple... They were all looking for *her* apple—the apple that her dog had been toting around in its mouth not long ago.

"She thinks we're talking about Atlantis!" Mrs. Carmichael cried. "She doesn't know Atalanta from Atlantis!"

"You usually keep your lady friends better informed, Mason," Angus boomed. "Isn't that right, Livvy?"

"Are you still harping on that, Angus?" Olivia carelessly waved a plump white hand. "Mason meant nothing to me. I've told you a hundred times."

"And never managed to sound convincing even once!" Angus's mustache twitched with agitation, and he pounded a large fist on the table.

Meanwhile, Mrs. Carmichael emitted her approximation of a laugh, and Mason's eyes turned to ice.

"Livvy is not and has never been my girlfriend," he said quietly. "I've told Angus that before."

"How dare you call her Livvy!" Angus thundered, jumping to his feet.

"Angus," Mason and Mrs. Carmichael hissed in unison. "Sit down!"

"What does it matter, anyway?" Olivia asked gaily. She set a soft little hand on Angus's forearm and yanked him back into his seat with a thud. "We're all here now, and we're all after the same thing. So who cares who used to date who?"

"Whom," Hayley said automatically. No one paid any attention; they were too busy sniping at each other. Letting the argument whirl around her, she put a moist palm to her forehead and tried to think and not think at the same time.

What should she do? She couldn't just tell them that she had the apple. They'd stampede her house and steal it, and that would be the end of that. Besides, making that kind of general announcement would put the thing up for grabs. *Carmelita* might end up with it. Her apple was not going to end up in that grasping palm, if Hayley had anything to say about it.

But on the other hand, how could she keep quiet? They were going bananas, looking for something that she already had! Was it fair—was it humane—to let them continue tearing their hair out, when she could solve their dilemma so easily?

"I don't know," she lamented, burying her face in her hands.

"What don't you know?" Mason asked kindly, obviously looking for a way out of the raging conflict.

Mrs. Carmichael's head whipped around. "Clearly, the dolt doesn't know anything. Let's keep it that way!"

I know more than you think, lady. And I could certainly take the air out of your balloon, now couldn't I? Hayley was so confused and so dazed that she considered announcing it right there and then, if only to see the look on Mrs. Carmichael's face.

Clearing her throat, Hayley waved a hand in the air to catch their attention. "Excuse me, can you stop fighting for a moment, please?"

Four pairs of eyes fixed on her, including one set of aquamarine eyes she knew she'd never be able to face again if she went ahead and blurted it out.

"Where did this apple come from?" she asked meekly. "And why do you all want it so badly?"

"It's mine!" Mrs. Carmichael and Olivia snarled in stereo.

"It belongs to history," Angus declared grandly.

Mason sat back. "It belongs to the person who gets to it first."

All she had to do was step forward and say, *Then I guess it belongs to me.* But she didn't. She thought of that beautiful little toy, of the way it felt warm and alive when she held it in the palm of her hand, of the way it shone softly in the darkness of her bedroom, casting a glow of well-being around it.

She thought of sweet little Harry, and the sparkle in his eye when he told her he was quite sure she was the right person to have the apple. If he was so sure, who was she to argue?

She kept her mouth shut.

At that moment Mason was abandoning that very strategy. When the evening began, he'd told himself that Hayley already knew far too much, and that his only chance of success was to stonewall her. Deep down inside, he'd hoped to enjoy her company for the few hours allowed him, before he had to resume the search, his number one priority. Now the beans had clearly been spilled, and it was too late.

He saw the conflicting emotions running over Hayley's features. She was starting to show the same zealous expression the rest of them wore every time they discussed the apple. Gold fever, perhaps. Whatever it was, it was instantly recognizable.

Shaking his head, Mason pushed his chair back an inch or two from the table. He'd seen enough of Hayley to realize that she was very stubborn and very determined. Now that she'd been bitten by the golden apple bug, she'd never give in and go away. It looked as though he had either a partner or another rival; the choice was up to him. Would he rather have Hayley for or against him?

He made up his mind quickly. "Hey, partner, how are you doing?"

"Fine," she whispered.

Oh great, she thought. *Now he turns nice and calls me his partner, just when I've decided to be a selfish pig and keep the apple to myself.*

She pushed away that ugly realization, reminding herself that the apple was hers; she didn't have to share it if she didn't want to. After all, what was Mason to her? She barely knew him. So what if for a few brief moments she'd labored under the misapprehension that he was her dream man? She'd been wrong. Anyone who couldn't remember her name was no dream man.

He knows your name now.

"Too bad," she said out loud. "That's just too darn bad."

"What did you say?" he asked, leaning closer.

"Nothing—just mumbling to myself."

"I'm a little worried about you. I thought for sure you'd be bombarding me with questions by now. What happened to all that curiosity?"

She nodded. He was right. The normal Hayley would've been interrogating the whole bunch of them. It wouldn't do to act differently and let on how confused and stupefied she felt. "So where is this thing from? You said it was Greek, and then you said Atlantis. I thought Atlantis was mythical, anyway."

"The whole thing's mythical," Angus allowed in a professorial voice. "And it's Atalanta, not Atlantis."

Mrs. Carmichael interrupted, "I already explained that. Or tried to, at any rate." She looked down her nose at Hayley.

"Cut it out, Carmelita," Mason said grimly. "Greek mythology isn't exactly something that comes up every day, so give the kid a break, will you?"

She wasn't sure she appreciated being called a kid, but the fact that he'd taken on Mrs. Carmichael on her behalf was gratifying. She smiled at him encouragingly, and he suddenly sat up as if she'd slapped him.

"I wish you wouldn't smile at me like that," he said gruffly.

She sobered immediately, although she hadn't the vaguest idea what his problem was. "Sorry."

"Look, Hayley," he continued, glaring at the tablecloth, "Atalanta is a name—a woman's name, in one of the classical Greek myths. The story was that she was the fastest runner around. So she said she'd marry any man who could outrun her, only nobody could, and they all were put to death when she beat them."

Her hazel eyes widened. "Nice lady."

He shrugged. "They didn't pull any punches in those days."

"It's only mythology," Angus interjected. "You know, fictitious, imaginary, as in mythic, as in those stories originating in preliterate societies, dealing with primordial beings and a primitive view of the world...."

"I know what mythology is!" Hayley fumed. "Now will you please tell me about the stupid apple?"

Mrs. Carmichael took up the story. "If we have to fill you in on the elementary details, you might as well hear them correctly, by which I mean, from *my* lips," she said grandly. "In any event, Atalanta won all the races, as you've heard. But then a youth named Hippomenes fell in love with her. He, too, would have to run the race, and most certainly lose. But the goddess Aphrodite—the goddess of love, I certainly hope you know that much—anyway, Aphrodite took pity on Hippomenes. She always had a fondness for young people in love."

Mrs. Carmichael smirked as she made the last comment, and Hayley blinked. The older woman was gossiping about these characters as if they were *real*.

"So," she continued, "Aphrodite gave Hippomenes three golden apples—pretty little things, you know—designed to catch the eye of an impressionable girl like Atalanta. And when young Hippomenes ran the race, he threw the apples off to one side to distract her. Indeed, she stooped to pick up the apples, giving Hippomenes enough time to win." She smiled happily. "Of course, I personally think that Atalanta was a little gone on him, too, and she let him win."

"Right," Hayley murmured, trying to maintain her sanity when everyone around her was acting extremely goofy. Did they really believe this stuff? Mason, too?

"Look, we know it sounds crazy," Mason said kindly, and Hayley relaxed a little. Whatever else, Mason had a strong aura of reality around him. "The next reference to a golden apple that I've found—I can't speak for the others—pops up in Renaissance Italy. The apple is painted into a portrait of a Venetian woman, and there's an entry in a monastic journal about it. The monk called it Atalanta's Apple, saying that it was one of the three Hippomenes had thrown in Atalanta's path, and that it came to this Venetian lady as a miracle. Any woman who owned it got three wishes. That's the legend, anyway."

"I—I see." Three wishes? As in, *only three, Miss Austin, only three*. As in Mrs. Carmichael and the busboy, and Mason sweeping her off her feet.

Hellfire and damnation, this was getting weirder and weirder. This kind of thing didn't happen to front-desk managers with perfectly normal lives. Why her? Why, out of all the people in the universe, did Hayley Austin get picked for this bonanza of weirdness?

"Of course," Angus pontificated, "there is some question as to the qualification that recipients be exclusively female. I myself wrote a monograph on that very subject in the *Journal of Historical Mythology*."

"We all saw it," Mrs. Carmichael grumbled. "Stuff and nonsense. I alone have pinpointed eight similar golden apple stories—all women. Anyone who pretends that that doesn't create a pattern is simply being obtuse."

"There is no reason a man couldn't claim the app—" Angus began, but Hayley cut him off. She didn't have the time or energy to waste on fine points.

"So far you've talked about Greece and Italy. But why are you all here, in Estes Park?"

Silence.

Mason stared at the tablecloth, Olivia batted her mascara-caked eyelashes at Mason, and Angus glared daggers at Olivia. Only Mrs. Carmichael seemed unfazed by the question. With a smug smile, she began to hum "Three Blind Mice" quite loudly.

"See how they run," she sang in an odd, tuneless soprano. "They all ran after *me*, you see, because I'm the only one who had the wherewithal to know where to go. They've all turned up here, hoping to catch at my crumbs, praying I'll lead them to the apple. So, you see, my dear front-desk person, they can't answer your impertinent question because they don't know why they're here."

"Mason, is this true? You don't know why you're here?"

"Unfortunately," he began.

Mrs. Carmichael cut him off cold. "Of course it's true! I was the first, wasn't I? And why do you think I was so angry when he arrived in that ridiculous Indiana Jones outfit?" Mrs. Carmichael was definitely on her high horse now. "I was righteously indignant, because he was horning in on *my* discoveries. It's totally unethical."

"But why not do your own work? Why follow *her*?" Hayley asked incredulously. "How can she possibly know more than the rest of you? I mean, he's written articles," she said, pointing at Angus. "And Mason, you run a museum. Shouldn't you be an expert?"

"I see Dr. Wilder hasn't told you that he is a lowly assistant curator at the Bendelow Museum of Western History. Have you ever heard of this museum? Of course not. No one has. And our dear Dr. Wilder catalogs miner's lamps and wheels off covered wagons. He is certainly no expert in antiquities!"

"Mrs. Carmichael, that's not fair," Olivia protested breathlessly. "Mason figured out about the apple being in Colorado, and that's how we all knew where to start looking, including you."

Mrs. Carmichael took a healthy swallow of wine, then cackled, "Wrong, wrong, wrong!"

"Well, if it wasn't Mason's story about the Colorado connection that brought you here, what was it?" Olivia inquired petulantly.

The others leaned forward expectantly, and Mason realized they had come to the point that everyone was waiting for.

"Why should I tell you?" Mrs. Carmichael asked with a smirk. "I know something—a big something—and all of you are in the dark. That's just the way I like it."

"You always did have the best sources," Mason offered sardonically. "Bribery and blackmail will do that."

Feigning boredom, Olivia pulled out a compact and reapplied her ruby-red lipstick. "She's lying. She doesn't know anything."

Mrs. Carmichael narrowed her beady eyes. "Ha! This is the discovery of a lifetime. I am proceeding on a tip of the first magnitude." She punctuated her words by jabbing her square index finger into the table. "No mere rumor, no mere gossip—but a bona fide *sighting*."

"Where?" Angus demanded. "Who told you? Where was the apple seen?"

"Oh, Angy, don't be so gullible. The old bat's making it all up."

"I have proof!" Mrs. Carmichael blustered.

Olivia examined herself in the mirror. "So prove it."

Much as she disliked the way Olivia looked and smelled, Hayley had to admit that the curvaceous brunette knew how to maneuver things to her best advantage. Frustrated and angry, with rusty color staining her cheeks, Mrs. Carmichael had grabbed her hefty handbag and was poking through it, obviously looking for the proof Olivia had demanded, the proof Mrs. Carmichael had planned to keep secret only a few seconds ago.

"Here!" she said, thrusting a crumpled postcard at them.

Mason jumped in and commandeered it first, while Hayley edged a little nearer, hoping to catch a peek. But when she leaned in, all she noticed was his delicious raspberry scent. A woman could get awfully attached to that smell.

He glanced at her as if he could read her mind, and she felt warmth suffuse her face.

"What is it?" he asked. "You look ill. Do you recognize something in the picture?"

Ill? She had let herself get lost in the smell of wild raspberries for three seconds, and he had the gall to say she looked ill. *Snap out of it,* she told herself angrily, and she focused on the item in his hand.

"It's a Stanley Hotel postcard," she said flatly. The dark green Stanley Steamer in the lobby was prominently featured on the front. She'd seen hundreds of that postcard come through the gift shop.

"The postmark on the back is Estes Park," Mason noted. "It was mailed in January. It says, 'Come and get it.' And it's signed, 'H. Peabody.'" Clearly suspicious, he looked at Carmelita. "So what?"

"Really!" Olivia sniffed. "It doesn't even say come and get *what*."

"You lured us up to this godforsaken place on the basis of that?" Angus's face was almost as red as Mrs. Carmichael's, and his shaggy eyebrows dipped toward each other in the center.

The older woman's breath was coming irregularly now, as if she were on the edge of hysteria. Obviously she didn't appreciate not being taken seriously. "There's more," she sputtered.

"I should certainly hope so," Angus grumbled.

"You are all Visigoths!" Mrs. Carmichael shouted. "Philistines! Infidels!" She retreated to her purse, this time coming up with a small Polaroid picture. "You'll all be singing a different tune when you see the pièce de résistance!''

This time Olivia grabbed it. Her neat, compact movements were quite unlike those of the fluttery coquette she'd been a few minutes ago. Chewing her flaming-red lips, she announced, "Looks like the genuine article, all right."

"The apple," Angus moaned. "My glorious apple."

"It could be faked, remember. It's just a picture," Mason warned. "What about these numbers? What do they mean?" He held up the Polaroid, showing the others its back, where the numbers 34 and 315 had been neatly printed.

"I didn't notice those before," Mrs. Carmichael gasped. "What can it mean? Room numbers, perhaps?"

As the others shared a heated discussion on the mysterious numbers, Hayley grew more and more impatient. She didn't give a fig about any silly numbers. "Can I see the picture?" she whispered. As Mason passed it to her, her heart sank. If she'd been holding on to any feeble hope that this could somehow be a different apple, she had to face facts when she saw the Polaroid.

It was definitely her apple—small, perfectly formed, radiantly gold. In the picture it was sitting on a small antique desk, the kind that graced half the rooms at The Stanley. Tourist flyers and brochures were scattered around it, and a patch of something green—a man's sleeve, perhaps—was just visible at the edge of the picture.

"Who sent you these things?" Mason asked the older woman.

"Well, I don't know," she admitted, losing a little steam. "They came in the mail—first the postcard, over a month ago, and then the photograph, in an envelope mailed from Estes Park. I'm certain that the person who sent me these things will show up here eventually and hand over the apple. To *me*, of course. Why else would he have singled me out like this?"

A postcard of the Stanley Steamer in the lobby, a picture of the apple, the suggestion of a dark green sleeve, *H.* Peabody...

There was only one person who tied it all together. "Harry," Hayley said bleakly.

"Harry who?" Mason asked quietly. "What are you talking about?"

Hayley opened her eyes in surprise. She hadn't realized she'd spoken aloud. "I didn't say anything."

"Look at her face!" Mrs. Carmichael cried, leaning across the dinner table to get closer to Hayley. "Do you know who sent me the postcard?"

"No," she protested, looking to Mason for help. "I don't know anything about anything."

Mrs. Carmichael's tiny eyes spit fire. "You'd better come clean."

On Hayley's left, Angus began to grumble. "If you're holding out on us, you'll regret it, lady."

She began to feel very nervous and very trapped. With Angus huge and angry on one side, Mason's blue eyes regarding her intently on the other, and Mrs. Carmichael blazing across the table, there was nowhere to run. Besides, they all knew by now that she worked at the hotel. Even if, by some miracle, she managed to escape now, they'd know where to find her.

So what could she say to pacify them? Her mind raced through possible stories, but never for one moment did she consider telling them the truth.

She couldn't give it up. She wouldn't give it up. It was as if the apple's spell continued to spin from a distance, pulling at her, wrapping her in unbreakable golden threads. It might be safe back at her house, but its impact was as strong as if it were here in the room with them.

Amid the tumult in her brain, one thought remained crystal clear. *It belongs to me.*

Wetting her lips, she managed to tell them, "The Stanley Steamer in the postcard reminded me of someone." Lying through her teeth, she added, "But I'm sure he doesn't have anything to do with your Atlantis Apple."

"Atalanta," Angus, Mrs. Carmichael and Olivia chorused.

Hayley bit back a smile. She'd called it Atlantis on purpose to distract them.

It didn't provide much of a respite. "Get on with it!" Angus demanded.

"Okay, okay." Hayley clasped her hands and tried to appear truthful. "There was a strange little man hiding behind the Steamer in the lobby yesterday. He hissed at me when I was on duty at the desk. And seeing the car in the postcard, I thought of him, that's all."

"He hissed at you?" Mason was gazing at her shrewdly, and she had the feeling that her innocent story hadn't fooled him one bit.

Mrs. Carmichael's ample chin quivered with excitement. "It must have been him. Don't you see? He was waiting at that car for *me*."

"What did he look like?"

"What was he wearing?"

"Did he say anything else to you, anything at all?"

"Is he staying at the hotel? Is he a guest?"

"Have you ever seen him before?"

As the three of them hurled questions at her, Hayley began to panic. Normally a truthful person, she couldn't think up lies that fast.

"Hold on, will you?" Mason interrupted. "We don't know this is your Peabody. In fact, it's quite a stretch even to throw that out as a theory."

"I'm sure!" Mrs. Carmichael bellowed. "I have an instinct about these things."

Olivia lifted her alabaster shoulders, exposing a dangerous amount of creamy bosom. "It's a start," she said ingenuously.

On Hayley's left, Angus managed to ignore Olivia's display of cleavage as he pushed closer to Hayley and grabbed her shoulder with a huge hand. "What did he look like?"

"Calm down," Mason commanded, "and take your hands off her."

The others treated him as if he didn't exist.

"What did he say to you?" Mrs. Carmichael asked, impatiently rising from her chair and shoving her way past Mason.

Olivia practically leaped over the table to join the fray. "Would you recognize him if you saw him again?"

"She's actually seen him! Do you believe it?" Angus shouted. "He has the apple and she's actually seen him! Quick—what did he look like?"

Hayley cringed under the onslaught of strange heads invading her personal space, loud voices ringing in her ears, and fingers poking at her. The guilt she was already suffering from only added to the burden.

"If you people don't back off, I'm going to scream!"

Mason muscled through the inquisitors. "I told you to leave her alone," he said angrily, prying Olivia away from Hayley's chair.

"I've had just about enough, of you, Wilder!" Angus blared.

"Calm down, Angus."

"No one tells me to calm down. Now take your hands off Olivia, you swine!" His face was redder than his hair as he tried to get a hammy fist on Mason's lapel.

Olivia went for Angus's arm, Mrs. Carmichael stamped her feet and shouted at them, Angus swung at Mason with a roundhouse punch, and Mason ducked at exactly the right moment, catching Hayley in one hand and their coats in the other. Bent like Groucho Marx, he pulled her safely out of her seat while the controversy raged on.

Still crouching, trying for cover, they angled between two tables and moved farther out of the way, but there was no way they could make it back past that rowdy bunch and out the door into the lobby.

It was Hayley's turn to take the initiative. After all, this was home turf to her, and she might as well use every advantage. Luckily, their position wasn't far from the door to the kitchen, and she knew that was the best way to make an escape.

"There's no time to lose," she called, leading him swiftly on a winding path through the kitchen and out the back door. She waved at the astonished chef, who stopped his preparation of a crepe in midflip. Amazingly enough, she felt like laughing.

They shrugged into their coats as they ran, hitting exhilarating, frosty air as soon as they cleared the kitchen door. Then she turned back to look at her companion.

"Well," he said with a cynical smile. "If we weren't partners before, I'd say we are now. That's two escapes we've made together, just in the nick of time."

"I owed you one," she said softly.

"Right." He took her arm and steered her away from the hotel and toward the smaller buildings that held employees during the tourist season. Wearing a fresh layer of snow, everything looked bright and clean, and the lights from the hotel cast tiny sparkles onto the white blanket around them.

Mason's expression was enigmatic as he gazed down at her. "Hayley, I think you'd better tell me. I distinctly heard you say the name Harry. What is it you're hiding?"

She shut her eyes. It was impossible to look at him and hold back.

A part of her actually wanted to tell him. But a stronger part kept presenting her with an image of Harry's face. *The apple is meant for you.* Her brain repeated the litany. *The apple is yours, and he'll take it away. He'll put it in an old museum. He'll lock it away forever.*

She couldn't share it. In her heart of hearts, she knew it wasn't right. So she made her eyes wide and innocent and quietly said, "I don't know anything more than I've already told you."

"I thought you wanted to be partners."

She met that chilly blue gaze with all of her courage. "Are you suggesting I'm lying to you?"

He considered a moment, then finally sighed. "I'm not sure of anything at this point."

"Look, I'll say this much." She paced on, listening to her footfalls in the crisp snow. "I wouldn't be surprised if he did have something to do with your search for the apple. He was definitely strange, and he was definitely hanging around the Stanley Steamer. That fits with Mrs. Carmichael's postcard, don't you think?"

Mason nodded. He slipped his hands into the pockets of his soft suede jacket, simply walking beside her as she circled down the hill toward the main road.

She almost wished he'd be curt and stuffy again, the way he'd acted after he'd carried her out of the dining room. That way she could shore up some righteous indignation and be angry with him. When he was acting so sweetly, it was difficult to dislike him. In fact, it was hard not to throw her arms around him and beg to be carried off again.

Oh, he was still big, intimidating, and occasionally infuriating, but there was something underneath all that size she really liked—something kind and maybe a little shy. But whatever she thought of him, it wouldn't do to get too attached.

She had the apple; he wanted it. And she wasn't giving it up. It was called "an irreconcilable difference."

She put the apple first and foremost in her mind and proceeded from there. "Mason," she said tentatively, as she led him down a snowy knoll, "will you tell me something?"

"I suppose."

"Why would this apple end up in Colorado?"

"Scottie MacPherson," he announced, as if that said it all.

"As in Olivia MacPherson?"

"Olivia is Scottie's great-granddaughter."

She stopped underneath a tall outcropping of rock, next to a pretty little pond. It was a peaceful place; sounds from the highway and the hotel were muffled by the ring of rock and the snow covering.

She gazed at the ice on the pond for a moment before continuing. She was weary of this apple business, yet still very curious about what exactly it was and where it came from. "Are you going to tell me about this Scottie?"

Mason shrugged. "She's the link. She's my claim to fame."

"I don't understand. Did you discover her or something?"

"Oh, no. She's an authentic, verifiable part of Colorado history. A lot of people know about her. I just connected her to Atalanta's Apple."

Hayley stood back and watched him, waiting for more. His features had once again taken on that intense, obsessed look she found so fascinating. She wondered if he realized how his face lit up when he talked about the apple.

"I was putting together an exhibit on Cripple Creek," he told her, "on the gold-mining days. And I kept running across all these odd stories about Scottie MacPherson. They sounded very familiar, especially when I got to the part about a golden apple that came with three wishes." Becoming absorbed in the story, Mason leaned closer to Hayley. His eyes glowed with a warm, inviting light, as radiant as the apple he was seeking, Hayley thought.

"Scottie MacPherson was a gold miner, and not a very good one. From all reports, she was a cantankerous, scrappy little thing. The way she dressed and behaved, half of Cripple Creek thought she was a boy. But then she hit a big strike, and overnight she was a millionaire. Suddenly she had a passel full of dresses straight from France, and a big house full of expensive things. Now everyone knew she was a woman—in spades. It seems Scottie was beautiful when she got out from under all those layers of dirt."

"She got rich because she had Atalanta's Apple?"

"MacPherson's Folly," Mason said softly. "That's what they called it—MacPherson's Folly."

"I don't understand."

"Apparently no one in Cripple Creek was smart enough to connect Scottie's apple to the one in the Greek myth. And because of the way her story ended, the newspaper boys dubbed her apple MacPherson's Folly."

"Sounds like her story doesn't end happily." Feeling edgy, she blew upon her hands and then shook them to try to keep them warm.

"Nope. No happy ending here. Scottie MacPherson fell in love." Absently noting that she must be cold, Mason took her hands between both of his, rubbing them gently. It was a gesture that meant nothing when he started, the kind of thing he would've done for one of his younger sisters. But when he touched her, when he felt her hands tremble inside his, he knew with absolute certainty that his feelings for her were not brotherly.

A smarter man might have dropped her hands right then and there—put temptation that much farther out of reach. But Mason held on more tightly. He felt the warmth of his hands flow into hers, the depth of his commitment to his mission communicate itself to her, as he continued his bittersweet story.

"Scottie made the mistake of confiding in her boyfriend about the secret of her great gold strike. She told him that she had been given an apple that came with three wishes, and that she'd only used two."

His voice was steady and low, its tone almost hypnotic. He was staring into Hayley's eyes as he spoke, and she was lost in that dazzling, aquamarine gaze. She was caught by the vision of the long-dead woman who'd wished on a golden apple, as she had. "And?" she managed.

"Not what you'll want to hear."

"Try me," she said, her breathy voice urging him on.

"The boyfriend—he stole the apple and lit out for Denver." He dropped his gaze. "He got caught in a snowstorm and froze to death."

"Oh, dear." It wasn't what she'd hoped to hear. "A-and the apple?" she asked softly.

"Disappeared. The legend says that they found the boyfriend's body with his hands outstretched in front of him, as if he were trying to hold on to the apple. But no one ever saw it again. Scottie lost the man she loved and the apple, too, because she chose unwisely, I guess."

She shivered, and he couldn't resist pulling her within the circle of his arm.

"That's creepy," she murmured, huddling a little closer.

He touched the tip of her nose with one finger. "That's how the old stories operate," he said lightly. "There has to be a moral, you know. At the time, they concluded that since he took something that wasn't rightfully his, he could only come to a bad end. Something to keep the kiddies from filching each other's toys, I guess. But oddly enough, that part of the story seems to recur in the other accounts of the apple. It's almost like a curse. Anyone who tries to steal it runs into tragedy in the end."

Hayley took a deep breath. What if the apple wasn't rightfully hers? What is she could only reap tragedy from it?

"Come on," Mason cajoled. "Don't look so stricken. It's all nonsense."

"Are you sure?"

"Of course I'm sure. People like to believe in magic and spooky old stories, because sometimes real life doesn't make a whole lot of sense. It's natural to turn to make-believe to sort it all out for you. But that doesn't mean it's true."

"But you believe in Scottie and the apple—you said so yourself."

"I believe that the apple exists, that it's very old and very valuable, and I know that the museum that owns it will be on the map. But it's not magic." The expression in his eyes softened. "I'm not looking for magic wishes, Hayley. All I want is to find Scottie MacPherson's apple and go back to Omaha."

Go back to Omaha? Was that what he wanted? Somehow, standing so close to him, she couldn't believe it was true. And when he raised a finger to stroke her cheek, she knew she was right. She couldn't look away from his striking, pale blue eyes. Now, as she watched, they seemed to shine with warmth and a strange kind of comfort.

"That's all you want?" she whispered. "That's all?"

He didn't answer. Instead, he leaned closer, as if he might kiss her. She held her breath and waited for the kiss to come, but as Mason edged nearer, one shoulder dipped. And over that shoulder she saw something—someone—clearly outlined in the soft moonlight. He was beaming at her.

Harry. Harry Peabody, in the flesh.

Chapter Six

Hayley murmured something indistinguishable and slipped away from him. Mason closed his eyes and swore at himself. What the hell had he thought he was doing? He wasn't the kind of man who kissed women he barely knew!

His affairs were part of a well-ordered life that included such niceties as dating and dinners and chaste good-night kisses at the lady's front door. "Thank you for a lovely evening." "You're very welcome." And then a sedate brush of lips that meant nothing to either party.

He couldn't remember the last time he'd kissed a woman purely on impulse, simply because he wanted to touch her and to feel her, simply because his emotions were running away with him. But that was exactly what had almost happened here, only seconds ago. If Hayley hadn't pulled away, he knew he would've been lost. Even now he felt a physical hunger, wanting the warmth and the closeness she offered, emotions he hadn't felt in a long, long time.

Hayley wasn't thinking. Full of unresolved longing and utter confusion, she was standing exactly where she'd spotted Harry. But once again, the little man had conveniently disappeared. "I can't believe this," she muttered, turning around. Mason stood where she'd left him, looking bereft and bewildered. "Oh, Mason." The memory of his finger on her cheek, the flutter in her stomach as he'd leaned down to her, repenetrated her consciousness. "Oh, *Mason*. Look, I'm sorry. It's just that—"

"No, no problem." He held a hand up to forestall her. "You're right. I should be the one who's sorry. I guess I got a little carried away." As he looked at her, he saw that her cheeks were flushed with the cold, the dark waves of her hair tousled by the chilly breezes. Her nose was pink, her eyes were wide and soft, and she looked wonderful. And he couldn't feel sorry that he'd almost kissed her, even if the timing had been deplorable and his priorities seriously askew.

He shoved his hands into his pockets. Somewhere along the line, his glasses had begun to steam over, and he jammed those into his pocket, too.

"Mason, it's okay," she told him, but it wasn't. When a rational person would've been packing her bags and taking a long vacation from the whole mess, she found herself enchanted by this man.

And what on earth had happened to Harry? Why had he popped up like that, and why had he disappeared?

"Maybe he didn't want you to kiss me," she whispered. "Maybe he's trying to tell me you're not the right man."

"What did you say?"

She smiled nervously. "Nothing. Just mumbling to myself." *Trying desperately to figure out what the heck is happening to me.*

"You seem to do a lot of that," he said thoughtfully. "Next time, speak up, okay?" He gave her a suspicious look. "I'm afraid of what I may be missing."

She gave him a dazed smile, feeling utterly confused. Pieces of their conversation floated through her mind, as hazy and as chilling as the mist from the mountains.

*MacPherson's Folly...that's what they called it—
MacPherson's Folly. No happy ending here...Scottie made
the mistake of confiding in her boyfriend about the golden
apple. She lost the man she loved and the apple, too, because she chose unwisely.*

Once upon a time, did Scottie MacPherson kiss a stranger
in the moonlight? Was that how it all began?

Hayley shivered and turned up her collar. Whatever she
did, whatever she decided about Mason, she was determined not to repeat Scottie MacPherson's mistakes.

"I THOUGHT we were supposed to be partners. Where have
you been for the last three days?"

Hayley pretended she hadn't seen him standing there on
the other side of the front desk for approximately five minutes. "I've been busy," she said defiantly, studiously sur-
veying the guest register. "And we never actually *decided*,
formally or otherwise, that we were going to be partners. I
brought it up and you refused, and then you assumed it was
all set, but we never *settled* anything."

"It was settled. You know it as well as I do."

"Come on, Mason, don't give me a hard time about
this."

She finally looked him in the eye, and was immediately
sorry. For three long days she had been staring at her apple
and thinking about Mason, trying to convince herself she
was doing the right thing by keeping her mouth shut and the
apple to herself. She hadn't exactly been avoiding him, but
she hadn't gone looking for him, either. She'd wanted to
figure it all out in her head before she had to face him again.

Seeing him again, staring into those aquamarine eyes, all
she wanted to do was ravish the man—now, before she had
a chance to think better of it. Wouldn't that be an attrac-

tive picture—the manager ravishing a guest over the front desk?

No swooning allowed at work, she ordered herself. Briskly she set about sorting the loose hotel keys, stuffing them into the appropriate cubbyholes with a vengeance. She turned back, saying, "It isn't like you need me or anything. You're an expert at this stuff, and I'm only a front-desk manager, as Mrs. Carmichael is so fond of pointing out."

Mason smiled wickedly. "She keeps calling you a 'lowly desk clerk,' but I don't suppose her inaccuracies are your concern."

Hayley set her lips firmly, ignoring his attempt at humor. "I have work to do, Mason. I applied for a promotion not long ago, and I have to work if I want them to take me seriously. I can't get embroiled in any craziness."

"Stop fighting so hard, will you?" He leaned over the desk far enough to catch her hand and to maneuver her around his way. "Since when does the manager file keys?"

"When there are keys to be filed."

"So delegate."

She jiggled the basket of keys noisily with her free hand, but didn't reply.

"I don't get this," he said slowly. "The last time I saw you, you were as caught up in finding the—" he glanced around quickly and dropped his voice "—the *apple*...as the rest of us. Don't even bother to argue. I saw the greedy look in your eyes. Carmelita, Olivia, Angus—even me—we've all got the fever, too, and believe me, I recognize the profile. But now you're acting like you've washed your hands of the whole thing. I mean, I've been looking for you since Tuesday, and you've been impossible to find. Now you pop up behind the desk, and you pretend not to be interested anymore. I don't buy it."

Watching her steadily, he tugged her closer, so that they were separated at the waist by the width of the desk, but at the head by only a few inches. She had no choice but to stand there, transfixed.

"Tell me the truth," he said flatly. "Are you looking on your own now?"

Her mouth dropped open. "Of course not. I wouldn't do that! I have some integrity, you know."

"Then what's the story?"

"There isn't any story. I needed some time to think, that's all. Lost antiquities and partnerships and moonlight encounters—it was all happening pretty fast, you know. Anyway—" she tried to change tactics "—you should be thanking me! You're the one who insisted you didn't want a partner in any way, shape, or form. Remember that?"

"Yes, as a matter of fact I do. But I changed my mind."

"And why exactly did you do that?"

He looked down at her and didn't say a word. It was a very good question, and he didn't have an answer. All he knew was that once he'd made up his mind that the two of them were going to operate as a team, a door had closed in his mind. Decision made; discussion ended.

He was opinionated and inflexible. He knew himself well enough to realize that, but he was also smart and extremely competent at the endeavors he undertook. If anyone had a right to be stubborn, he did.

"I don't know why I changed my mind," he said finally. "And I don't care. I refuse to drive myself crazy, trying to figure out what I think. I think it, that's all."

"Well, you can think it all you want, but that doesn't mean I have to." Hayley tried to maintain a certain businesslike rigidity as she pulled her hands away from him and retreated to safety on her side of the desk.

"So you've decided you don't want in on the search for Scottie MacPherson's apple? I can't believe you're serious."

"I'm not!" She shook her head. That made no sense at all. She *was* serious; she simply wasn't sure about what. "What I mean is that I haven't decided anything yet. You have to admit, it's been very strange so far. It's not the kind of thing a person jumps into without some serious consideration."

Mason sent her a wary glance. "I don't get it. You were more than willing to jump in headfirst the first time I met you. You didn't seem to need to take the time for serious consideration then."

But that was before she knew he was looking for her apple. That was before he almost kissed her....

"I know it sound preposterous," he told her, "but Scottie MacPherson's apple is perfectly real. I have all sorts of documentation to prove it. The other stuff—whether it's Atalanta's Apple, whether it's magical—well, I can see where you'd find that incredible. I do myself. But don't you see?"

His voice dropped into a rougher, more persuasive register. "We have to get our hands on the apple if we want answers. Hayley, we can be a part of history if we find this thing—even if it's just Scottie's apple, not Atalanta's, even if it's just a lump of gold and not magical at all. How can you pass up being a part of history?"

"Easy."

"Not for me," he said fiercely.

Once again she was surprised by his intensity. "Why is this so important to you, Mason? What do you think you'll get if you find the apple?"

"Let's just say I have personal reasons for wanting it." He stood in profile, with the sun from the lobby windows lighting him from behind. It was quite an appealing picture. "I want it, and I'm going to have it."

"That's fine for you. But why me?"

Her mournful question carried several extra levels of meaning that he couldn't possibly understand. Why had she been given the apple in the first place? Why had she been the one to meet this man at this time? Why had she been the one to get sucked into this thing against every scrap of better judgment she possessed?

"You're the only one who's seen Peabody," he said flatly. "If he's got it, you and I will have an edge in finding him."

"I should've known it wasn't my fatal charm."

"Excuse me?"

"Nothing."

"So?"

"So what?"

"Are we partners or not? Will you help me find Peabody?"

"All I saw was a weird little man named Harry. I told you, I don't think he's your Peabody."

"You're lying," he said calmly. "Something about Carmelita's Polaroid made you sure Harry was Peabody. I knew it the moment I saw your face."

He was right, and she was tired of arguing. "Meg," she called out to the girl behind her, "I'm leaving. Cover the desk."

Slipping out the back door, she met Mason in the lobby.

"Okay," she announced, before he could open his mouth. "Have you ever seen *Miracle on Thirty-fourth Street*? Good. Harry looked just like Santa Claus—short, plump, white hair and a full beard. Twinkly eyes, round cheeks, the whole shot. He didn't say he was staying at the hotel, but the Polaroid was taken in a room here. I recognized the kind of desk the apple was sitting on, plus it was next to the brochures we leave for guests. And as for Harry..." She took a deep breath. "I made the connection because of a green section in the bottom corner of the picture. I'm pretty sure it's Harry's sleeve. He was wearing a dark green corduroy suit the day he was hiding behind the Stanley Steamer." The same day he'd given her the apple and started this whole mess.

"I was sure you knew something." Mason winked at her. "I knew it! This is a big jump on the others. Have you seen him again since then?"

She shook her head.

"Maybe you could look him up in the hotel records, check on when he was here, get his home address, that kind of thing?"

"I don't think so. It sounds very unethical." She could almost see a snappy retort forming on his lips, and added, "If you're done with me, I'd like to get back to work."

"Done with you? You can't leave. We're only getting started."

"This is your battle, Mason, your hunt for ancient treasure, your search for fame and glory." Oh, how she wished she were telling the truth. "This has nothing to do with me."

There was silence between them for a long moment.

Finally Mason said coolly, "It's because of the other night, isn't it? You don't want to help me because I almost kissed you."

"That has nothing to do with anything," she returned angrily, getting stirred up and ornery, the way she did only when her back was against the wall. What was it about Mason that brought out her worst impulses? "I'm just not the kind of person who falls for cockamamie stories about magic apples and cockamamie men from Omaha! I want my normal life back, if it's all the same to you."

"If it's the apple that's bothering you, I don't believe it's magical any more than you do."

"I don't know what I believe," she muttered.

He shook his head. "I don't understand any of this. What was that about Omaha? What difference does it make where I'm from?"

"It makes a difference where you're going back to."

"Oh." His eyes narrowed at her as comprehension dawned. "Isn't it a little early to worry about that?"

"I prefer not to play with fire," she responded politely.

"How about if I promised nothing personal would happen between us?"

"I don't care what you promise." As a bright, intelligent woman, she knew it when she saw the handwriting on the wall. If the Scottie MacPherson story was any indication, if Mason was indeed the misbegotten answer to a wish, she wouldn't have a choice. She would fall for him, hand him his apple on a silver platter, and end up just like Scottie, with no apple and no lover.

"Why don't you look at the proof I've got?" he asked gently. "You won't think this is such a crackpot idea, once you see all the history behind it."

"I assure you, I don't think it's a crackpot idea."

"Then come up to my room and see what I've collected on it. It's fascinating, irresistible." He couldn't believe he was pushing this hard. Wasn't he the one who'd said he wouldn't want a partner in a million years? So why was he trying so hard to convince her? He hadn't the vaguest idea. "Hayley, when you see the pictures of this apple, you won't be able to say no. You'll want to find it as much as I do."

Against her will, the apple's image invaded her mind. She could see it sitting in the palm of her hand, glowing and inviting. She could feel its warmth, its amazing aura of spirit and life.

"I would like to see the pictures," she said slowly. "I'd like to know where it came from."

"Then what are you waiting for?"

"Mason," she ventured, "this isn't like going up to see your etchings or anything, is it?"

But he had already started up the stairs; she followed reluctantly. She was in relatively good shape, so it was annoying to be huffing and puffing by the time they hit the fourth floor.

"What have you got against taking the elevator?"

"Didn't want to wait," he said absently, opening the door to his room.

It was a pretty room, one of Hayley's personal favorites, sunny and bright, with a great view of the mountains off its tiny breakfast nook. White wicker chairs and a glass-topped table were wedged into the small space.

The Stanley's rooms had always appeared spacious to Hayley. Handing out keys across the front desk, she'd never had the slightest qualms in assuring guests that they were getting accommodations with elbowroom to spare. But Mason's room suddenly seemed tiny and stuffy, even claustrophobic.

Was it because he was so large, or because he was there at all? Crossing her arms over her chest, she took a few deep breaths and hovered by the door.

"You realize this is the floor we get the most complaints about, don't you?" she asked, watching as he dragged file folders out of a bulging leather briefcase. "As far as being haunted, I mean."

Mason shrugged. "I don't believe in ghosts."

"I didn't use to."

He glanced up at her. "You do now?"

"Working here—" she smiled ruefully "—it's hard not to." Her eyes skittered around the room that looked perfectly serene in the bright light of day. But she'd been up here after dark, and she knew things seemed very different then. "This place has such a sense of the past," she murmured. "I don't know how to explain it except to say that I've always believed in *possibilities* here, like the possibility of magic or ghosts, even when I was a little girl."

"Then I guess it's the perfect place for Atalanta's Apple to show up after all these years."

"Ah, yes, the apple."

He reached out to hand her a large, glossy photograph, obviously taken of a painting. Depicting a comfortably plump lady half reclining on a salon chair, the original painting evidenced the rich color and dramatic strokes of a Renaissance master. The woman in the picture wore a low-cut, high-waisted gown of opulent emerald-green brocade, and glorious, red-gold hair spilled carelessly over her creamy bosom. Even in the photo, the fabric of her dress seemed thick and luxurious, and there was a glimmer of humor in the sedate smile she had focused on the artist.

It was a wonderful portrait, full of life and color. But its focal point was what she held in her hand.

The apple, of course.

It managed to outshine the beautiful Renaissance lady, her splendid clothes, jewels and hair. Hayley's finger traced a circle around the small place in the photograph where the golden orb beamed so brightly.

"It's caught you, too." He leaned over her shoulder to gaze at the picture. He felt inexplicably pleased to share the apple with someone, to share his research and his evidence, and to feel that even in a small way, someone else understood. "Does it look like you expected?"

She looked up, surprised at the question.

"Most people expect it to be bigger, for some reason," he explained.

"Oh, no," she said with an ironic twist. "It looks exactly like I expected."

Quickly he laid out a series of photographs and drawings showing the apple and its path through history, and beckoned her to sit beside him on the bed to peruse the evidence. Without thinking, Hayley abandoned her safe place near the door and joined him on the edge of the bed.

She wanted to see it. She wanted to see who'd owned it before.

Her eyes flashed past a pen-and-ink sketch of a woman with powdered hair and small, greedy eyes—she held the apple between both her hands, as if she were guarding it jealously—to a rather murky reproduction of another painting. This one featured a sullen young girl cowering under a tall ivory comb and lace mantilla. The apple wasn't in the picture, but the girl wore a tiny replica on a chain around her neck. And then there was a drawing of a plain lady with a sensual smile that belied her severe Puritan dress.

Hayley scanned the array of pictures around her. Each lady was different, yet they shared a common golden thread.

"They're all young, they're all female," she whispered, "and they all look..." There was only one word for it. "Hungry." She had the immediate desire to look at herself in the mirror, to see if that rapacious appetite marked her face, too.

Mason couldn't understand her sudden display of concern. "Oh, yes, they're all female. Regardless of what Angus says."

She found his eyes. "Mason, is that the reason you want me along?"

"I'm sorry. I don't follow you. Is what the reason?"

"The legend!" She knew she wasn't being particularly enlightening, and she tried to slow down. "The legend said that a person would reap only tragedy if it wasn't rightfully his, right? And you aren't female, after all.''

"And?''

"And I am. Female, I mean.'' Intent on getting her message across, she turned and laid a restless hand upon his arm. "I know you say you don't believe in the magic part of the apple, but I think maybe you do, deep down. I think maybe you're afraid you'll find it, and end up like Scottie MacPherson's boyfriend, frozen to death in a snowbank somewhere. Or something equally ugly,'' she added hastily.

"Hayley, that's crazy.'' A slight smile curved his narrow lips. Of all the reasons he'd wanted her along on the search, escaping the curse was not one of them. "It's only a little gold apple. I just want to put it in my museum. How can you think I'd be worried about some silly curse?''

"How can you not be worried about the curse? You have a brain, don't you? Look what happened to Scottie MacPherson's boyfriend.''

"He was stupid. He went out in a blizzard. People die in blizzards all the time. It has nothing to do with curses or legends, just pure stupidity. And luckily,'' he said lightly, covering her hand with his own, enjoying the idea that she might be concerned for him, "I'm not stupid.''

"I know.'' She sighed and maneuvered herself away from him, picking up a picture at random from the pile on the bed.

Whatever his reasons for wanting her as a partner, whether it was because she was a convenient female to nullify the curse, because she'd seen Peabody, or even because he liked her company, he obviously *did* want her along.

It was sort of flattering. He'd shared his precious papers with her, he'd offered to bring her in on something that was of vital importance to himself, and she felt touched. For a moment she almost wished she'd never seen the apple, so that she could throw herself into the search for it with complete abandon.

Permitting herself one last, small sigh, she glanced down at the photograph she'd picked up. It was Scottie Mac-Pherson. It had to be. She was a small woman, posed formally in a chair, with an open book in her lap. Her eyes were dark and rather sad as she stared unsmiling into the camera; her dress was severely wasp-waisted and high-necked, with huge puffed sleeves and lots of drippy ruffles. Inside the stiff, elaborate dress, the woman looked skinny, desperate, defiant.

Harry, you idiot, how could you give the apple to her? Hayley thought indignantly. Anyone with a particle of sense could tell that this miserable woman would only squander her wishes.

"Good heavens." She dropped the picture and sat back on the bed. "I'm really starting to believe that Harry trips along from century to century, handing the apple out like a good-conduct medal. I've started taking it for granted that the thing gives wishes. I must be losing my mind."

Mason slid a comforting arm around her shoulders, giving her a small squeeze. "Don't worry. It happens to the best of us. I don't know whether it's the thrill of the hunt or a lust for gold, but all of us go a little overboard where the apple is concerned. It's only a momentary lapse—a momentary loss of perspective on reality."

"I haven't seen you doing any lapsing."

"Well, then, look at Carmelita. I still can't believe she came after me with her umbrella like that."

"I don't want to have anything in common with Carmelita Carmichael, thank you very much."

"It's too late," he told her softly. "You already do. You see the apple in the pictures, and you're consumed by it, just like Carmelita and just like me. You don't have a choice anymore. You're in on the hunt."

"It's a toy, Mason." She focused on the picture of the sulky Spanish girl with the miniature apple around her neck. "Why should it control us like this? It's only a toy."

"It's a very valuable toy."

She rose from the bed, letting Mason's carefully assembled exhibits tumble to the floor. "You could at least tell me why it's so important to you." She sent a quick glance in his direction. "And don't bother to tell me it's the money, because I don't believe it. You're not the type to expend all this effort for pure greed."

He smiled but didn't offer further information.

"It might be competition. You do seem to be keen on beating out the others." She considered. "Naah. I just don't think that's enough of a reason to send you racing up here from Omaha on the off-chance there might be a clue."

Once again, all she got was an enigmatic smile.

"Come on, Mason," she said impatiently. "I'm a good listener. You said before that you had personal reasons, that you wanted to be a part of history. What did you mean?"

He shrugged. "It's exactly what I told you then. The museum that gets Atalanta's Apple will be famous—infamous, even. Personally, I'd be at the pinnacle of my profession. It's like uncovering Troy or King Tut's tomb or finding the Dead Sea Scrolls. What's so hard to understand about wanting that?"

"You. You don't fit that picture." She began to pace in front of him, her arms once more folded across her chest. "You're the guy who hauled me out of the dining room like a hero and then beat a hasty exit because you didn't want to be the center of attention. You were the one who blushed when I told you you smelled like raspberries. These are not the actions of a man on a collision course with fame and glory and the spotlight of the historical world."

"Stop pacing like that. You're driving me up the wall," he muttered. When she didn't stop, he stood up and yanked her back onto the bed.

"Tell me why!" she persisted.

"None of your business."

"I'm your partner, aren't I? I deserve to know."

"I said it's none of your business."

"I don't accept that."

"Hayley!" He reached around to shake her, but only got as far as clasping her shoulders before he gave in. His voice sounded gruff as his fingers twined around a loose strand of her chestnut hair. "You are the nosiest woman alive."

"I prefer to call it curious," she whispered.

Dimly she wondered why she'd never noticed how sexy a man could look wearing wire-rimmed glasses. Her gaze wandered to his narrow, sensual lips. They were slightly parted and he was breathing unevenly.

Damn. Desire ran through her body like warm honey. She tried to breathe, but all she got was raspberry-scented air. She tried to speak, but no words came out. She had no weapons against this kind of erotic onslaught.

Who wanted weapons? At the moment, she was more than willing to beat her sword into a plowshare.

"Are you going to kiss me?" she asked breathlessly.

"I'm thinking about it."

"Don't think too long."

His better judgment might have decided it was all for the best that he hadn't kissed her before, but this time he didn't plan to behave so nobly. With a groan, he lowered his mouth to hers, kissing her fiercely, demandingly.

He seemed dangerous, hungry, hot, as if he knew exactly what he wanted and how to go about getting it. Hayley had never seen him like this—except when it concerned the apple.

They were all ruthless on that score.

She blocked that picture out of her mind. This was the wrong time to think about the apple. Temptation, yes—apples, no.

The remaining photographs and drawings scattered off the bed as Mason pulled her back into the pillows and fitted her up against his long, lean body. He slid elusive, clever hands along her back, branding her through the silk of her blouse, tracing the line of one shoulder, the edge of her jaw. His fingers framed her face as he paused, gazing into her eyes.

Without realizing what she was doing, she slid his glasses off his nose and dropped them over the side of the bed on top of the mass of papers.

"I like you when you're being forceful," she murmured.

"I like you all the time."

Still holding her face between his large hands, he angled over her and met her mouth with his own. He tasted delicious, liquid, tantalizing.

She took the kiss as ardently as it was offered, wrapping herself in the golden glow of sensation. But he murmured her name and brushed his lips over her cheek, and guilt began to cast shadows around the edges of her desire.

"Mason, I—"

"Hmm?"

"About the apple—"

He propped himself up on one elbow, absently sketching the curve of her ear with one fingertip. "What is it?"

He was warm, he was gentle, he was so sweet it knocked her socks off. She was alive, she was melting, and everything else—including the damned apple—would have to wait.

''The hell with it.''

She pulled him against her, kissing him with every ounce of pent-up energy and passion she'd been holding on to for years.

Chapter Seven

Crash. Bang. Boom.

Hayley realized that the exaggerated pounding was not her heart only when Angus's voice blasted through the door, following hard upon his knocks.

"Wilder—open up in there!"

Mason groaned and rested his forehead against hers, but made no move for the door.

She took his face into her hands and tried to reconstruct the intimacy of a moment ago. "Don't answer," she whispered.

"Wilder, answer the door! I know you're in there! And she's with you, isn't she?"

His long body grew very still, and Mason stared blankly at Hayley. "What could he want with you?"

"He means Olivia, you fool, not me."

"I heard voices! Open this door or I'll kick it down! This is important, you fool!"

"I don't like being called a fool twice in five seconds," Mason said ominously.

"Don't answer the door," she hissed.

"Wilder?" Angus continued. "This is crucial, vital, of the utmost significance. We must talk at once!"

Mason drew back from Hayley's arms. "It must be about the apple," he said tersely.

"Who cares?" Actually she did. A lot. Not about what Angus had to say about the apple, but about Mason's apparent willingness to drop everything in its pursuit.

She felt like belting him one. Instead, she grumbled, "So go. Leave me behind like a TV rerun. Find out what Angus has to tell you about your precious apple."

He was already halfway to the door.

The second the handle clicked, Angus came storming in, "Where is she?"

Hayley sat up on the bed and hugged her knees. "Hi, there," she said gloomily.

"You!"

"Expecting someone else?"

"But I thought—Olivia said—" He scanned the room as if he still believed that Olivia might be hiding under the desk or behind the drapes.

"She's not here, Angus." Mason came up behind the other man with a steely glint in his eyes. "If you had any sense, you'd have known that before you came barreling in here like a bat out of hell."

"Since when do bats barrel?" Hayley put in snidely.

Mason glared at her, too.

"If she's not here, then where is she?" Angus muttered, missing completely the tension crackling between the other two people in the room. "I haven't been able to find her all day."

"So," Hayley speculated, "the bit about utmost significance was just to get in here to find Olivia, right?"

"It's not what you think." Angus drew together his mighty eyebrows. "I admit, I was jealous. If Olivia and Mason were, you know, *doing it* together, I wanted to know."

"Doing what exactly?"

At this point, Mason's eyes were little slits. "Hayley," he warned.

"No, I want to know. What did you think Mason and Olivia were doing together?"

"Going after the apple, of course." Angus clenched his hands into hammy fists. "The ultimate betrayal."

You people are obsessed! she wanted to shout. Everything revolved around the apple—even their love lives.

"Angus, I'm getting very tired of this. How many times do I have to tell you I'm not interested in Olivia?"

Angus gave him a pained expression, reflecting his disbelief that anyone could escape the lure of Olivia's charms. "Well, if she's not with you, then I guess she's on to something by herself."

"Like what?" Hayley ventured. "A new shade of nail polish?"

"Don't be absurd. If she or Carmelita found that man Peabody while I stewed around this hotel, I'll...I'll..." Angus's face flushed red. "I don't know what I'll do."

"So you can't find Carmelita, either?" Mason set his jaw. "Both of them missing. This looks bad."

Angus nodded vigorously. "They may know something we don't."

"Peabody may have contacted Carmelita."

Watching Mason get further and further entangled in the elusive puzzle of the golden apple, Hayley began to feel exceedingly cranky. "Mrs. Carmichael is hardly Harry's type," she declared. "Hungry, maybe, but young and female—ha!"

"What?" Both heads swung her way.

"Nothing."

Mason frowned at her. "You always say that."

"And I always mean it." She stood up and slipped past him on her way to the door. "Have fun, boys."

"Where are you going?"

"As far away as I can get from the local meeting of the Fanatics' Union."

Mason followed her. "You can't leave now," he whispered roughly as she edged through the doorway.

"Why not? What should I stay for, Mason? Fun and games with you and Angus?" She shook her head. Berating herself more than him, she directed her comments to the hallway wall. "I almost gave in. I almost decided I didn't care if you were fixated on that damn apple the rest of the time, as long as you were willing to spare me a few minutes. But forget it. I'm not living in Never-Never Land, even if you are. So long, Mason. Oh, and don't drop by the desk anymore to harass me, okay? I don't need the aggravation."

She stalked down the hall before he had a chance to change her mind. Behind her, Angus called out, "Mason? Where did you get the picture of the Spanish girl? She isn't on my list."

Mason allowed himself one last, grim look at Hayley's retreating backside—it was a very nice backside—before forcing himself to return to Angus and the search for the golden apple, that obscure object of desire that was making his life hell.

Remember your priorities, he commanded himself.

It was stupid to waste precious moments fooling around with Hayley, when it meant giving Carmelita and Livvy the edge. It was also stupid to waste precious energy trying to make Hayley see things his way. If she didn't want in, if she couldn't understand the way it had to be, then he didn't have room for her on his team.

Remember the apple, he told himself. It was the answer to everything. It would give him all he'd ever wanted, if he could only hold on and go for it.

"Eyes on the prize," he said out loud. "Everything you ever wanted."

So why did that ring false, even to his own ears?

HAYLEY HUNG UP the receiver after the latest in a series of unsatisfactory phone calls from her mother. Since her parents had retired to Florida, she didn't hear from her mother all that often, and when she did, she usually ended up feeling frustrated, guilty, or plain old depressed.

For the past few months especially, her mother's calls had been pretty grim. The routine was always the same. They'd barely get past the hellos before her mother got down to business, and where Fern Austin was concerned, the only business that mattered was her son Dan.

"Have you talked to your brother?"

"No, Mom."

"Have you talked to Nicki?"

"No, Mom."

"Are you going to talk to Nicki?"

"About Danny? I don't think so, Mom."

"Why not? Don't you care about your brother?"

No comment.

"Don't you care that he's all alone in Los Angeles, while his wife is a thousand miles away? He can't be eating right."

As if the only thing in the world Hayley had to worry about was the status of her glowingly healthy brother's diet.

"I don't want to interfere," she'd say, after it had gone on for several minutes.

At that point her mother would shout, "Someone has to interfere! What can Nicki be thinking of, leaving poor

Danny like that? Destroying a marriage is a serious mistake...."

And on and on, until Hayley would prop the receiver between her ear and her shoulder and clean the kitchen, murmuring, "Mmm-hmm," at appropriate intervals. When her mother called on a regular basis, Hayley had the cleanest kitchen in three states.

Unfortunately, this call had ended differently. This time, Fern Austin had somehow managed to talk her daughter into interfering.

"I can't believe I agreed to this," Hayley told Fluffy bleakly. "What am I supposed to say? 'So, Nicki, how's it going? Thought about divorce lately?' If she wanted to tell me, she'd tell me, and she hasn't said anything."

Fluffy put down his front paws and began to yip loudly. As far as he knew, the kitchen meant food. He didn't care about Hayley's mother or possible conversations with Nicki. He wanted a snack.

"Okay, okay," she said with a laugh. As Fluffy stuck his mangy gray paws on the cabinet door and propped his chin on the counter, she flipped a treat his way.

Hayley leaned back against the counter, musing as she held on to the box of doggie treats. "You know, Fluffy, I thought I was used to it."

The dog woofed sympathetically.

"But this time, I just wanted to say, 'By the way, Mom, *I'm* fine, not that you asked,' Or," she decided, picking up speed, gesturing with the Snausages box for emphasis, "maybe I wanted to say, 'By the way, Mom, I'm *not* fine. I met this guy I think I might like, but his affections are otherwise engaged. No, Mom, it's not another woman. It's an apple.' That'd throw her for a loop, wouldn't it, Fluff?"

Fluffy indicated that he'd prefer another Snausage before commenting.

"And then she could give me some motherly advice on what to do about Mason. Isn't that what's supposed to happen between mothers and daughters? But then, how would *I* know? The only advice my mother ever gave me was on how to improve my jump shot. Or maybe that was Dad. It isn't easy having coaches for parents." She laughed humorlessly and slid to the kitchen floor, pulling Fluffy into her lap.

"I guess I should face facts, Fluff, old boy. With my mother and with Mason, I'm strictly an afterthought. I'm not even in the running! Hayley Austin, also-ran, low woman on the totem pole, bottom of the barrel."

Whining piteously, Fluffy snuffled up to her face and began to slurp at her chin.

She giggled as she always did when her dog grew affectionate; it tickled. "I get the message. I'm feeling sorry for myself, and I'm no fun, right?" Pushing his tongue away from her chin, she ruffled his scruffy topknot. "Okay, pooch, you get your way. One more Snausage—and I promise not to snivel anymore, all right?"

The dog concentrated on his treat, and Hayley smiled and shook her head. "What's wrong with me, anyway? After all, I should be on top of the world. I've got the apple that all those people would give their eyeteeth for. It's safe and secure on my bookshelf." She'd been checking on it on an average of once every five minutes. "And I've even got a wish left. Of course, if my third wish goes as well as the other two, I'm in big trouble."

Remembering the phone call from her mother, she mused, "I suppose I could wish that Nicki and Dan would patch things up. I'm sure that's what Mom would do if she were in my place. Anything for Danny Boy..."

So saying, she piled about ten doggie treats onto a plate and left them on the floor for Fluffy, then dashed upstairs to pull on a jean skirt, boots, and a thick sweater the same pale blue as the skirt. She figured she'd better get dressed and over to Nicki's stables before she changed her mind.

No time like the present to get this painful obligation out of the way, she reminded herself as she walked past the hotel and out to the stables.

Nicki was going to kill her.

Actually, Nicki seemed very glad to see her. Looking beautiful even in worn jeans and a flannel shirt, she was brushing down a big white stallion when Hayley ventured in. As soon as she heard someone enter the stables, she turned and smiled, tucking a tendril of silky black hair back into her long, loose ponytail.

"Hayley—what a nice surprise! I haven't seen you since we had brunch. Don't tell me you came down to borrow a horse?"

"In your dreams."

Hayley didn't like to ride, which Nicki well knew. They'd managed to remain best friends as kids through thick and thin, but one of the thinnest spots had been when Hayley admitted to her horse-crazy friend that she preferred to stay home and read *My Friend Flicka* rather than make friends with the real thing.

Even standing in the same stable with ten or twelve large horses was making her very nervous. Immediately she recognized Major, the black Percheron Nicki had had since they were small. Nicki insisted that Major was as gentle as a lamb, but Hayley wasn't taking chances with anything whose foot was bigger than her head. "Is Major growing, or was he always that huge?"

"Always been that huge." Nicki smiled. Reaching over into the next stall to stroke the enormous Percheron's coarse mane, she called out to Hayley, "So what's up? Are we arranging another brunch for the girls?"

"No, nothing like that. I tried to reach you at home, and when you weren't there, I figured I'd try the stables. Just like you to be working on Saturday."

"Horses need to eat, even on the weekend."

"I'm really sorry to barge in on your work like this, Nick."

Hayley's apologetic tone must have given Nicki a hint, because she dropped her hand from Major's back and wearily turned to face her friend. "This is about Danny, isn't it?"

"Unfortunately, yes," Hayley allowed. "I promised Mom, Nick. Otherwise you know I'd never push."

Nicki dropped the brush she'd been using and let herself out of the white stallion's stall. "So what does Fern want?"

"She's worried about Danny. You know how she is about Danny."

"Everybody loves Danny," his estranged wife said dryly.

"Well, you know how he is—Mr. Message Machine—and I'm sure she's called him a million times and he won't return her calls. She's frantic he's not eating properly, not taking care of himself. You know the routine. So she keeps begging me to talk to you, to see what's happening between the two of you."

Nicki smiled bitterly. "Nothing's happening between the two of us."

"You're still married to him, Nick."

Nicki didn't answer; she retreated into the back room and returned whistling tunelessly and hefting a large bag of feed.

"I guess you're trying to tell me the subject is closed," Hayley said softly.

Nicki methodically measured feed into pails, maintaining her silence, until Hayley finally gave in.

"Nicki, I'm sorry. I'll tell my mother it's none of her business, okay?"

Standing up, Nicki dusted off her jeans and gave Hayley a determined smile. "Hayley, we've been friends a long time. I refuse to wreck it over Danny *or* your mother. So, let's talk about something else, okay? You can see what my life is like—scooping oats and shoveling out the stalls. Your life has got to be more interesting than that. So," she said firmly, "how's it going, kid? Last time I saw you, you'd just gotten hauled out of the MacGregor Room by Indiana Jones. What happened with ol' Indy, anyway?"

Hayley raised her hands and backed off. "Nothing happened with ol' Indy. The man's a kook."

"Hayley!" Nicki's mouth dropped open. "I was only teasing, but I can tell by the look on your face something *did* happen. Don't tell me. He took you looking for the Lost Ark and dropped you in a pit of snakes."

"Something like that."

Nicki cleared a space on the bench and pulled Hayley down next to herself. "You mean you're seeing this guy? Seriously?"

"Not really. Well, I mean, I did see him—once. Or twice, if you count yesterday. Not that I think yesterday should count."

"This is beginning to sound interesting."

"Well, it's pretty funny, anyway." Hayley fixed a smile on her face. "After I met him, he asked me to dinner, and I thought, sure, okay, why not? But it was a bust, a disaster. You know how my dates always turn out, and this was weirder than most."

Recounting the story of that unforgettable evening, Hayley retreated behind the veil of humor she always used to cloak her feelings. "You should've been there, Nick—it was hilarious. I'm supposed to be having dinner with Mason, right? Oh—that's his name—Mason. So we go to the MacGregor Room, and what happens? All these hysterical pals of his show up. There's Olivia, the clinging vine, wearing enough perfume to choke all twelve of your horses. And then Mrs. Carmichael—you remember her—the human tank, including artillery. And last, but not least, Angus.'' She pronounced his name as if it were Frankenstein. ''He's huge,'' she went on, ''almost as big as Major over there, with really grizzly eyebrows and this droopy mustache that hangs over his mouth when he talks. He likes to glare at people.''

She demonstrated one of Angus's sneers, and Nicki began to laugh. ''Why did these people invade your date?''

Hayley shrugged. ''They're all crazy. They don't need reasons to do things. Besides, you can't really call it dinner, because we never got around to ordering. We did do away with some champagne, though. So Angus is sitting there staring a hole in Olivia, the clinging vine, because he's gung ho for her, only she's being coy and cutesy and batting her eyelashes at Mason, who's so caught up in being Indiana Jones that he doesn't even notice Olivia is drooling all over him.''

''And are you drooling on Mason, too, throughout all this?''

''Heavens, no,'' she scoffed. ''What do you take me for? So Angus gets fussy and throws a punch at Mason, and Mason grabs me, and we go flying out of there through the kitchen, do you believe it? Hans, the chef, was in the middle of flipping a crepe, and I came dragging Mason through the kitchen. I just hope Hans didn't say anything to Mr. Normali about my strange behavior.''

She went on in some detail about pots and pans and kitchen personnel in an uproar, until Nicki was roaring.

''And then what?'' her friend prompted.

''Well, then, nothing. I mean, we escaped.''

''Yeah, but then what?''

"I told you, nothing."

"Hayley's blushing!" Nicki cried. "Okay, I get it. You make this daring escape, he sweeps you up in his arms and takes you up to his room and tosses you on the bed and—voilà!"

"Nicki! Nothing like that happened. We went through the kitchen, remember? We were outside. It was freezing."

"Moonlight," Nicki added. "You were trembling with the cold and the aftereffects of the champagne. He took you in his arms to warm you up. He kissed you—"

"He didn't kiss me. Not then, anyway."

Nicki's eyes widened. "So he *did* kiss you. I knew something was going on."

"A kiss is nothing."

"It is for you."

"Oh, that's flattering." Hayley gave her friend the evil eye. "What do you think, I never have dates, I never kiss men?"

"Not very often. At least not that you tell me about."

"I didn't want to tell you. You pried it out of me."

"Well, was it a good kiss at least?"

"Oh, yeah." Hayley's voice softened. "Definitely."

Nicki tipped her head as she studied her old friend's uncommon reaction. "So what's the problem?"

Hayley stood and wandered over to Major's stall. "Do you have any carrots or anything else to feed this beast?"

"Leave Major alone and come back here. You must really like this guy, and that must have been some amazing kiss, or you wouldn't be changing the subject."

"Mason and me together is a disaster, Nick, a joke."

"Everything's a joke to you," Nicki commented wryly. "So what? I know you too well to let that bother me. Usually, the more you ham it up, the more you have to hide."

Hayley ran her fingers over the stiff brush Nicki had used on the white stallion. "Even if I were hiding something—which I'm not—I'm not going to see him again, so what's the difference?"

"Why can't you see him again? Has he left the hotel?"

"No, he's still there." Her voice became low and miserable. "But I told him to leave me alone."

"He kisses you—you melt into a puddle at his feet—and you tell him to leave you alone." Nicki's wide eyes expressed disbelief. "Are you out of your mind?"

"There's more to it than that." She couldn't think of any way to turn this into a funny story, so she related it straight, without embroidering it. "When he kissed me—yesterday—we were in his room together."

Nicki cleared her throat. "His hotel room? Alone? Just the two of you?"

Hayley rolled her eyes. "Nothing happened, believe me. We were alone together for all of five minutes. And I was really starting to feel like he was special, and I thought he was really starting, you know, to be attracted to me, too. But then Angus came bursting in, because he thought Olivia was in there with Mason, and Mason suddenly forgot I even existed."

"Because of Olivia?"

"No, because of. . ." Her voice trailed off; she remembered that Nicki didn't know about the apple's importance in all of this. "Because of this *business* that he has with the others. He's totally consumed by this business project to the exclusion of everything else."

"Including you?" Nicki added.

"Especially me." Hayley let out a breath of air. "I don't know. Maybe I'm being unrealistic. I mean, we just met, so I can't expect to shoot to the top of his priorities list. But on the other hand, I can't see myself falling for him under these circumstances.''

"Because he's got this other thing he's so attached to, you mean."

"Exactly."

"Hmm." Nicki pondered. "You know, you haven't given him much of a chance. Maybe if you let it go a little further, he'd wise up. He'd see what a jerk he's being to let a terrific person like you slip away, and he'd stop being all obsessed with this...whatever it is he's obsessed with."

"Business," Hayley supplied softly.

"Right, business. So, what do you say? Why not go see him and knock his socks off and show him what's what?"

"I don't know," Hayley said reluctantly.

"What have you got to lose?"

"A lot."

"I can't believe I'm hearing this. What happened to the woman with the positive approach, the woman who believes in magic, the woman who has more confidence and fewer insecurities than anyone I know?"

"Yeah, but—"

"Hayley, snap out of it," Nicki said sternly.

"But he drives me crazy! I don't need the hassle."

"I know you." Nicki tossed her hair back over her shoulder. "This man is obviously important to you. If he weren't, you wouldn't be talking to me about him."

Hayley glanced at her friend. "What do you mean?"

"Hayley, old pal, you haven't confided in me about your romantic problems since the sixth grade. In fact, I never thought you had any problems! You collected and tossed away boyfriends with a smile on your face—no sweat—all in fun—no big deal."

"Maybe it was no big deal," Hayley said innocently.

"I was there, remember? You had as many heartaches as any other teenage girl. You just didn't like talking about it, that's all. You preferred to make jokes."

"Better a smile than a frown," she said gloomily.

"Well, Hayley," Nicki said, rising and joining her friend near Major's stall, "you haven't cracked a joke in the last ten minutes. The only thing I can figure is that you're in a bad way."

"I'm not! I'm fine. I swear!"

"You're miserable."

Hayley met Nicki's warm, chocolate-brown eyes. "I'm miserable."

Nicki hugged her oldest friend. "What you need to do is go find this Mason character and wake him up."

"Yeah, right." Shaking her head, Hayley laughed. "I can get at least a minute and a half alone with him before one of those dodoes interferes."

"So get him alone, away from the distractions. Drag him off somewhere." Nicki's smile was crafty. "You're a creative person. Make it somewhere good, where all he has to think about is you, and none of his friends can possibly find you."

"That's not a bad idea." Her mind sifted through the possibilities. "Maybe that's exactly what I should do."

"Go for it," Nicki advised with a laugh. "I think you're driving yourself bananas, because you keep thinking about him at the same time you're trying to convince yourself to stay away. Trust me. You can't be any crazier with him than you are now."

"Thanks a lot," she said sardonically. Nonetheless, she draped an arm around her tall, lithe friend, and suddenly remembered that she hadn't begun this conversation for the purpose of pouring out her heart about her own predicament. She'd come in here to listen to Nicki's problems.

"Nicki," she ventured, "is that what it's like for you, too? Does it drive you crazy to be away from Danny?"

"Honestly?" Nicki let out a long breath. Quietly she said, "Being away from Danny, all I feel is relief."

Hayley was shocked. She hadn't realized things had gotten that bad. "And you're counseling me to go after Mason?"

"Hayley! What went wrong between your brother and me has nothing to do with you and this Mason guy. With Danny and me it's over." Her eyes became deep and dark. "With you and Mason it hasn't even begun."

"Oh, it's begun all right. The question is what happens next." Wheeling abruptly, Hayley made for the door.

"What are you going to do?" Nicki demanded.

"I don't know yet." Hayley laughed as she strode out into the fresh, invigorating early-spring air. "I'll let you know as soon as I figure it out."

"You'd better!" Nicki called after her.

MASON WAS GOING STIR-CRAZY. Ever since he'd arrived at The Stanley in pursuit of Carmelita, he'd been skulking around behind pillars and posts, spying on his adversaries and doing his best to stay one step ahead of whatever they were plotting. Unfortunately, they didn't seem to be plotting anything. All four of them were spending their time spying on each other.

He was grouchy, tired of poring over his pictures, diagrams and notes, and he wanted to get out of the hotel, even if it meant losing his edge in the hunt. Outside the mountains beckoned. Rocky Mountain National Park was only a few miles away. And what was he doing? Watching Carmelita watch the Stanley Steamer, while Olivia watched him and Angus watched Olivia. It was downright depressing. He wanted action. He wanted the hunt for the apple to move forward.

More than that, he wanted to see Hayley.

He glared at himself in the mirror as he pulled down the brim of his beat-up fedora over his forehead. He wasn't supposed to be thinking about her.

Oh, he'd passed the front desk a few times when she was on duty, and she'd purposely looked the other way. He had, too. At the time, he'd figured she'd apologize if she wanted to, and he might, being a magnanimous sort of guy, let her back onto the team, because he really had enjoyed her company, no question about that.

Pacing around the hotel alone for several days at a crack had convinced him that having a partner was a lot more fun than going it alone. Hell, even Olivia was starting to look good.

But Hayley was different, and it was Hayley he wanted. He'd known that from the moment he met her, when she'd thrown herself in front of Carmelita's umbrella to protect him. She was stubborn and inflexible, exasperating at times, but then, so was he, so it hardly mattered.

On the practical side, she was smart and a veritable expert on the subject of The Stanley Hotel, which could come in handy, since their search was centered here. She also noticed things he didn't—like the sleeve in the corner of the Polaroid—and all things considered, she'd make a great partner.

On a less practical note, she was warm, sweet and alive. She made him want to hold her and kiss her until they both turned blue from lack of air. She made him want to lock the door of his room, forget about the golden apple, and make love until next winter.

She made him crazy.

"The hell with all of it," he mumbled. "I'm taking a day off."

It was Saturday, there was more than a touch of spring in the air, and he was damned if he'd hang around the hotel playing cat and mouse with a bunch of lunatics, when he could be out looking for Hayley.

It was a good bet she lived in Estes Park. Now all he needed was a phone and a phone book.

HAYLEY WAS FEELING much better. There was nothing like a shopping spree and a new crop of lingerie to perk her up. Clutching a large paper bag full of teddies and camisoles, she edged down the main street of Estes Park, enjoying the ambience of the small shops and the lack of crowds in this, the off-season. She was debating whether to get an ice-cream cone when she saw him.

The shoulders were unmistakable from the back, even if he hadn't been wearing his Indiana Jones hat. The Estes Park natives generally ignored tourists, but Mason was getting a few curious stares. Hayley smiled to herself. As usual, he was oblivious to the attention he commanded, not even noticing the sighs and giggles directed at him from a group of teenage girls.

Her smile turned into a frown, and she ducked into the nearest store, a print-your-own T-shirt place, as her nerves tingled uneasily. The man was gorgeous, no question about it, and emotions she hadn't been aware she was capable of jumped into life every time she saw those shoulders. She wanted to see him, but she was afraid. What if he told her to go far, far away because he was too busy? What if she blurted out the truth about the apple?

"Chicken," she chided herself.

"Is that what we're having for lunch?"

Her heart leaped into her throat, she spun around and into Mason's suede bomber jacket.

"What are you doing here?"

"Well, I might get a T-shirt," he said thoughtfully, looking over her head at the choice of imprints.

She put a hand up to her chest to calm her erratic heartbeat. "You scared the pants off me."

His mouth quirked into a half smile. "That I'd like to see."

This conversation was so unlike him that she began to feel suspicious. Since when was he charming and glib, with cutesy comments dripping from his tongue? The Mason she knew was mostly preoccupied, usually grim, and never cutesy.

"What's in the bag?" he asked.

Glancing down, she felt her face grow warm at the thought of pulling out the jazzy red teddy she'd just bought and showing it to Mason. Which one of them would be more embarrassed? Instead, she changed the subject. "What are you doing here?"

"Okay, I admit it. I'm not here for a T-shirt." His smile widened. "I saw you come in and I followed you."

"Why?"

"Because I wanted to talk to you."

"About what?"

"Not very trusting, are you?"

"We didn't exactly part on the best of terms," she reminded him.

"I thought maybe we could fix that."

She started to unbend. "Oh, yeah?"

"Yeah. Call a truce. Have lunch together. Act like normal people for once."

She took a deep breath and looked up into those aquamarine eyes. "I'm not saying I'm completely convinced, but, well, that might be okay."

"Great. Where to?"

"How about my house, Mason? It's quiet there." And there was little chance of being disturbed by the others. Of course, if Mason happened to get the urge to paw through her bookshelves, he might find the apple, but then, what was the likelihood of that? "Might as well live dangerously," she said out loud.

Mason gave her an odd look as he followed her out of the T-shirt store and onto the sidewalk. "What's so dangerous about lunch?"

If he only knew.

Chapter Eight

He liked her house immediately. It was small, with a sharply inclined roof, rough-hewn siding, and a crooked porch that gave it character. Flowerpots that would undoubtedly be full of blossoms later in the spring hung cheerfully from the overhanging roof, and a mailbox in the shape of a swan proclaimed "Austin." But it had been quite a hike from downtown Estes Park to this sprawling, hilly neighborhood. "Do you walk this every day?"

"It's a lot shorter if you don't go through town," she explained as she slid her key into the lock.

"Still..."

"Well, it keeps me in shape," she said with a smile. "And I really like to start my day with some fresh air—get out and see the world." Suddenly she realized how goofy that might sound. A few miles of Estes Park was hardly the world.

But Mason was on a different track. "Walking for exercise—that's different. It seems like everybody I know belongs to a health club. And then they drive around in circles, looking for the closest parking space before they'll go in and work out."

"Duck," she called out, and he dipped his head to avoid hitting the low front doorway as he followed her into the house. "I'm not much for health clubs. I don't own the right wardrobe."

Fluffy immediately bounded up and threw himself at her, barking vigorously and madly waving his tail. After rubbing his head and murmuring words of welcome, she introduced Mason to her pooch.

Mason stretched out a hand, and was soon treated to the same rough-and-tumble greeting Hayley had received. "Friendly, isn't he?" Mason observed, subtly trying to remove large paws from his abdomen.

She grabbed Fluffy's collar and dragged him away. "He isn't much of a watchdog, but he's good company."

"And does he accompany you on all these walks you take?"

"Nah. If Fluffy goes, it turns into a run. I like to walk. But I take him when I ride my bike, when the weather gets a little warmer."

As she tugged Fluffy into the kitchen and then let him out the back door, Mason trailed along, feeling a little self-conscious in such a small house. The beamed ceilings were low, perhaps only seven feet, and he had to keep ducking as he went through the curved archways that led from one room to the next. "Funny, I didn't picture you as the athletic type."

"What a joke. I am absolutely not athletic."

Courtesy of the telephone call from her mother, the kitchen was neat as a pin, but not really large enough for two people to loiter. The way she and Mason were standing, they were practically knee to knee, so she quickly decided to take him into the living room.

Hayley kept up a steady flow of chatter. It was weird having him in her house, and she knew she was babbling, but she couldn't stop herself. Anything to bridge the silence, anything to keep from looking at him, to keep from getting to the heart of the matters between them.

"I'm a real klutz," she continued, fluffing a pillow on the sofa and motioning that he take a seat. She settled into a maple rocker with red plaid cushions. "And believe me, it's tough to be a klutz when both your parents are coaches and your brother is a natural at anything that requires referees and fans. Danny—my brother, that is—plays to the crowd, and he's very good at it. But not me. Put me at bat and I shrivel up and die! So I take long walks. It gives me time to think, it doesn't require coordination, and it kept me out of wind sprints when I was a kid."

Mason folded himself onto the sofa and surveyed the room. The living-room ceiling was higher than those in the rest of the house and therefore more comfortable for him. He didn't have to worry about bumping his head if he stood up too fast. A rough stone fireplace dominated the whole front wall, giving a log-cabin feeling to the room that blended well with the red and white quilts and pillows thrown over the dark blue print sofa and love seat. It was small, intimate and very cozy. All it needed was a fire in the fireplace.

On one side, a narrow stairway led to an open loft, where Hayley presumably slept. Since there weren't any doors left unaccounted for, he could only assume this was all there was. Compact and functional—a one-person house.

He drummed his fingers on his knees and wished he knew what to say. As usual in conversations more personal than professional, he wasn't sure where to begin. His natural inclination was to get down to business, but he knew most people didn't operate that way. They ditzed around with chitchat and polite comments until they could work up to whatever it was they were really trying to say. Since this was intended as a conciliatory meeting, however, he figured he'd better go by the rules.

"So your parents are coaches?"

"Right. Well, they *were*, anyway. My mom coached volleyball and basketball, and my dad did football. My brother was the star quarterback on one of my dad's teams. But they retired after Danny got married and moved away. I'm kind of surprised they didn't go to California—that's where he is—but they're in Florida now." She clasped her hands in her lap. Mason didn't say anything, and she felt compelled to keep the conversational ball rolling. "I used to think I was a changeling. You know, left by the gypsies," she joked. "I mean, I like to *watch* sports, but I never played on a single team. Well, I was on a softball team once in college, but that's it."

"Just the opposite of me," he commented.

"Don't tell me you were a jock?" She was frankly surprised. She'd always thought of her brother as the typical athletic type, and Mason's personality was nothing like Danny's.

"No," he said with a wry smile. "I just wanted to be. I always wanted to play baseball, but my parents thought it was too dangerous."

This was so far out of her range of experience that Hayley didn't know what to say. She'd never heard of parents who thought sports were dangerous. "What I would've given for parents like that!" she offered lightly. "They might have actually let me stay inside and read when I wanted to, instead of forcing me outside to catch passes with Danny to keep his arm warmed up."

"I would've traded in a minute," he told her with a laugh. "But I was supposed to be a smart kid, you see, and my parents thought it was too risky for a smart kid to do sports. Like I might get hit in the head with a baseball and lose all capacity for high-energy physics. Anyway, they enrolled me in one of those magnet schools for brainy kids. They didn't have teams, so I was supposedly safe."

"Supposedly?"

"My parents didn't know I was so baseball-crazy I conned some of the other guys into playing in the chemistry lab. We broke quite a few beakers before anybody found out. That was the end of my baseball career, and I went back to being just another brainy nerd."

She looked him up and down, from the broad shoulders to the narrow hips and long, lean legs. "Mason, I'm sorry, but you don't resemble a brainy nerd in the least."

He raised an eyebrow. "Tell that to my parents. 'Brainy nerd today, Nobel Prize winner tomorrow,' was their motto."

"But what about all the virtues of being on a team? I heard about teamwork and sportsmanship and learning when to lead and when to follow until I wanted to barf! I thought it was the American way."

"Not in my house. The only team I was allowed to be on was the chess team."

"The only team I wanted to be on *was* the chess team." They were both smiling and she realized they hadn't mentioned the apple in a long while. It felt good. Very good.

"Lunch," she said suddenly. "I was supposed to be giving you lunch."

She didn't like leaving him alone in her living room, when the apple was hidden on the bookshelf, not five feet from where he was sitting. On the other hand, she felt like a rat, letting thoughts of the apple intrude upon what had been a nice interlude.

"Why don't you come and help?" she asked with every bit of girl-next-door charm she could muster.

"Great."

And he smiled at her, and she felt even more guilty.

He seemed happy chopping vegetables for a salad, and she made sandwiches, trying not to back into him on her way to the refrigerator or to brush his arm when she reached for plates.

They sat down at the tiny kitchen table to eat, but Hayley was not in the least hungry. Gazing at him, she thought he looked wonderful; somehow the food they'd prepared tasted like dust. He was in his Indiana Jones outfit again, though he'd abandoned the hat and suede jacket when he came in. He really looked terrific. Serious, maybe even solemn, but terrific.

She took a few half-hearted mouthfuls of salad, so he'd know there wasn't anything wrong with it, but she wasn't really aware of what she was eating.

Mason had no such problems, it seemed; he made short work of his lunch and then sat there, looking at her.

After picking up and putting down her sandwich several times, she asked edgily, "Mason, was there something you wanted to talk to me about? You did say you'd been looking for me. It's not that I think we have to talk about anything in particular, but if you had something in mind..."

"Well, sort of."

This was awfully tentative for Mason. "Okay." She smiled encouragingly. "Go ahead."

"I, well, I really wanted to apologize. About when Angus came in." His voice was deep and low, and the look in his eyes was very serious. "You were right. I've been obsessed with the apple, and it's a stupid way to behave."

"Thank you for the apology," she said slowly. "I appreciate that."

Her mouth had gone on automatic pilot, but her brain was doing a tap dance. Good heavens! Could it be this easy? Nicki had told her to give him another chance, that he'd see the error of his ways. But she hadn't expected it to happen with no effort whatsoever on her part.

"I like you, Hayley, and I...I don't know. I guess I'd like to get to know you better and find the apple, too, and I..."

His lean cheeks had started to redden slightly, and he was looking at the wallpaper behind her head instead of meeting her gaze. He was obviously embarrassed at having to come right out and say all this. She could've saved him by jumping in and talking about the weather, but she was rather enjoying it. It wasn't every day a man told her he liked her. He liked her! It was adorable.

"Well," he managed, "I wondered if that were possible—seeing you *and* looking for the apple." His eyes narrowed slightly as he gazed right at her. His voice dropped even deeper. "We could be a great team—I know we could."

"I think you're right," she whispered.

"So you're saying yes, then? You'll help me look and we can spend some time together?"

"I—I guess so."

Rat fink! her conscience shouted. *How are you going to help him look for it, when you've already got it? Or maybe you're planning to throw him off the scent, send him in the opposite direction?*

She felt like the scum of the earth. So she busied herself clearing away the lunch dishes and making small talk as he helped her fill the dishwasher and wipe off the table.

Don't be so nice! she felt like snapping at him. Why couldn't he tell her that he thought dishes were women's work or something equally ugly, so she could lump him back with that group of men who were irritating by virtue of their extra X chromosome, and go on cheerfully deceiving him?

Instead, he continued to be nice as they went back into the living room. He played games with Fluffy, throwing dog biscuits behind the sofa for the mutt to fetch. When Fluffy finally tired out, Mason turned back to Hayley. His eyes were still earnest.

"There was one other thing I wanted to tell you. It's what you asked before, about why I'm so obsessed with the apple."

He clenched his jaw, giving his face a pensive, determined line. She got the feeling he wasn't enjoying confiding this, but that he was hell-bent upon getting through it.

"I thought if I told you the reason I want the apple, it would be like a symbol of good faith between us," he explained.

"You'd do that? You'd tell me just like that?" she asked, awed.

"Absolutely."

She swallowed, leaning forward and taking his long hand in her own. "Okay. I'm ready."

"Come on, Hayley, it's nothing tragic." A smile played about his narrow lips. "And you already know part of it, anyway, since we were talking about my family before."

"Your family?"

Her mind was suddenly spinning with the possibilities of irrefutable family obligations. Something sweet, uncomplicated, and absolutely binding, like a deathbed wish.

"Will you promise to find the apple for me, my son?" his mother gasped, desperately clutching his hand.

"If it's the last thing I ever do, I'll get that apple for you, Ma," he promised with tears in his eyes. And then his mother's frail hand slipped from his grasp. It was all over.

"Oh, come on," Hayley muttered. The imaginary dialogue playing in her brain sounded like something from a bad movie. Personally, she always hated it when they killed off somebody to propel the hero into action. She decided that she ought to be thinking along more positive lines.

Trying to be sensible, she said, "The only thing I know about your family is that they didn't want you to play baseball. What does that have to do with the apple?"

"Nothing, really, except for the reason they didn't want me involved in sports. Do you remember me mentioning high-energy physics?"

"Vaguely. But I still don't get it. Physics and a golden apple? What's the connection?"

His expression asked her to bear with him as he gravely continued. "Both of my parents are physicists. Very well-known physicists. They work with the particle accelerator at Fermi Lab, outside Chicago. What they do is so hush-hush, they can't even tell me. And also I have two sisters. One is a physics grad student at the University of Chicago, and the other one works with my parents. And my grandfather was Mason Samuel Wilder, Jr. You may have heard of him. He won a Nobel Prize for his work at Los Alamos on the atomic bomb."

Her mouth fell open. "Your grandfather invented the atomic bomb?"

He shrugged. "He was part of the team. And then there's my great-grandfather. He discovered some new subatomic particle. I forget the details. I never did like physics," he said grimly.

"Okay." She nodded, letting the facts sink in. "What you're telling me is that your family is really into atom bombs and atomic particles, but you're not."

"Right."

"Okay." But she didn't have a clue as to the significance of this information. Confused, she glanced at him. "So what?"

He rubbed his jaw and leaned farther forward. "Most kids are brought up on Dr. Spock. I was groomed on the quantum theory."

"Well, that's different."

"But I turned my back on it, Hayley."

He seemed to be getting impatient and frustrated. She could understand that; his parents sounded like real jerks, forbidding their son to play baseball and making him study neutrons and protons instead. They couldn't exactly be happy memories.

"It's okay, Mason," she said kindly. "It's a long time ago."

He shook his head. "Remember what you said about being a changeling, left by the gypsies? Well, that's me, too. My parents were sure I could be the second Nobel Prize winner in the family, but I went into history instead."

"And I'm lousy at sports. We all make our own choices, Mason." She gave him an upbeat smile and patted his hand. "You like what you do—you don't like physics—you made the only choice you could."

He shook his head. "You don't understand. This isn't about not choosing physics. This is about not choosing physics and then becoming a mediocre historian and an assistant curator at a mediocre museum."

"Mason, you're not mediocre." In fact, she thought he was pretty special.

"To them I am."

Suddenly it all became clear. "And if you have the apple, you become a big-shot historian and show all the folks at home that you're just as good as they are, even though you don't split atoms for a living."

"Something like that."

"Oh, Mason," she said sadly. From her own experience, she knew what it was like to be the one who didn't fit in, the one who didn't meet parental expectations. But that was all so long ago....

"This is very important to me," he said quietly. "I have something to prove. Can you understand that?"

"Of course. I mean, there's a part of me that would love to get married and have football prodigy babies, so my dad would finally notice I'm alive. But it doesn't work. You can't live your life trying to prove something to other people. And you can't set your heart on finding a magic apple, because you think they want you to want it." She broke off. "Look, I'm sorry. I know that last part didn't make much sense. I only meant—"

"I know what you meant." His eyes were very chilly, very blue. "I'm trying to prove something to myself, not to them."

"But, Mason—"

"No," he said flatly, "it's true. Okay, so I have a family that demanded excellence from the moment I was born. But whether they know it or not, they inculcated that in me, too. I demand excellence from myself. And in this case, that means getting the apple for my museum. That means making my name in the world."

She could already see the *Time* magazine cover. "Historian Mason Wilder and the Golden Apple. Is It for Real?" The Carson Show, maybe even Letterman. A movie made about the dashing historian, starring Harrison Ford. Or maybe Kevin Costner. No, he was too short.

"Are you sure that's what you want?" she asked softly.

"Oh, yes." He got up from the couch and jammed his hands into the pockets of his khaki pants. "Hayley, this is very important to me, not just because of my family, but because of *me*."

"Yes, I can see that."

As he paced the length of her living room, he was clearly on a roll. "Scottie MacPherson's apple is the key to everything. Funding for the museum, academic acceptance, my own career—it's all on the line." He ran a hand through his hair. "There's just no other way. I have to find the apple."

His body was a taut line of frustration, and her heart filled with sympathy. Mason was smart and good at what he did, but it wasn't good enough. He wanted to be the best.

She knew what that was like. She knew what it meant to settle for the middle of the pack, when everyone around you expected nothing but first place. In sports she'd given up long ago. In her career she was still grappling for her rightful place. But in her personal life, she'd already decided she couldn't accept second best again.

It was all part of the same problem. Inside Hayley Austin, everybody's pal, lurked a woman who wanted to be the most important thing in someone's life. Inside Mason Wilder, competent museum curator, hid a man who wanted to be *somebody*.

Oh, yes, she understood only too well. And she realized for the first time that she had in her possession the one thing that could make Mason truly happy. She possossed the apple of his eye.

It would take so little on her part to give him what he wanted. After all, she had no real right to the apple herself. With more conviction than she'd felt in days, she knew what she had to do. The only question was how.

"Mason," she said carefully, "there's something I have to tell you."

He glanced at her with an air of distraction. "What is it?"

"It's..." Her voice trailed off. *Say it,* she commanded herself, but no words came out. How in the world was she going to accomplish this, with her tongue stuck to the roof of her mouth, as if she'd been eating peanut butter?

She was also feeling a little wary of Mason's reaction. Would he be furious? Or too happy to know where the damned thing was to care that she'd purposely deceived him?

"This is hard," she admitted, and tried to start again. "All right. I'll just come right out and say it. I—"

The phone rang. Saved by the bell.

"Don't go anywhere, Mason. I'll take this call, and then I'll be right back, okay?"

"No problem."

He wandered over to her bookshelves and began to peruse the titles as she waffled between the living room and the kitchen, where the phone was ringing away. All she needed was for Mason to be a James Fenimore Cooper fan and blunder across the apple hidden behind the books, before she had a chance to tell him she had it. But he chose a biography of Catherine the Great and retreated to the rocking chair to look at it, so she figured she was safe for a while.

Anxious to tell him and get it over with, yet still uneasy about her decision, she answered the phone.

"Hello, Hayley. This is Kate."

"Hi." She was relieved that she had something else to think about for a moment. "How are you? Everything okay in Boulder?"

"Well, yes, I suppose so." Kate paused as if she were deciding how to broach a particular subject. "I don't quite know where to begin."

"Is something wrong?"

"No, of course not. Well, not exactly. This is about you, Hayley."

"About me?" What one earth was this all about? Kate's voice was grave, her words carefully chosen.

"Do you remember the gold apple that strange little man gave you at the hotel the day we met for brunch?"

"Of course I remember," she muttered. How could she possibly forget? She glanced over her shoulder, but Mason was still in the living room, safely out of earshot. "What about it?"

"I don't know if you'll recall this, but when we were discussing the general idea of three wishes in fairy tales and all that, I mentioned that it reminded me of something, but I couldn't quite put my finger on what. Do you recall that?"

"Yes, I think so," she returned, wishing Kate would get to the point.

"It's been nagging at me ever since that day. I finally traced it. I went through some notes Martin had collected for a book he planned to do, but never finished." Kate hesitated. "I haven't really looked at Martin's papers since he..."

"I understand," Hayley said quickly. It was obvious that Kate had been avoiding her late husband's papers since he died, and it was difficult for her to talk about it.

"Anyway," Kate continued in a determinedly brisk voice, "I felt I simply had to find out what this is all about. I kept having this feeling that Martin's research was the key, and I'm afraid I was right."

"About what, Kate? What was he researching?"

"Colorado legends and lore."

Hayley muffled a sigh. She knew what was coming.

"He had a section on a particular Colorado legend, Hayley, and I found the substance of that legend so disturbing and so unbelievable, I'm still not sure what to think." Kate's tone became even more cautious. "You see, the legend involves a miner who was supposedly granted three wishes. Hayley, this miner... well, the story says she had a magical golden apple. And it sounds exactly like yours."

Hayley bit her lip. "Kate, I already know all about it."

"You know?" Kate demanded. "What do you make of it? Don't you think it's strange?"

"Well, yes, I do," she said in a rush, trying to cover her tracks, "but I'm sure the old story isn't important. It has nothing to do with my..." She ventured a glance around the corner into the living room, then lowered her voice to a whisper. "It has nothing to do with *my* apple."

There was silence for several seconds. "Hayley, are you lying to me? What exactly is going on?"

"Why would I lie to you?"

"I haven't the vaguest idea. I admit, it's pretty hard to tell over the phone, but I'm very familiar with students who practice evasion when their papers are late or suspiciously like someone else's, and I recognize deceit when I hear it."

"Hayley?" Mason called from the living room. "Are you going to be on the phone much longer? Didn't you say you had something to tell me?"

"Just a minute," she called back, and then, "Look, Kate, I'd love to chat, but I really have to go."

"Hayley, don't you take one step before you tell me what's going on!"

"To tell you the truth, I don't know what's going on or what I'm going to do about it. But don't worry, and don't do any more research," she told her friend firmly. "It's my apple and I'll handle it. I'd appreciate it if you wouldn't say anything about this to anyone in the meantime."

"All right. But you'd better get up here and see what I've found before you decide anything. It's an absolutely fascinating story."

Hayley put a hand to her head, but made no comment.

"Do you hear me?" Kate prompted. "Before you do anything with that apple of yours, you have to come up to Boulder and go through the file Martin compiled, so you can see for yourself what I'm talking about. Okay?"

"Yeah, yeah, okay," Hayley murmured. She hung up with a sense of apprehension, wondering if Kate's file could possibly contain anything she didn't already know. She remembered her previous impulse, to unburden herself and tell Mason the truth. But Kate had warned her not to do anything until she saw the complete file. What should she do?

She didn't have long to ponder the question. A gentle tapping at her kitchen window caught her attention, and her gaze shot automatically to the glass.

Harry. Her entire body went numb. Harry Peabody was waving at her from the other side of her kitchen window.

It wasn't possible. She put her hands over her ears and shut her eyes, as if that would make him go away. But when she could stand the suspense no longer and uneasily opened her eyes, he was still there. His sweet, round face reflected a gentle concern, and he was shaking his head, as if to give her a firm negative answer to a question she didn't recall asking.

"Harry?" she whispered. "What are you doing here?"

"Came to see you," he told her, mouthing the words and gesturing with his hands. He broke into his familiar cherubic smile and pointed at the back door. "May I come in?"

She shook her head. She could hardly invite Harry in for tea with Mason camped in her living room. "Come back later?"

"Oh, no," he said calmly. "Now." He pointed at her door again, indicating that she should let him in.

"I'll come out," she decided. "Wait there." After an apprehensive peek into the living room, where Mason was quietly reading his book, she tiptoed through the kitchen and eased herself around the edge of the door.

"Hello, Harry," she said, not knowing whether to hug him or belt him one.

"Hello, my dear," Harry said happily. Then he seemed to remember his mission and adopted a sterner expression.

"Miss Austin," he said in mild rebuke, "I know what you were about to do, and it isn't allowed. I've arrived in the nick of time, I presume."

"Excuse me?"

"In the nick of time," he repeated. "You haven't told him, I hope?"

"No, I . . ." Her eyes narrowed; she regarded him suspiciously. "How did you know I was thinking about it?"

He ignored the question. "It's yours alone, my dear. You mustn't share it."

"Good grief." She tried a different approach. "Harry, you have to tell me why you gave me that apple and what I'm supposed to do with it. Do you know there are a whole bunch of people looking for it?"

"Oh, certainly," he returned easily. "There are always people looking for it. It's quite valuable, you know. But it isn't meant for them, and you mustn't give it to them. It's yours, my child, and yours alone, until you've taken your three, of course, and then I'll come to fetch it."

"Oh, Harry . . ." She sighed. "This is all so weird, and I haven't the vaguest idea what to do."

"Why, you're doing just fine, Hayley. I certainly wouldn't worry about it. Just fine, my dear."

"I'm not fine! I feel like I fell into the twilight zone."

He clucked his tongue in mild reproach. "Atalanta's Apple should bring joy, young lady, and if you use it properly, that's what you'll find. Twilight zone, indeed. Atalanta would be insulted."

Her head was spinning. She took a deep breath. "Are you saying it really is Atalanta's Apple?"

"Well, of course."

"But Atalanta is a myth," she insisted.

"Yes," he returned. "She is that."

"But you think she's real."

"Well, she's that, too."

Hayley lifted her hand to her forehead. "I'm so confused. I don't know what to think."

"Don't think," he responded gently. "It will make it a lot easier for you, my dear."

How could she not think? Ideas were tripping over themselves in her fevered brain, with one notion front and foremost. Mason. "Are you sure the apple wouldn't be better off...?" She paused, not sure she should mention Mason. Harry already knew far more than she was comfortable with, and she didn't want to spill all the beans. "Would it be better off with someone else, someone who knows more about all of this than me?" she asked hopefully.

"Oh, no, you mustn't think that. You must trust me, my dear. It's your alone, not Mason's or anyone else's."

She stiffened. "How do you know about Mason? How do you know about everything before I tell you? Who are you, Harry?"

"No, no, I haven't time for meaningless questions. The apple is yours, and there simply isn't time for discussion."

"But why me?"

Harry shrugged, lifting his small shoulders. "You're right for it," he said simply. His voice dropped into a lower, more persuasive register. "Think of it, my dear. Picture it in your mind."

"No, I don't want to," she said stubbornly, not wanting to be manipulated like this. But he continued, and she couldn't hold off the image of the apple that began to tease her from the periphery of her thoughts. "No," she repeated, but it was futile.

"It's beautiful, isn't it?" Harry persisted. "Can you honestly say you're willing to give it up?"

Flickering in her mind, its image was golden and mysterious. It was warm, shimmering, as alive as if she held it in her hand this very moment.

"It's so beautiful," she whispered.

The essence of it was irrevocably etched upon her consciousness, and she couldn't think of anything else, no matter how hard she tried, no matter how firmly she tried to conjure up Mason's image, or anything else that might dissolve this crazy obsession.

"I can't give it to him," she said suddenly. "It's mine."

She felt guilty and disloyal, yet at the same time compelled to keep the apple. She'd been backed into a corner; she had no choice.

"There now," Harry offered brightly. "I knew you'd be sensible."

"Sensible?" Nothing about any of this was sensible.

"Oh, dear me. Now I've almost forgotten. I did want to explain the confusion over the first one. I hope you didn't mind, but I truly didn't think you meant to harm Carmelita seriously, and so I altered it a bit."

"Altered what?"

"The bus. I substituted—"

"Busboy," she murmured helplessly. "You substituted busboy. Oh, Harry..."

"Well, I did want to explain that and to remind you to be careful, because I really ought to be doing what you ask, and not trying to finagle things around to what I think you mean. You do understand that, don't you?"

"I don't understand anything!"

"But of course you do." He laughed, with a cheerful little piping sound that danced in the air around them. "And now I really must go."

"Harry, please don't go. I have so many questions!"

"Oh—one other thing, my dear. Look at the numbers on the photograph I sent to Carmelita. I thought it would be so clear to a young woman of your intelligence, but you don't seem to have deciphered it yet, so I suppose I must tell you. It's your deadline. I'll be back to see you then, my dear, and not before."

"Deadline, did you say? You haven't told me yet why you sent Mrs. Carmichael the photograph."

"All part of the plan, my dear." Harry chuckled and patted her hand. "I like to make it interesting, you know. Keeps my work entertaining. But don't you worry your pretty head about the details. Harry Peabody has it all worked out, and everything is proceeding on schedule."

"What do you mean, Harry?"

He squeezed her hand gently, and for that fleeting moment she felt comforted. "Your wishes, my dear. To get Mason, I had to get Carmelita, so he could think he was coming of his own free will." He clucked his tongue. "A man like Mason doesn't take kindly to being plucked up and dropped somewhere without rhyme or reason."

"Good Lord," she said weakly. He was telling her that Mason was the answer to her wish, that any feelings they had for each other were the result of magic, fantasy and trickery. It was horrible.

"Quick—Mason's coming," Harry muttered. "Remember, mum's the word. You go back inside now, and I'll talk to you again when the time is right."

"Mason's coming?" She whirled toward the kitchen door, half expecting Mason's broad shoulders to come barreling through. There was, however, no sign of him, and she spun back to ask Harry what he was talking about. But there was no sign of him, either. Once again, Harry had conveniently disappeared.

She had no choice but to retreat into the house and hope for the best. But she was so confused!

"Hayley, are you still on the phone?" Mason called out, as she closed the back door with a muffled crunch.

She tried to keep the panic out of her voice. "No. I just hung up."

She took a step in the direction of the living room, feeling like a first-class jerk. How could she face Mason, when she wanted so desperately to give him the apple he coveted, yet knew she couldn't? How could she confront him, when she was experiencing so many conflicting emotions about him?

In her heart she felt warmth and joy. She truly *liked* Mason, and felt so special when she was with him. And there was more. She thought of being with him, of his knee accidentally touching hers, of his fingers brushing her cheek. She closed her eyes and moaned softly.

From her fingertips to her toes, Hayley burned with desire. She wanted to hold him and feel him and wrap herself so tightly around his heart that he could never break free.

But in her mind . . . in her mind, the apple held sway and there was only selfishness, greed and canny self-preservation. *The apple is mine.*

As she drifted a few inches closer to the living room and the inevitable decision about Mason, the front doorbell rang. She stopped in her tracks. If it was Harry again, she didn't know what she'd do.

Mason got to the door first, swinging it open just as Hayley reached the hall.

It was Olivia, dripping with mascara and reeking of perfume. "Hi, Holly!" she announced breathlessly.

Chapter Nine

"Not Holly, Hayley," she and Mason chorused.

Olivia waved away the challenge. "Whatever."

"What do you want?" Hayley asked.

"Looking for Mason," she trilled, pinching his cheek. "I had a hunch I'd find you here!"

"Lucky me."

Olivia tripped in, dragging her fur behind her and revealing a clingy red dress that molded to her ample curves. "Cute place, Holly."

"My name is *Hayley*," she managed between gritted teeth. "And I don't recall inviting you in."

"Oh, that's okay. Mason invited me." Olivia crinkled her nose at him. "Didn't you, sweetie?"

"Well, actually I did," Mason admitted.

Hayley shook her head at him. "Any why exactly did you do that, Mason?"

"I didn't want to miss out if she learned anything important," he explained in an undertone. "Don't worry. We'll find out what she knows and get rid of her."

Meanwhile, Olivia had wiggled into the living room and ensconced herself upon the sofa. "How quaint," she cooed, looking around and peering up into the loft. "I never met anyone who had a bedroom like a hayloft. A real country girl, huh?"

"Okay, that's it." Advancing on the dippy woman, Hayley clenched her hands into fists. "I'm giving you exactly five minutes to state your business and get out of my house."

"Simmer down, sweetie," her nemesis replied. "I have a clue, a lead, you know, on that Peabody guy. Of course I ran right over to share it with Mason." She bestowed a gooey smile upon Mason. "Ready to go looking for Mr. Peabody with me, Mason?" Gaily she added, "Olivia's chauffeur service leaves in five minutes."

Simmering, Hayley asked, "Why didn't you share your clue with Angus, Olivia? I'm sure he'd love to hear all about it."

The curvacious woman pouted. "Angy can be such a drag."

But Mason edged next to her on the sofa—how he got that close without being asphyxiated by her perfume was a mystery to Hayley—and asked intently, "What's the lead, Livvy? Did you see Peabody?"

"Uh-huh. He was at the hotel," she said coyly, batting her eyelashes. "I saw him by that car thing in the lobby, and I told him to stay put until I could get you and come back."

Hayley raised an eyebrow. "And the mysterious Mr. Peabody supposedly agreed to this?"

"Well, yeah," Olivia breathed. "I can be awfully persuasive, if you know what I mean."

Hayley rolled her eyes. "We know what you mean."

"I think he kind of likes me," Olivia confided girl to girl. "You know, *that* way."

The thought was enough to make Hayley feel queasy. "And you came right over here after you talked to him?"

Olivia nodded vaguely.

"So you saw him at The Stanley, oh, five or ten minutes ago?"

Again, Olivia nodded. "He was sitting in that car in the lobby not five minutes ago. And if we hurry, he'll still be there."

Hayley frowned. Now she knew for certain that Olivia was lying. Harry certainly couldn't have been chatting with Olivia at The Stanley when he had been standing in Hayley's backyard. Even Harry couldn't occupy two places at the same time.

Mason stood up and looked around for his coat. "Okay, let's get going. There's no time to waste."

"Mason!" But he was already on his way to the door, with Olivia prancing right behind.

Hayley took his arm and pulled him aside. "Look, she's got to be lying. Peabody's no more at the hotel at this moment than I am."

"What makes you think so?"

"I'll prove it," she whispered. Directing herself to Olivia, she said innocently, "This is all so exciting, Olivia, that you've actually seen the mysterious Mr. Peabody, I mean. And what exactly does he look like?"

Clearly sensing a trap, Olivia narrowed her eyes and proceeded cautiously. "He's very... nondescript."

"Oh, come now, there must be something about him you remember. Old or young? Handsome or ugly? Tall or short?" Hayley insisted.

"Older, distinguished, tall—"

"That's it—she's lying. Mason, I told you what Peabody looks like, and she's not even close."

"Aw, Livvy," he said gruffly. "Why did you make all this stuff up?"

"Angy," she said sweetly, as if she were perfectly justified in lying through her teeth.

"What about him?"

"He's not jealous anymore." She shrugged and re-wrapped herself in her fur. "I thought if I got you back to my room and then lured Angy over while you were there, he'd, you know, think the wrong thing about you and me."

"Livvy, you're hopeless," he told her. "Now go back and talk to Angus like an adult, and stop playing all these silly games."

"You better remember you have to be nice to me, Mason," she whispered, loudly enough for Hayley to hear. "Great-granny's apple *is* rightfully mine, after all. And if you find it, I *may* be willing to sell it back to your museum. *If* you're nice to me." Without further ado, Olivia flounced out the door.

"You treat her a lot better than she deserves," Hayley complained as she followed Mason into the living room. "What a ninny."

"Me or her?" he asked dryly.

She crossed her arms over her chest. "Both."

"So how did you know she was lying?"

"Other than general principle, you mean?" She met his gaze squarely. She was trying to muster some fury; after all, he had practically kowtowed to Olivia. And then he'd professed willingness to run off with her on a wild-goose chase without even thinking about his supposed partner! It was outrageous. "Maybe I gave Mr. Peabody credit for having a brain," she said icily. "I knew he'd never go along with Olivia."

"That's the lamest thing I ever heard." He eyed her suspiciously. "What else is going on here? How did you know Olivia was lying?"

"I told you."

"No," he said angrily, "you didn't. I've had the feeling you've been holding out on me since the very beginning, and the feeling just got a hell of a lot stronger.'' Advancing toward her, he held her face in his hands and forced her to look him in the eye. Finally he demanded, "That was him on the phone, wasn't it?"

"Don't be ridiculous. It was Kate."

"You're lying to me."

"I am not!"

"You talked to Peabody."

"Well . . ." It was very hard to lie to his face.

"So it was Peabody on the phone." His face was drawn and grim. "And you weren't going to tell me."

"Mason, you've misunderstood. I would've told you." She broke off. No, she wouldn't have, and it wasn't Peabody on the phone. It was Peabody in person. Even worse.

"I can't believe you were going to keep this from me. I have to think." He moved away, burying his hands in the pockets of his khaki pants. "So what did Peabody say? He must have had a reason to call. And why call you?"

"Maybe he likes me," she returned. "Maybe he respects me. Maybe it's a good thing *someone* does."

Mason raised a narrow eyebrow. "Is that slam directed at me?"

"Yes."

He clenched his jaw tightly and studied Hayley's face. Softly, dangerously, he said, "Here I thought I was the one who was furious with you. Are you telling me you think *I* did something wrong?"

"Damn right you did," she responded. "First you invited Olivia to my house, without bothering to inform me. Then you let her tromp in here under the pretext of some absurd story. You were ready to follow her right out the door, without asking a single question *or* caring what I thought about it. Then you assumed I was withholding important information from you, without even giving me a chance." She knew she was lashing out more from guilt than anger, but it didn't seem to matter at the moment. "I thought we had it settled, Mason. I thought you understood. If we're going anywhere together, I have to count. I have to *matter* to you."

Tell me it's not just the apple, that it's not make-believe, her heart pleaded. *Tell me you feel something that's tangible and ordinary and real. Tell me I matter in your life.*

"You do matter," he grumbled. "I told you that. And I wasn't going to go along with Olivia without you."

"Well, you sure didn't act like it," she muttered. "You hung on every little word that dropped from Olivia's lips. The things I tell you are like afterthoughts—maybe you'll listen, if you don't have something better to do."

His mouth dropped open. "That's not true."

"Oh, yeah?"

"Yeah," he said roughly. And then he grabbed her.

"Don't you dare," she warned, looking at the fire in his blue eyes and feeling very afraid of what she'd started.

"Dare what?"

"Kiss me when I'm mad at you. It's not fair."

"How about if I kiss you when *I'm* mad at *you*?"

"Worse," she whispered.

"Too bad," he growled. "I'm furious with you, and I want you so badly I can't stand it."

He bent his tall frame, crushing his lips against hers, sweeping her up against him, holding her so tightly she could barely breathe. Kissing her senseless, he toppled her onto the couch and covered her body with his own.

He was hard and strong above her; his mouth tasted hot and hungry. Angry, she gave as good as she got, fastening her arms around his neck and kissing him back with all the subtlety of a Mack truck. Her whole body felt taut, as if her passion were spring-loaded and ready to explode.

This wasn't lovemaking. It was a battle, a fight to the finish, to see who could kiss harder and longer without calling uncle. It felt harsh, mean and ferocious, and she'd never been more turned on in her life.

But he changed the temper of the tryst. And it undid her.

He whispered her name and started to brush small, soft kisses over her cheek, her ear, the column of her throat. Hayley shivered, unable to hold on to the stark feeling of desire this way, with the puffs of his breath warm and sweet on her cheek. She began to remember who it was she was with, and what exactly was happening.

She closed her eyes and tried to recapture that angry, raw current of sensation that had felt so cleansing. Instead, she smelled wild raspberries.

"Damn your sister for giving you that soap," she whispered.

But the damage had already been done. Inside she was trembling, scared, ready to run for her life. Her face felt hot and flushed; her hair was no doubt a mass of tangles, and she was seeing stars from not getting enough air.

Managing to extricate herself, she pushed him off the couch and onto the floor with a loud thud. "You shouldn't have done that," she whispered.

"Why the hell not?" he demanded from his place on the floor.

"Because it's not fair! Because we were having an argument, and you kissed me in the middle of it, and that's not fair!"

His voice became low and gruff, but there was a spark of cynical humor in his eyes. "It's a hell of lot more fun than arguing."

Smoothing her denim skirt and adjusting her sweater, she sat up and covered her face with her hands. "I wish I could think."

"Think on your own time." He scooted next to her, taking up much of the couch and settling one long thigh against her leg, entirely too close for comfort. "Right now I want to know what Peabody told you."

"God, you have a one-track mind."

"I want that apple."

"Gee, what a surprise. I'd never have guessed." She stood up to leave, but he yanked her back down again. With fire in her eyes, she declared, "Do you know how insulting it is for you to bring up that damned apple at a time like this?"

"As far as I'm concerned, we have two choices. We can get back to what we started on this couch, or we can discuss your pal Peabody." A smug smiled lifted one corner of his mouth as he reached out a finger to play with a stray tendril of her chestnut hair. "What'll it be?"

She knocked his hand away. "I guess we'll talk about Peabody."

"Great."

She didn't know which annoyed her more, her blazing reaction during the episode on the sofa, or Mason's ability to block it out and get on with his search.

"So," he prompted, surreptitiously cleaning his glasses. "What did he tell you?"

Rising, she carefully picked her way over his long legs, trying to think. Had she ever admitted she'd talked to Harry? Mason was acting as though she had, but she couldn't remember.

"Tell me," Mason repeated.

"Look, I really did talk to Kate most of the time," she told him. "Harry—Mr. Peabody—that was just for a second. He was very evasive. I asked him what was going on, but he wouldn't tell me. He did mumble something about the numbers on the photograph he sent."

"Carmelita's Polaroid? He told you what the numbers mean?"

"No, not really. Not that I remember, anyway, but he said to look at it."

"First we have to get it." Mason stared into space for a moment. "I guess we'll have to steal it."

"You're kidding, right?"

"Well, it wouldn't be stealing if you took an extra key to her room and let yourself in, would it?"

"Mason, that's illegal! Not to mention unethical and downright rude. I could get fired."

"Okay, so you don't have to break into her room. We'll figure out a way to get the picture."

"No funny business in my hotel," she ordered.

"We'll discuss that later. What else did he say?"

"Nothing." *Nothing I can tell you, anyway.*

Expelling a long breath, he stretched out his legs. "So what's our next move?"

She glanced at him, surprised. "*Our* next move?" So they were back to being partners, after all, and he was soliciting her advice, instead of acting like a lone wolf.

What should she do? She was not in the mood to give him the apple, even though she'd been so sure she'd wanted to only an hour ago. But she also wasn't willing to throw him out and go back to square one. Damn it, there *was* something between them. Now all she had to do was figure out which it was—fact or fantasy, magic or mistake.

Nicki's words came back to her. *Get him alone, away from the distractions, where all he has to think about is you, and none of his friends can possibly find you.*

Then Kate's words echoed softly in her mind. *Before you do anything with that apple of yours, come to Boulder and find out the whole story.*

"Boulder," she said aloud. It was pretty, romantic, awa
from the hotel and the apple bunch, and she could find ou
what Kate knew that was so important. She could also sub
ject Mason to Kate's scrutiny, and see what her older, wise
friend thought of him.

"Boulder?" Mason joined her eagerly. "Did Peabody sa
something about Boulder? Do you think we should go t
Boulder to look for him?"

"I think that's a great idea," she answered slowly, wit
only a twinge of guilt.

One way or the other, she swore, she'd find out in Boulde
what this attraction was all about.

ANOTHER DAY, ANOTHER DOLLAR. Hayley studied the res
ervations cards, trying to figure out how busy they wer
going to be next week, and how many people she shoul
schedule for the various shifts. But she was really thinkin
about the postponed trip to Boulder. Chewing a pencil, sh
stared at the calendar on her desk and absently flipped th
pages.

From the vantage point of Monday morning, with
whole week of work looming ahead, she knew she couldn
take off on a day trip until after she'd settled some from
desk business. Besides, Mason was determined to get hi
hands on Mrs. Carmichael's photograph before he did any
thing else. Hayley kept trying to talk him out of it, but h
was stubbornness personified when he chose to be.

"I don't see any point in heading off to Boulder blind,
he'd told her. "Let's get the picture first, and see if it give
us a clue as to where in Boulder to go."

How could she argue? She had no real reason to take hi
to Boulder, anyway. It was a fake, a fib, a ruse to get hi
away from Olivia, Angus and the damned apple. But wha
was one more deception piled on top of the others?

Aware that her conduct was bordering on impropriety, she nonetheless slipped up to the front desk and pulled the hotel folios on Mason and his rivals. She knew she wouldn't find much more than addresses and credit card numbers, but she wanted to get what information she could.

Mrs. Carmichael's and Angus's registrations yielded no surprises. Mrs. Carmichael had filled in a Southern California post office box as her address and guaranteed her reservation with an American Express card number. Angus, on the other hand, called himself a professor and asked that his bill be directed to a university in Cincinnati.

With a pang of guilt, she turned to Mason's card. Mason Wilder, Bendelow Museum of Western History, Omaha, Nebraska. Paid the first night's room in advance with cash.

Slim pickings.

She went again to look for Olivia's records, but there was nothing listed under MacPherson. The hotel wasn't all that full, so it was relatively easy to scan the entire register, to see if the daffy brunette had been misfiled. But the only Olivia in the house was a Smith.

"Olivia Smith?" Hayley murmured, retreating with the folder to her desk in the back. Maybe she had registered under Smith for tactical reasons.

She inspected the folio, and indeed, the fat, round handwriting fit her picture of Olivia. Olivia Smith, Milwaukee, Wisconsin. Driving a rental car. Paid with Master Card. Also in the name of Olivia Smith.

That was odd. It was one thing to register in a hotel under a fake name. But to carry around a credit card in that name, too?

"I hate to interrupt, Hayley," Meg broke in, "but I wanted to warn you."

She snapped the folio shut, feeling very nosy. "Warn me? Not Mrs. Carmichael again, I hope."

"Nope. It's the boss. In fact, both of them."

The owners of the hotel weren't difficult to get along with
but they did set high standards for their operation. The ten
sion level among employees always crackled a little highe
when the Normalis were around.

"Is something wrong?" Hayley asked, vowing to put th
guest folders back the first moment she could.

"Not as far as I know. But they're meeting in the lobb
with some carpeting man—they're comparing samples an
things—and I wanted to warn you that they were here, i
case you wanted to put in an appearance out front."

"Good idea." She handed the folios to Meg, with a dis
tracted, "Refile these, will you?" Then she tucked in he
blouse and straightened her short wool jacket. She wa
wearing her hair pulled back today, tied with a large bov
and she felt confident that she projected a professiona
positive image.

Although she hadn't thought about her promotion i
days, she knew she needed to make a good impression on th
big bosses if she was going to have a shot at the assistar
hotel manager position. Whatever happened with Maso
she wanted that promotion.

She strode briskly up to the front desk, waving to th
Normalis over the desk when she caught their eyes.

"Hayley," Frank Normali called out, walking toward th
desk, one hand in the pocket of his expensive suit. "I hea
you want a shot at Assistant Manager."

Smiling assertively, she nodded. "Think I have
chance?"

Mr. Normali grinned back at her. "Everybody has
chance. You better than most, I'd say. You're very famili
with the hotel, after all, and we already know you do a goo
job with the desk. But we haven't made up our minds ye
We have some very good applicants," he reminded her.

"Keep me in mind," she answered.

He tapped a hand on the desk. "Will do."

Her smile faded as she saw Angus swaggering toward her wearing a thundercloud expression. Luckily, Mr. Normali rejoined his group with the carpeting samples, and they ducked into the billiard room before Angus opened his large mouth.

"Where is he?" he demanded.

"'He' this time? Not 'she'? Not Olivia?"

"No!" he roared. "I want to know what's become of Wilder."

"Keep your voice down, will you? I don't know where he is."

"I don't believe you," he boomed.

"Well, it's the truth."

But Angus wasn't buying it. He seemed to be gathering steam for his next assault on her ears, and disaster loomed on the horizon. The bosses and their group were leaving the billiard room and heading back into earshot.

"I, uh, do know where Mason is," she improvised. "I remember now. He said he was going to the Estes Park Historical Museum. They have something on Scottie MacPherson that he thought might be useful."

His mighty red brows drew together. "Was Olivia with him?"

"That I don't know." She lifted her hands in defeat. "Sorry."

"Thinks he can outsmart me," he rumbled, and off he toddled in hot pursuit.

Of course, these were more lies laid at Hayley's door, but she had averted disaster and wasn't sorry. The Normali party had settled into a group of chairs not far from the Stanley Steamer, and Hayley scanned the lobby, determined to keep peace at the front desk if it was the last thing she ever did.

No more than three minutes had passed before Olivia cozied up to the desk. This time Hayley didn't even hesitate before spinning another story.

As Olivia opened her mouth, Hayley jumped in and cut her off. "Yes, I saw Angus. The Estes Park Historical Museum." She handed her a brochure. "If you hurry, you might be able to catch him."

"Right," Olivia whispered, winking one heavily made-up eye at Hayley. "Thanks for the tip."

She wished she'd remembered to ask about the Smith business, but it slipped her mind until after Olivia had departed.

Hayley watched the movement of the second hand on her watch, waiting for Mrs. Carmichael's appearance. Right on cue, the iron matron and her sturdy pumps clumped toward her.

"Don't even think of playing coy with me, Ms. Austin. Where have they all gotten off to?"

She didn't bother to tell her, just handed over another brochure for the museum without a word. Away lumbered Mrs. Carmichael, and Hayley felt like collapsing. How many close calls was she going to have to endure, with her bosses sitting some twenty feet away? At least all the loud people were now accounted for.

As she contemplated that fact, the phone rang, which was not an unusual occurrence at the desk. Nonetheless, Hayley jumped when it went off right under her elbow. Calming herself, she answered crisply, "Front desk."

"Hayley Austin, please," a hard, deep voice requested.

"This is she."

"My name is Charles Darban, from Darban, Darban and Sidney in Denver. You've heard of us, I'm sure."

"I'm afraid not."

"Attorneys," he said haughtily. "Personal injury specialists."

An attorney had to be bad news, especially when he spoke in that funereal tone. "And what can I do for you?" she asked, glancing over at the big bosses where they sat chuckling about carpets.

"This involves a slip-and-fall case we're handling. The plaintiff is Mrs. Carmelita Carmichael."

"Oh, my God. She's suing? Who?"

"A suit has not as yet been filed," he responded cautiously. "We're simply investigating our options at the moment."

"She's going to sue the hotel, isn't she?"

"That's not clear at the moment. But you are familiar with Mrs. Carmichael, I take it?"

"As a matter of fact, I just saw her. She was dancing through the lobby, looking none the worse for her slip and fall."

"Yes, well, laymen know so little about damages." He cleared his throat meaningfully. "I'm calling to inform you that one of our junior partners will be arriving there shortly to take your deposition."

"My what?"

"Your deposition. You were a witness, as I understand it."

"I guess so. Although I wasn't watching during the part where she actually fell down."

"Yes, well, you can tell that to Skip Sidney. He'll be there momentarily. Goodbye then," he said cheerfully, and hung up.

"Lawyers," she moaned. Coming to The Stanley... What if the hotel got socked with a lawsuit because of Mrs. Carmichael? What was she going to do?

She remembered one occasion when her brother had been sued for a traffic accident. When dealing with lawyers, Danny had said, the only smart thing to do was get one of your own.

Karen, she thought with a grim smile.

Karen Larsen was the only female attorney in Estes Park. She was also thin as a rail, smart as a whip, the snappiest dresser in town, and a tough cookie with a reputation for taking no prisoners when it came to her cases. With Karen Larsen at her side, Hayley knew that the firm of Darban, Darban and whoever could do its worst, but wouldn't be able to push her into saying anything incriminating.

Karen was there in five minutes, in a drop-dead Joan Collins suit and stiletto heels. She immediately came around to the back room for a powwow.

"I can't believe they called and told you the guy was on his way," she griped. "What way is that to do business? They thought they'd scare you into giving them all kinds of ammunition. Well, sweetheart, never fear. Your legal counsel is here."

Together they went step-by-step through the incident in the dining room, until Karen waved a hand in the air. "Time out," she said. "You didn't see her fall down, then?"

"No. I heard this big crash, but that's it."

"Listen, kid, there is not a reason in the world for them to depose you. You don't know anything and there must've been a hundred people in that restaurant who saw the whole thing. So why are they hassling you?"

"Because of Mrs. Carmichael. She doesn't like me."

"Tough. She can dislike you till the cows come home, but that doesn't mean she needs to get you involved in her spurious lawsuit." Karen leaned over and patted Hayley's hand. "This is going to be a piece of cake."

"Let's hope so."

As if that were his cue, Skip Sidney poked his head into the back office. He was thirtyish, with a receding hairline and a very self-assured manner. "Ms. Austin," he said happily, extending a hand in the direction of both women. "Skip Sidney. So nice to meet you."

Karen stood up and placed herself between Skip and her client. "Karen Larsen. I'm Ms. Austin's attorney," she said coolly.

Skip's chin quivered slightly, but he appeared to regain his composure quickly. "I wasn't aware you'd have counsel present, Ms. Austin."

"Ms. Austin wasn't aware anyone was going to interrupt her at work for unnecessary depositions."

"Unnecessary?"

"She didn't see the accident."

"We'll just take her statement," Skip said with an unctuous smile, and set up a small tape recorder. "And then we'll all know what she saw or didn't see."

He began his questions. They went from who she was and what she did to where she was exactly in the dining room, whom else she remembered seeing, and on and on, until she wanted to scream. *Why don't you ask me about Mrs. Carmichael falling down and get this over with?* she wondered.

"Can we get to the point?" Karen interrupted, as Skip posed a question about what Hayley had eaten for brunch. "My client is on duty, and she can't spend this much time away from the desk."

Skip glared at her. She was obviously ruining all his fun. He went back to his list of questions.

Letting her mind wander, Hayley gazed wistfully at the open doorway. As if by magic, Mason's large frame appeared.

"Hi," he said in his low, careful voice. A small smile played around the corners of his lips.

Hayley sighed with satisfaction.

"Ms. Austin," Skip broke in. "I asked about the restaurant that morning. Would you say it was busy, not busy, what?"

"I don't know," she snapped.

Skip cleared his throat. "Next I suppose you'll try to tell me that you weren't there at all?"

Karen leaned forward and said calmly, "Don't answer that, Hayley. He's being argumentative."

Meanwhile, Mason came striding into the office with a dangerous look on his face. "Who are you, anyway?" he demanded of Skip. "And what gives you the right to talk to her like that?"

"I am an attorney," Skip blustered. "I'll talk to her any way I please." Obviously not appreciating the attack on his authority, he turned back to Hayley. "Are you going to answer the question, or are you hiding something?"

Mason bent down from his towering height and grabbed the lawyer's lapels. Hoisting the smaller man to his feet, he muttered, "I suggest you watch your mouth, buddy."

"This is assault!" the attorney screeched, trying to get his collar out of Mason's hands. "You're all witnesses!"

Another possible witness squeezed himself into the small office. "You lied to me!" Angus roared dramatically. "Wilder was here all along!"

Olivia was hot on his heels. "Really, Holly, I'm ashamed of you," she said in her highest, fluffiest voice.

"Outrage!" thundered Mrs. Carmichael. "Deception! Subterfuge! Treachery!"

"Oh, God." Hayley closed her eyes.

"Who are all these people?" Karen demanded. "And what are they doing here?"

"The large lady in the olive drab suit is Carmelita Carmichael, the one who hired Skip over there."

For once, even Karen Larsen was speechless.

"And the tall guy who's choking Skip, that's Mason Wilder. He and I are, well, dating, sort of."

"He's energetic," Karen said weakly, watching as Mason released Skip and started to argue with Mrs. Carmichael. "Uh-oh. Did you notice who's standing in the back, looking horrified?"

"In the back?" She thought Mrs. Carmichael had come in last. Standing up, peering over the crowd, Hayley got a clear view of the man on the edge of the melee, the one with the horrified expression. "The manager," she said, sinking back into her seat. "My life is a nightmare. The manager of the hotel is standing here, witnessing this entire mess."

Even as she spoke, the manager was working his way through the passel of irate guests. "Ms. Austin, can you tell me what's going on here?"

"A misunderstanding, sir," she tried.

"Are any of these people guests of the hotel?"

Her heart sank into her shoes. "I'm afraid so."

He nodded. "I think you'd better take the rest of the day off. Perhaps a few days, Ms. Austin. This is not the way we run our hotel." Pitching his voice louder so as to be heard above the din, he announced, "Excuse me, everyone. I'd like to offer you all a drink on the house, so we can sort this out. Come with me, all right?"

The manager was a forceful person, and he succeeded in getting Olivia's allegiance immediately. Smiling at him, she took his arm and let herself be led away from the disturbance. Where Olivia went Angus followed, of course, so he was also disposed of. And Mrs. Carmichael was thrilled to hear that she'd get a drink on the house.

Skip managed to extricate himself from Mason, and pleading a conference with his client, fled after Mrs. Carmichael.

That left Mason and Hayley sending significant looks at each other, and Karen, who was still baffled by the recent turn of events.

"No charge," she told Hayley, picking up her briefcase and showing every indication of slipping out the door. "I don't get this kind of entertainment often. If you hear from what's-her-name's lawyers again, let me know."

Hayley nodded dully, in shock. "That was the manager, Mason," she whispered. "I'm probably going to be fired. Booted out on my ear. Promotion? Ha!"

He patted her arm helplessly. "I'm sorry I got you into this."

"You didn't. Not really. I mean, I'm the one who told Angus and the others to go to the historical museum. It was a lie, a way to get rid of them for a few hours, and it backfired. It's my own fault."

"Well, there's one good thing."

She raised her eyes to his. "What's that?"

He smiled wickedly. "I got Carmelita's picture and her postcard. I went through her purse while she was yelling at Olivia."

"Oh, Mason . . ." she groaned. "How could you?"

"Now we can go to Boulder."

Boulder. She'd completely forgotten about Boulder.

"I do have the rest of the day off, after all. I may even have the rest of my life off, as far as this hotel is concerned." And it would get Mason and his dangerous tricks away from her hotel. Smiling bravely, she stood up and put her hand in Mason's. "I guess we might as well go to Boulder. My calendar has been forcibly cleared."

Chapter Ten

Hayley made a quick call to Kate, warning her not to say anything about the apple in front of Mason, then joined him near the hotel parking lot. For a long moment they stood and looked at each other, each waiting for the other to make the first move.

"I didn't think about how we were going to get there," she admitted. "You don't have a car, do you?"

"Not here, I don't. I took a shuttle from the airport."

"I was afraid of that. Look, we can use my car. I guess." She thought of her ancient Volkswagen Bug, with its bad tires and tricky starter. They'd be lucky to get to Boulder, and even luckier to get back.

Noting the dubious expression on her face, he suggested, "Why don't we borrow Olivia's rental car? I think it's a big Buick or something."

"Right." She narrowed her eyes at him. "I suppose you plan on borrowing it the same way you 'borrowed' Mrs. Carmichael's picture. Theft is what I'd call it."

"Lucky I didn't ask you." He gave her an exasperated look. "Olivia wouldn't care."

"*I'd* care."

So they hiked over to her house, and Hayley backed the tiny VW out of the garage. It was another lovely spring day, with signs of a thaw everywhere, so she tried hard to be cheerful as she took the wheel and Mason folded himself into her front seat.

While she was busy praying that the car would make it to Boulder, Mason scrutinized the photograph and postcard he'd so slyly swiped from Mrs. Carmichael's purse.

"I don't see anything here to get excited about," he concluded. "We know it's the apple, we know it's Mr. Peabody's arm, we know it's The Stanley.... What help is that?"

"He said something about those numbers on the back."

She concentrated on keeping the car's bad tires on the twisting mountain road as he flipped over the Polaroid picture and took a look at the numbers.

"34," he mused, "and 315. We know they're not room numbers, because there's no room 34 at The Stanley."

"If I could just remember what Harry said," she muttered.

Mason took a gander out his window at the dramatic scenery dropping away from the road. It was beautiful; he saw tall trees dusted with snow, deep valleys, craggy rocks, dangerous curves and deadly cliffs. Meanwhile, Hayley's car swung through each hairpin turn at what seemed an excessive rate of speed, buffeted by a brisk wind to boot. He had visions of toppling over the side into some vast ravine and never being heard from again.

"You pay attention to the road, okay?" he said uneasily. "I'll figure out the numbers."

"Tell me the numbers again," she returned impatiently.

"34 and 315. Will you watch where you're going?"

"I am watching where I'm going. Three-four and three-one-five. Hmm..."

"Thirty-four and three hundred fifteen," Mason tried.

"Three-four and three-one-five . . ." Sitting up abruptly, she muttered, "Three-four. Deadline, he said. He said it was a deadline. Why not? Mason, what's the date today?"

"The twelfth, I think. Why?"

"March 12. Three-twelve, get it?"

"Dates," he said tersely. "They're dates?"

"Exactly. And here's the neat part."

As she sent him an excited glance, he spared a few anxious looks of his own, out the car window at the vertical drop next to the road.

"I saw Harry at the hotel a week ago yesterday. The date? The fourth of March," she said triumphantly. "Three-four!"

"And what about three-fifteen? What happens on the fifteenth?"

"A return appearance."

He considered. "Makes sense to me. The numbers tell us when to watch for him."

"Exactly!" Her triumph faded as she understood what that meant. Why would Harry return on the fifteenth, except to take back the apple? Maybe he was trying to tell her to get her last wish in by then, or lose it.

"Now all we have to do is figure out where he'll show up on the fifteenth," Mason said slowly.

Hayley was doing the opposite. She wanted to know where Harry *wouldn't* be. That was where she planned to hide out on the day in question.

"So why are we going to Boulder?" Mason inquired. "If Harry's not showing up until the fifteenth, why are we going to look for him in Boulder on the twelfth?"

"I don't know. I thought it was your idea."

"My idea?" Mason tried to sit up, but succeeded only in whacking both his knees on the dashboard of the tiny car. "You told me Harry dropped a hint about Boulder."

"I don't remember what I told you. Besides, we still don't know where in Boulder we're going. You thought the picture would give us a clue, remember?"

Mason muttered something indecipherable. After a moment, he said coolly, "You're obviously headed somewhere. Where were you planning on going?"

"Well, the Hotel Boulderado for starters. We're meeting my friend Kate for lunch there." By way of explanation, she added, "She's a professor of Colorado history. I thought she might know something about the MacPherson legend that we don't."

"Oh, no!" Mason shook his head vehemently. "We're not bringing more people into this, especially not a history professor. Your friend will want it for herself, and where will we be then?"

"Not Kate," she protested. She declined to tell him that Kate had not only heard about the apple, she'd also seen it. For all Hayley knew, Kate was already preparing the first draft of a monograph on the subject. "No," she repeated. "Not Kate."

"That doesn't settle what we're going to do in Boulder."

"We're going to have a nice lunch with my friend, and then we'll decide on our next move." Hayley's tone was decidedly testy.

"Okay, okay—settle down." He fiddled with the lever on his seat, trying to give his tortured legs a little more room. No luck. Instead, he decided to broach a subject he'd been wondering about for the past hour. "Hayley, will you tell me something if I ask you?"

She shot him a curious glance. "Maybe. It depends."

"I wondered what was going on at the hotel—the lawyer, the guy in the suit who told you to take the day off—it upset you pretty much, didn't it?"

"Well, yes, I suppose so."

"Why?"

"It's my job." That wasn't much of an answer, and she tried to do better. "The guy in the suit was the manager, Mason. He saw the whole thing, which means my bid for a promotion went down the drain."

"But it wasn't your fault."

"I screwed up," she said softly. "I've been doing a lot of that lately. Usually I'm very good at being front-desk manager, but mostly what I do is put out fires. Well, there was a biggie blazing behind the desk today, and I was lighting the matches."

"But you're still good at what you do, and your boss must recognize that." He gave her a slow smile. "I wouldn't rule out the promotion if I were you."

"Think positive thoughts, huh?"

"Hayley, you're like a ray of sunshine in that hotel. No boss with an ounce of sense is going to pass you over." He couldn't believe the words coming out of his mouth; he wasn't the type to run over with compliments. He'd just told her she was a ray of sunshine. Sheesh! He sounded like a real drip.

But when she looked at him, her eyes were the color of warm honey. "Thank you, Mason. I appreciate that."

He nodded. Silence loomed between them as she pulled the car to the curb and pointed out their destination.

The Hotel Boulderado was about the same age as The Stanley, but it had a very different look. Where The Stanley was elegant and mysterious, the Boulderado was square and solid. Red brick and green awnings marked the historic structure from the outside; inside it was all dark wood and soaring stained glass.

Mason's legs were stiff from riding in the cramped car, and he limped slightly as they headed into the small, cozy restaurant off the lobby. White tablecloths and stained glass in different shades of green greeted them as their eyes adjusted to the dimmer light.

"There she is," Hayley announced, then called, "Kate!"

Kate rose to meet them. As always, her regal carriage made Kate seem taller than the five foot six Hayley knew her friend to be. She raised a hand to tidy her auburn hair, worn in its customary chignon, and then held out her hand to Mason.

"Kate Norris," she said gravely.

Mason shook her hand, equally somber in mood, as Hayley quickly performed the introductions.

"Kate, this is Mason Wilder, a friend of mine. He's the assistant curator of a museum in Omaha. He's involved in the history of the West, which I know is right up your alley."

Keeping silent barely long enough for their waiter to fill the water glasses, Kate braced her long, slim hands together and fixed a speculative look on her younger friend. "I'm glad you're here, Hayley. I think this is too important to let go another moment."

Hayley tried to remind her that she was *not* to mention the apple, but Kate was a difficult woman to derail when she had decided upon a particular course of action. Warning or no warning, Kate would do exactly as she pleased when it came right down to it.

She pulled a fat folder out of her briefcase and slid it across the table toward Hayley. "I assumed you'd want to see all of Martin's notes."

"Kate, really," Hayley exclaimed, then said meaningfully, "I'm sure Mason's not interested in this. Just a project Kate's late husband started that we're carrying on," she told him quickly.

Kate shook her head in obvious disapproval. Hayley knew her friend well enough to realize that Kate did not cotton to duplicity. "Mason," Hayley ventured. "Do you think you could do me a big favor? I think it might be a good idea...to have a newspaper," she finished on a momentary inspiration.

"A newspaper?"

"Trust me," she said sweetly, winking at him on the side Kate couldn't see.

"Right." His expression was wary, but he excused himself politely and strode back into the lobby in search of the suddenly important newspaper.

"Newspaper?" Kate inquired dryly. "Why did you do that?"

"I needed to get rid of him long enough to try to convince you that I'm right. He can't know about the apple, Kate."

"Hayley," Kate said reprovingly. "I don't like the kind of game you appear to be playing with that man."

"It's not a game. This is very serious."

Kate pressed her lips together. "Explain," she commanded, much as she'd done years ago when Hayley was a student in her American History class. If a student gave a half-baked answer, Kate would skewer him with a stare and demand a more complete explanation. It signified that the student wasn't going to get off the hook that easily.

Rather than beat around the bush, Hayley came right out with it. "Yes, I've got the apple. No, I haven't told Mason. How can I? He wants that apple more than anything in the world. He thinks it will make his name in the world of history. But I can't give it to him! So how can I tell him I've got it? He'll want it, he'll take it, and he'll be back in Omaha in two seconds flat."

"But he knows you're aware of its existence?"

"Oh, yes. He told me himself. That's how I know the whole Scottie MacPherson story." She laughed sadly and propped her chin in one hand. "I'm supposed to be helping him look for it. Isn't that hilarious?"

"Not really." As Kate shook her head, a few more recalcitrant curls slipped away from the chignon and wisped around her temples. "The poor man."

"I know." Hayley heaved a deep sigh. "But what else can I do?"

"You could try the truth. Tell him you've got it, and explain that you want to keep it. Surely he'd respect your wishes."

"In your dreams," Hayley muttered. "He's obsessed with it. Once he knows where it is, I'm dead meat."

Kate folded her slender hands on the edge of the table. "I must confess, I'm surprised that you're so anxious to keep the apple. As I recall, you were none too thrilled when you received it. Why has it become so important to you?"

Because it's beautiful. Because I held it in my hand and I felt the warmth and the power of all those years and all those women, and I couldn't give it up.

"Because it's real," she answered simply.

"In what sense do you mean that?"

It came home to Hayley for the first time that she had accepted the notion of the apple's magical powers somewhere along the line. "Kate, I know this sounds crazy, but that apple is real—it's magic. There is something in it that I can't explain."

"History repeating itself," Kate murmured.

"What do you mean?"

"Scottie MacPherson believed the same thing. It caused a great stir, as you might imagine. There were claims that she was a witch, that she was possessed, that kind of nonsense." Kate leaned forward and placed her own hand over Hayley's. "Scottie MacPherson came to a very tragic end because of that apple. I don't know what it is or isn't, Hayley, but I do know one thing. It is never healthy to become obsessed with something, whether it's a man or money. Or a golden apple.''

"But Mason's the one—''

"No," Kate interjected quietly. "Mason is not the only one. I can read you like a book, child, and I can see the warring emotions on your face. You're very attracted to Mason, and yet you can't quite shake the hold that infernal apple has over you." Her expression grew solemn. "No, Hayley, I don't believe it's magic, no matter what the stories about Scottie MacPherson purport, no matter what you think in your current dazed state." Hayley moved to object, but Kate refused to yield the floor. "I'm worried about you, Hayley. You're usually so levelheaded and so reasonable. But this thing has hit you hard. Don't let it control your life. Don't become another Scottie MacPherson.''

"So you think I should just turn it over to Mason and forget about it?''

"No, not necessarily.''

"You're maddening!" Hayley told her older, wiser friend. "All right. What do you think I should do?''

"I don't know. That's up to you. It *is* your apple, after all.''

Back to square one. The apple of desire, the apple of knowledge, the apple of discord... "Now I know why apples are a recurring theme in everything from the Bible to the movies," Hayley complained. "They're nothing but trouble.''

"So what about Mason?" Kate asked, with a glint of humor in her blue eyes. "I gather you're rather attached to him as well.''

"I could be. Maybe I am. He can be so sweet and yet such a turkey." She smiled wistfully. "Do you know he almost choked a man at The Stanley for harassing me?''

The glint turned into a full-blown sparkle. "That sounds promising."

"It would be, if it weren't for the fact that he's ranting and raving about the apple every time I turn around. My rival is a piece of metal fruit!"

"What did you hope to accomplish by bringing him up here to see me?"

"I don't know." She smiled softly. "Or maybe I do know. Maybe I needed a friend. I told myself that this trip was to get him away from the mess at the hotel for a little while, but all I've done is bring the mess with me. But the trip is hardly a waste," she added wryly. "I know you'll be blunt enough to tell me what you think of him. You've always critiqued my choices of men in the past."

"And found them severely lacking," Kate reminded her.

"Well? What do you think?"

"He's very nice to look at, and I have a weakness for men in the field of history," her friend returned promptly. "Anything else?"

"So you like him?"

Kate smiled. "Hayley, my dear, I like him a lot. He seems kind and intelligent, and most important, there's something in his eyes when he looks at you that says he thinks you're very special, too."

"I wish I could believe you. If it weren't for the apple..."

"Obviously, I've only just met the man," Kate said briskly. "So I'm not really speaking from any base of knowledge here. But from the way he looks at you, well, I'd say you're safe."

"When was he looking at me?"

"The whole time he's been standing over there, pretending to read that newspaper." Kate waved to him, signaling that the private chat was at an end. "Let's let the poor man have a seat, shall we?"

"Here you go," Mason offered, handing her the paper and sliding into the booth next to her. Quirking an eyebrow at her, he said darkly, "I had to walk to a drugstore to get one. Four blocks, Hayley."

"Well, it was important," she said glibly. "I suddenly thought that maybe Peabody left a message for us, you know, in the personal section."

"Right." Mason's tone indicated he wasn't fooled. "You told her about the apple while I was gone, didn't you?"

"Well, yes, but—"

"I thought we agreed that wasn't a good idea."

"Mason, you're embarrassing Kate, and I told you I was going to tell her." She shot Kate a look, imploring her to keep her own counsel about certain crucial details. "Kate knows a lot about Scottie MacPherson, Mason. We need her expertise."

"As a matter of fact," Kate cut in, "Scottie MacPherson is part of a book my late husband was compiling, on colorful stories in Colorado history. I find it very interesting that you're planning an exhibit on her and her mythical apple for your museum. Isn't that right, Hayley?"

She nodded nervously, silently thanking Kate for running with the ball.

"Although Martin—my late husband—was the one who did the work on the MacPherson chapter, I've looked over his notes, and I am now quite familiar with the story. If you need any assistance, I'd be happy to help."

"I'm quite satisfied with my own research, Mrs. Norris, but thank you, just the same." Under the table he kicked Hayley lightly, as if to chide her for spilling the beans in his absence. "Tell me, do you believe the apple was magical?"

Kate sent a startled glance at Hayley. "Why, no, I don't," she told him. "I'm afraid I don't believe in magical spells and that kind of gobbledygook."

"Neither do I," Mason assured her. "Do you think it's possible the apple still exists?"

"It's possible, of course." Again her eyes darted to Hayley. "Of course, no trace was found after John Mason died in the blizzard. Scottie swore he'd stolen it, and they found his body frozen in a snowbank, but there was no sign of the apple. As far as I know, it was never found."

"That was his name?" Hayley gasped. "John Mason?"

"Why, yes. I thought you told me you knew the story."

"I knew that her boyfriend died tragically after he took off with the apple." There was a long pause before she added softly, "But I'd never heard his name."

"Why is that so important?" Mason asked curiously.

"His name was Mason, don't you see?"

"It's a coincidence, Hayley." He laughed at the anxiety reflected in her wide hazel eyes. "There are a lot of Masons in the world, including Perry. Yet I've never felt the slightest inclination to try a case."

"Don't joke around." She shifted in her seat and gazed straight into his eyes, trying to convince him. "Don't you see, Mason? You're just like John Mason, and I'm just like Scottie."

"Don't be silly. You're nothing like Scottie Mac-Pherson."

"Oh, yeah? Well, we have one very big thing in common that you don't know about." She knew her next words would give away her secret, but she couldn't stop herself. Mason deserved to know if he was on the verge of tragedy. "Just like Scottie," she said in a rush. "*I* ha—"

Her mouth fell open. Staring at Mason, she'd also caught a glimpse of a familiar figure in the corner of her eye. She leaned sideways to get a better view. A small, round man with a full beard, wearing a green corduroy suit. "Harry!" she cried.

"Peabody?" Mason jumped up, dumping his napkin onto the floor. "Where?"

"He just darted out the door into the lobby. I'd swear it was him."

"You wait here. I'll find him." Mason charged off in hot pursuit of the elusive Mr. Peabody.

"I'll be happy to wait here. I'd be thrilled never to see Harry again as long as I live."

"What was that all about?"

"Harry—the little man who gave me the apple—keeps turning up when I least expect it. Actually, it's every time I almost let something slip about having the apple. This is getting downright scary." She shook her head firmly. "He either has every single item of my clothing wired for sound, or he *is* magical. Take your choice."

"'There are more things in heaven and earth, Horatio, than are dreamt of in your philosophy,'" Kate quoted softly.

"Excuse me?"

"Shakespeare," she supplied. "In other words, there are a lot of things we can't explain in this world."

"I'll buy that. But where does that leave me?"

"With yourself and a very nice man tied up in knots."

Hayley's expression softened. "You really think he's nice?"

Kate couldn't stop a small smile from creeping onto her lips. "He's smart, he's great to look at, and you obviously think the sun rises and sets on him. Who am I to quibble?"

"Well, I do like him quite a bit. But I have to admit, his passion for the apple bothers me." After a moment of reflection she added, "A lot."

"Is this that 'I want to be the center of his life' stuff? I don't know. He seems to jump up like a jackrabbit every time you tell him to. Seems to me you've got him pretty well under control."

"But is it me or the apple he wants?"

"I can't answer that, child. You're the only one who knows."

"I wish I knew."

"What does your heart tell you?"

"My heart is confused. It wants Mason, but my brain keeps telling it to shut up. My brain says, 'It's my apple, and I'm not sharing it with anyone.' Meanwhile, my heart says that Mason is getting a raw deal and I should give it to him immediately."

"So you're torn."

"In two."

Kate patted her friend's hand. "What's the worst that can happen either way?"

"I'll give it to Mason, he'll get stuck in a snowbank and freeze to death," she lamented.

"Hayley!" Kate laughed out loud. "I don't think you need to get so melodramatic about it. History doesn't usually repeat itself that precisely."

"Who says?" Hesitating a moment, Hayley twisted her fingers together. "Will you tell me the rest of what happened to Scottie and John Mason, Kate? If I'm going to relive her story, I might as well be prepared."

"You're not reliving her story," Kate declared in her best no-nonsense tone. "I was trying, in my tactful way, to warn you not to get greedy, like she did. But I don't think you're in any danger of turning into her overnight. For one thing, the two of you couldn't be more different. She was a bad-tempered little ragamuffin who struck gold and found herself suddenly desirable, when no one had ever looked at her twice. Does that sound like you?''

"Well no, not really. I don't think I'm all that bad-tempered, and I've always had plenty of dates."

"This woman was a shrew, Hayley, and that's not you. On top of disagreeable, Miss MacPherson got snobby when she got money. She built herself a fancy house and hooked up with a no-good cardplayer. As you know, he died in a blizzard, and that's pretty much the end of the story. Townsfolk had never been crazy about mean little Miss MacPherson, and they didn't mind gloating when she lost it all."

"What do you mean, lost it all?"

"The mine dried up, no more suitors came calling, and Scottie's temper didn't improve. They said she was a witch, the town's children threw rocks at her—that sort of thing. She died a few years later, friendless, holed up in that big house of hers. It's very tragic, really."

"What happened to the child? Was it John Mason's?"

Kate raised a delicate eyebrow. "Who said there was a child?"

"But I've met Scottie's great-granddaughter. So there had to be a baby," Hayley concluded.

"I don't know whom you've met, but that person isn't any relation to Scottie," Kate informed her dryly. "If she'd had any children, her estate wouldn't have reverted to the state of Colorado. That's when most of the stories about her were printed, when she died without an heir. They ran stories about the mysterious apple and the whole crazy story, hoping to find some distant relative, because apparently there were items of value left in her house. But they never found any heirs."

"But Olivia..." Was a Smith, she remembered with a jolt. Was it possible that Olivia had concocted a phony identity in order to create a claim on the apple? Surely Mason, with his piles and piles of research, would've caught it if Olivia were lying. Wouldn't he?

"Your young man is returning empty-handed, with storm clouds hovering about his head," Kate remarked.

"If he looks cranky now, wait till I tell him Scottie MacPherson had no children. He's going to blow a gasket."

"Discretion is the better part of valor, my dear," Kate whispered. "In other words, I'd wait to tell him, if I were you. He doesn't look like he's in any mood for bad news."

Hayley looked up apprehensively. Indeed, Mason's lean face was a study in frustration.

"Nobody saw hide nor hair of Peabody," he admitted, tossing himself into the booth. "The thing I don't understand is what he was doing here today. The clue said the fifteenth, not the twelfth, and this little visit certainly didn't serve any purpose."

She took his hand and squeezed it gently. "I'm really sorry you didn't find Harry."

"Aw, I don't know if I'm sorry or not."

"What did you say?"

"For a whole week I've been putting myself through the wringer with this thing, and I'm no closer to the apple than I was when I started. What good does it do for me to keep bashing my head against a brick wall?"

"You may be closer than you think," she said, trying to stop cringing with shame. Why was Mason being so nice all of a sudden? Could it have something to do with the fact that Harry Peabody had been running around? *Everything is on schedule, my dear,* Harry had told her. Maybe pushing Mason in the right direction was part of the plan....

Repositioning her fingers so that he held them gently inside his, he brushed his thumb back and forth across the back of her hand. His deep voice lowered a notch, sounding husky and heartfelt. "To tell you the truth, I'd like to forget about it for a while, concentrate on something more positive than a needle in a haystack. What do you think?"

As the steady rhythm of his thumb insinuated itself into her consciousness, as she felt the light touch reverberate throughout her body, she found herself not caring if Mason's good mood was a result of supernatural intercession or a plain, old-fashioned whim. "What would you like to do?" she asked meekly.

Mason smiled. "I suggest we forget about Harry and the apple for the rest of the day. We can make a pact not to mention either one. And then we can finish our lunch like normal people who enjoy each other's company."

She responded to his slow grin with one of her own. When he focused all of his attention on her, as he was doing now, she felt herself mellowing and warming, like brandy over a candle. "It sounds lovely, Mason."

His eyes never left hers as he raised her hand to his lips and pressed a soft kiss into her palm.

"Oh, Mason," she breathed.

"Ahem." Kate cleared her throat and gave them each an indulgent smile. "It's been a long time since I played chaperone."

Hayley felt her face flush with warmth. She'd completely forgotten there was a third party at the table.

Still holding on, Mason slid their clasped hands below the edge of the table. "So," he said casually, launching a standard conversational gambit, "how do you two know each other?"

While Kate told him about their shared past, filling him in on the American History class she'd taught that Hayley had aced, the ace in question breathed a sigh of relief. She hadn't expected Mason to be the one to suggest a quiet, romantic day away from the hunt. But now that he had, maybe they could make it a day to remember.

She tightened her fingers around his. Maybe she could discover what these intoxicating, maddening feelings were all about.

"NICKI KNEW we were up to something. I mean, she knew darned well we wouldn't let her engagement go without a big splash!"

Hayley was filling in the next chapter in the continuing saga of the three friends. Kate had gotten it started at lunch, and now that Mason and Hayley were alone, dashing in and out of the small, fun shops on Boulder's cobblestoned mall, she was regaling him with more stories. As she laughed at the memories she was sharing, dancing slightly ahead of him on the wide sidewalk, he gazed at her with rapt attention. When he saw the sparkle in her eyes and the sunny smile curving her lips, all he could think of was how much he'd like to kiss her.

"But she wouldn't leave our dorm room, no matter what ruse we came up with, because she could tell something was in the wind," she continued. As she got further into the story, she began to gesticulate with the hand not looped through his arm. "So Kate, who is really cool and the last person Nicki expected to fool her like that, told her there was this huge spider in the bathtub and that Nicki had to come and kill it. Nicki was always the brave one," she added wryly. "So when Nicki got into the bathroom, Kate and I shoved her into the shower—here she is in a flannel shirt and jeans, with rollers in her hair, dripping wet—it was hilarious. Kate got everybody lined up outside the bathroom, so when Nicki came out all wet, all of our friends yelled, 'Surprise!' and Nicki almost had a heart attack."

"And Nicki married your brother, right?"

"That's right. They were the perfect couple. Danny Touchdown, the golden boy, everybody's idea of the perfect guy, and Nicki, so sweet, a great friend. It's funny. Danny's not that handsome, but everyone always thinks he is, because he's blond, clean-cut and kind of cocky. I mean, he thinks he's a hunk, so people assume he's right. And Nicki's gorgeous, although you don't really notice it because she's so down-to-earth."

"The perfect couple," he echoed.

Her voice became more subdued. "Well, they used to be, anyway. They're not together now. I ... I'm not sure why."

"But Nicki's your friend," he said softly. "She hasn't told you why?"

"No, not really." She shrugged. "The last time I talked to her, she said it was definitely over, but I find that so difficult to believe. I guess it's hard to handle when the perfect couple breaks up." Forcing a wide smile onto her face, she glanced up at him. "Aw, who cares? Breakups happen all the time. They probably couldn't agree on how to squeeze the toothpaste, or something. They're probably better off apart, anyway."

"Not necessarily." Although they were supposedly talking about her brother and Nicki's relationship, they both knew better. "Sometimes people have to put up with a few obstacles, because it's worth it to be together."

"Do you really think so, Mason?"

He nodded. "I really think so," he said quietly.

The mood was quickly becoming too deep to navigate. Carefully casual, she laughed again and took his hand, steering him toward the Mrs. Field's Cookies kiosk directly ahead of them. "There's only one way to make a great day better," she told him. "Mass quantities of Mrs. Field's Cookies!"

Pulling at her hand, he hauled her back and against his chest. "I can think of something better." He slid one finger under her chin and tipped her face up close to his. Gently, very gently, he touched his lips to hers. "Kiss me back," he whispered.

Closing her eyes, she opened her mouth to him, right in the middle of Boulder.

Chapter Eleven

Her life had become as magical and as beautiful as the golden apple itself. Who could've guessed it could turn out so well?

Sighing with contentment, Hayley lay on the sofa in her living room, her hands folded behind her head, staring at the high, beamed ceiling as if it were a night sky full of stars.

She didn't expect Mason for several hours, but she was already dressed in a long suede skirt and a bulky cream sweater—an outfit she particularly liked—for their proposed day together in Denver. They hadn't made specific plans for what they'd do or where they'd go, but she didn't care. Like everything she did with Mason, it was going to be great fun.

Two whole days, she thought happily, two whole days till Harry reappeared, two whole days till she had to worry about anything. In the meantime, she planned to enjoy the company of the sweetest man she'd ever met, be very circumspect around the hotel, and stay out of trouble on both fronts.

"So what do you think, Fluffy? Is there any way I can juggle all this without something falling on my head?"

The dog woofed a very negative-sounding answer, and she tried to haul him onto the couch with her. She succeeded in lifting about half of him, and a very wiggly half it was. "Don't be such a pessimist. I'm not Scottie MacPherson. I can handle the apple."

As Fluffy wriggled away, barking sharply, she sat up and followed him. "What is it, boy? What do you want?"

He stopped underneath her bookshelves and began to howl, shaking his head from side to side.

"It's that lousy apple, isn't it? You know where it is, and you want me to take it out, so you can play with it. Get serious, dog."

But Fluffy refused to give in. The howling grew louder and more prolonged, until she finally relented and moved aside James Fenimore Cooper to get the apple.

"I'd forgotten how small it was," she said softly.

Holding it in her hand, it was everything she remembered. It was only an insignificant piece of sculpture, yet the moment she held it or looked at its radiant surface, it managed to weave its spell, to bind her in invisible golden threads.

Why did it affect her this way? She trailed a finger around the widest curve of the apple, near the top, pondering what it was and what it meant.

"My third wish," she mused. "I haven't used my third wish."

Bringing the apple with her, never taking her eyes from it, she cautiously sat down on the sofa. The apple rested in the palm of her hand, glowing and shimmering, warming her by its very presence. Fluffy, too, was entranced. He perched at her feet, his head tipped to one side, clearly fascinated by the tiny golden toy.

"I've never seen you this quiet for this long," she remarked dryly. "I bet you think I should wish for a lifetime supply of chew bones."

The dog didn't even woof, just kept his eyes fixed on the apple.

Slowly, Hayley shook her head from side to side. "If only I knew what it was that made this thing so mesmerizing. When I'm looking at it, I can't think about anything else, and I don't like the feeling."

She was not a woman who gave in easily to that kind of control. "I will look at you," she told the apple firmly, "and I will think about something else. I will think about Mason." Her lips curved into a smile. "Mason. He makes a very nice mental picture, I must say."

Fluffy suddenly jumped up, bumping her hand and knocking the apple to the ground, where it rolled under the ruffle on the couch.

"I'm being punished for not paying enough attention to the precious apple? Is that it?" she asked angrily, getting down onto her hands and knees to retrieve the apple. Fluffy tried to look innocent, but Hayley was becoming suspicious of her dog's behavior. "First you beg me to take it out, and then you knock it out of my hand. If I didn't know better, I'd think you were in cahoots with Harry."

It was absurd. Accepting that theory, the man would not only possess magical power, but also the ability to communicate with dogs and command them to do his bidding. *Yeah, sure!*

She almost had the elusive apple within her grasp when the phone rang.

"If it's Harry, I'm leaving town, dying my hair, and assuming a new identity," she threatened under her breath. Leaving the apple under the sofa, she tramped into the kitchen to answer the telephone.

"Hello," she snapped.

"Hi. It's Mason." His tone was confused, as if he were asking, "Why are you angry, when I haven't said anything yet?"

"Oh, hi. Look, I'm sorry if I sounded snippy. I've been fighting with Fluffy." It was the best she could do on the spur of the moment.

"Well, forget about Fluffy. I have news." His voice dropped to a whisper. "Big news."

She stiffened. "What's that?"

"Carmelita," he said slowly, a current of excitement running through his voice. "She found some ancient woman who lives near Hygiene, wherever that is, and this woman remembers Scottie MacPherson from when she was a kid. She lived in the house down the street from her or something."

"Mason—" she began warily.

He cut her off. "Wait until you hear the rest. This woman told Carmelita that she definitely recalls seeing the apple among the things that were auctioned off after Scottie's death. She says her older sister bought the apple, and it's been in her attic for fifty years. Carmelita would've kept it to herself, but Olivia followed her and also talked to the old lady, so now it will probably go to the highest bidder. Or whoever can sweet-talk the old lady the best. I figure I win on that score."

Hayley tried again. "Mason, this is hardly credible. The woman must be a hundred years old, and you're buying this story? What about Peabody and the photograph?"

"Look, Hayley, the others are ready to leave. I'm sorry you won't have a chance to go with me, but the old lady told Olivia she's got the merchandise and she's ready to deal. If they get to her ahead of me, I may lose my shot at the apple forever."

"Mason—" she said for the third time, but she was talking to a dead phone.

It looked as though she could kiss goodbye to her afternoon and evening with him. She wondered if he even realized that he was standing her up.

"He probably thinks I'll understand that the damned apple has to take first priority. Again."

Damn the man! Just when she thought she had his full attention, he was off on another wild-goose chase.

Anger began to stir in her heart. What did it take to get him to look at her, see her, and notice that his obsession was driving her crazy? Was it too much to ask for him to put her first for once?

You could wish for it, a little voice whispered inside her head. *Wish Mason to fall desperately and madly in love with you, forever and ever.*

And why not?

The apple was like a magnet, drawing her back into the living room, and she raced in there, poked under the couch and reclaimed her prize.

"I'll do it!" she said out loud. "I'll use my last wish, and I'll make the creep fall so hard for me, he'll never escape."

She sat on the floor with the apple in her lap and stared at it, determined to construct her wish so perfectly that there could be no loopholes. It had to be permanent, the real thing, and he had to forget about the apple and everything else in this all-consuming passion she was going to conjure up.

"Yuck," she groaned. "All-consuming passion? It makes him sound like my love slave or something, like all he'd do all day is mope around after me. I mean, I'd have to live with this totally devoted, sloppy person following me around and drooling on me."

And if she really wanted a love slave, what business did she have going after Mason?

The things she liked most about him were his intelligence, his stubbornness, his independence. Wishing him into some passive toy of a man would destroy the person she loved.

"Oh, God." Pulling her knees up, she let the apple roll onto the rug. "I love him. I really do."

She loved the person he was, not the person she'd thought he might be in some goofy pipe dream about total devotion.

"I don't want to change him," she whispered to herself. "And I don't want to wish him in love with me, either."

It had suddenly become very clear.

"What kind of life would that be?" she asked the dog. "I'd look at Mason every day and know that the only reason he cared was because of some damned wish I made thirty years ago. What was I thinking of? To wish him in love with me—it would be wrong, it would be wicked—it would be downright *creepy*."

Fluffy barked, and she grinned at the dog, feeling strangely strong and confident.

Defiantly standing up, she hoisted the apple into the air, like the Statue of Liberty with her torch. "I'm too good to *wish* a man in love with me, damn it! Who says I'm so pathetic I need wishes, anyway? Mason Wilder will fall in love with me the old-fashioned way, because of me and who I am, or not at all," she vowed.

She certainly hoped it would be the former. She wasn't sure she could handle "not at all."

Covering the apple with her hand, she clasped it close to her heart. "I have to give it to him, Fluffy. If I love him, I can't keep it from him. It's wrong and selfish and...something Olivia would do.'' She raised an eyebrow. ''And I certainly don't want to be like Olivia.''

She waited for a moment, half expecting Mr. Peabody to appear in a puff of smoke and demand the apple back, since he'd told her she couldn't give it away. But he'd also said it was hers, and if it was, she could do what she damn well pleased with it.

Laughing to herself, she set the apple on the coffee table. Now that her head was clear, its golden beauty didn't seem quite so enticing, so magnetic, so alive. It was still luminous, still breathtaking, but perhaps a little cold, a little heartless. ''I'm not like the others,'' she told herself bravely. ''I'm not going to let an inanimate object pull my strings.''

It was time for action, time to break the spell she'd been suffering under, and get moving, like the positive, energetic person she was.

She would have to think of the perfect time and the perfect place to tell him she'd had it all along. Of course, she could lie and say she'd just gotten it. No. Honesty was the best policy, she decided. But she'd tell him how she felt about him first, to soften him up for the shock. She wondered if he already knew how she felt. Mason? Ha. Mr. Oblivious.

''Forget about that,'' she said aloud. ''What I need to do is come up with the time and the place.'' Her mouth lifted in a self-satisfied smile. ''And I have to look so dazzling, he won't care that I lied to him about the apple.

''For once, *I'll* be the forbidden fruit.''

WHEN THE NIGHT of their date finally rolled around, Hayley didn't know whether to be thankful that the anticipation was over, or even more nervous because the time had come to tell him. As usual, she buried herself in the everyday concerns of her toilette.

She had never been in doubt as to what she'd wear. That racy little black number that she hadn't worn the first time she and Mason were supposed to have dinner. She'd been waiting ever since for a chance to wear it. Luckily, the weather was unseasonably warm, and she thought she could get away with it tonight without freezing, although the night air was going to be brisk on her bare arms.

There wasn't much to the dress. Strapless, it skimmed the line of her body over her waist and hips and stopped a few inches above her knees. The only ornamentation was a line of bows up the middle of the back.

From the back it was whimsical and fun. From the front it was simply black and simply stunning.

She hummed to herself as she piled her hair on top of her head and added long, dripping jet and rhinestone earrings. As she pulled on elbow-length black gloves, she smiled at herself in the mirror on her closet door and murmured, "Voilà!"

It wasn't the normal, carefree, everybody's pal Hayley who looked back at her, but a sultry siren. "Mason will have to notice," she whispered to her reflection.

There was a certain sense of anticlimax as she covered up all that glamor under a vintage opera cape and wedged herself into her little VW to set out for the hotel. She'd considered hiring a limo, but that seemed a little excessive. Mason might think that she was planning to propose or something, when all she wanted was a romantic, sensational evening to put him into a good mood before she broke the news.

Maybe he'll be thrilled, she thought as she pulled her Bug into the hotel's parking lot. *After all, he gets what he wants.*

But there was one potential problem—Harry Peabody. She was a little surprised that Harry hadn't called or dropped by to try to dissuade her from giving away the apple. Of course, The Stanley was the most dangerous spot, since she knew Mr. Peabody hung out there from time to time, but if she could just avoid him until after she told Mason, all would be well.

It's only the fourteenth, she reminded herself. *Harry won't be back until tomorrow.* She hoped.

"Mason," she called, waving a long, black glove and slipping her cape to one side to give him a better view of her dress.

"Hayley?" He felt as if he'd been kicked. She looked gorgeous. Since when did Hayley—the Hayley he knew—waltz around in tiny dresses and gloves up to her elbows? "Wow."

She beamed at him; the wide-open, sunny smile was something he recognized.

"You look terrific," he told her.

"You don't look so bad yourself." He was wearing a black suit that made him look elegant and slim, broad-shouldered and very tall.

Looking serious, he held out a small nosegay of spring flowers. She swallowed a lump in her throat. "For me?"

He nodded.

Her smile grew misty. "How sweet, Mason. I didn't expect you to give me flowers."

"My pleasure." He extended his arm in a gentlemanly gesture, and she laughed and took it, leading him toward her dilapidated little car.

"What is tonight in honor of?" he asked her as he tried to settle his long legs somewhere between the seat and the dashboard.

"Oh, I don't know," she returned lightly. She handed him the bouquet to hold as she slid into the driver's seat. "I wanted to get away one last time before Harry's deadline. It's tomorrow, you know."

"Yes, I know."

His tone was pensive, and she reached over and gently patted his arm. "I'm really sorry the old lady didn't work out."

He managed a derisive laugh. "Yeah. She had a glass pig full of pennies and a cracked cup from the Saint Louis World Fair. She thought we'd all be dying to get our hands on her treasures."

"But she told Olivia and Mrs. Carmichael she had the apple. Why?"

"Attention, I guess. She wasn't very coherent, but it turns out she really did live down the street from Scottie Mac-Pherson when she was a child." He shrugged. "So Peabody remains our only lead, although I imagine you'd prefer not to talk about any apple business tonight."

Her voice had an ironic tone when she commented, "Oh, I expect we'll get around to it sooner or later."

The night slipped past them, black and mysterious, as she headed the small Volkswagen down the mountain to the restaurant she had chosen. She'd picked this particular place for several reasons. First, it was obscure and private, so there was little chance of interruption from anyone they knew. Second, the food was wonderful and the atmosphere intimate, which she thought might aid her in informing Mason as painlessly as possible. After all, he hated scenes, so he couldn't very well shout at her in a tiny restaurant full of elegantly dressed people.

"We're here," she announced, with a hint of nerves in her voice. She tried twice to unlatch her door in a vain effort to get out of the car.

Finally he swung the door open for her, handed her the flowers and escorted her to the restaurant. She smiled at him weakly, feeling as if she were coming down with some dread disease. Her heart pounded in an erratic rhythm, and she

felt warmer than her skimpy dress allowed. But she knew he
symptoms had nothing to do with illness or the weather.
was simple. The time was rapidly approaching when sh
would share her heart with Mason. She wasn't sure whic
idea was more petrifying—telling him about the apple, o
telling him she loved him.

Café Varennes was painted white, with blue-and-white
striped awnings and gay flower boxes along the front.

"Pretty place," he murmured.

"Yes," she said inanely, trying to think of a way aroun
the conversation she knew she had to pursue.

"Don't look so anxious, will you?" he told her gently. "
promise I'll like the place and we'll enjoy ourselves."

She laughed self-consciously and held on to his arm fo
dear life. The maître d' led them to a quiet, secluded corne
table partially hidden by a large potted palm. *Will this be th
last time I touch him?* she wondered, as her fingers burne
into the dark sleeve of his suit. *Will he hate me after I te
him?*

She tried to get herself back on track. After all, her pla
was direct and uncomplicated, and she made herself review
it as Mason studied the menu. Nothing would mar thei
dinner, but over dessert she'd tell him—first that she ha
deep feelings for him and that she couldn't lie to him any
more, and then that the apple was sitting in her living room
waiting for him. If he drove her home, she'd hand it ove
immediately. And allowing for the fact that he might b
upset about her deception, the long drive home would giv
him time to cool off and forgive her. She hoped.

"Hayley, you look like you're a condemned woman cor
templating your last meal," he commented. "I hope tha
isn't the effect of my company."

"Heavens, no." She took a long sip of wine for fortifi
cation, then fastened on her most charming smile. Raisin

her glass, she offered a toast. "Here's to a perfect evening."

Mason's glass clinked softly against hers. "To the evening . . . and to us."

"To us," she echoed. It was a heady thought.

Candlelight flickered on the pristine white tablecloth, casting a warm glow that reached out and surrounded them, and a simple floral arrangement spread a faintly spicy aroma from the center of the table, intensifying the dreamy atmosphere. Everything in the restaurant was decorated in deep rose and pale blue, and she felt calmed, yet stirred at the same time. Mason smiled his slow, careful smile and edged his chair nearer to hers, and she found herself relaxing into the quiet, expansive mood of this perfect evening.

The meal passed quickly. Conversation seemed to flow between them as smoothly and as easily as the elegant cuisine they were sampling.

"So then I was promoted to assistant curator," he said in his deep, rich voice. "The head of the museum didn't like it, but he didn't have much of a choice."

"You like it then, the museum business?"

"Yeah," he allowed, his lips quirking self-consciously. "I never really thought about it in those terms, but I guess I like it a lot."

"So it's what you'll do forever and ever?"

"I wouldn't go that far. Not in Omaha, at least. After this caper, if I return to the Bendelow Museum empty-handed, I may just end up without a job." He stretched his long legs under the table, and once again she was indelibly reminded of his masculine presence, so close to her, so different from her. "I don't know that it would break my heart to lose the job in Omaha." He gazed at her with an intense, focused expression. "I always wanted to open my own museum, set it up the way I want, collecting everything from that Ju-

deen flask I saw at the hotel's gallery to Mickey Mantle's ol
glove.''

"The Mason Wilder Collection," she said agreeabl
"Renowned all over the world for its eclectic taste and ir
comparable style."

"Exactly." Smiling at her, he enjoyed the fantasy of th
mythical museum, enjoyed the way she looked by candle
light. He had never felt so comfortable with a woman, ha
never waxed so loquacious about his thoughts and feeling
"Is it the wine or the company?"

"What do you mean?"

"I'm feeling rather relaxed."

"It's the company." She laughed. "Definitely the con
pany.''

"Okay, now it's your turn."

She tipped her head slightly. "My turn for what?"

"For sharing your secrets."

"Who says I have any secrets?" She concentrated on th
dancing reflection of candlelight on the pale liquid in he
glass.

"That Mona Lisa smile says you have secrets."

"Maybe I do."

"So share them. Tell me what Hayley the front-desk lad
is all about."

"Hayley the front-desk lady?" She shook her hea
loosening a few dark tendrils from the dramatic upswee
and swinging her long, glittering earrings from side to sid
"I don't really define myself in terms of my job. Don't g
me wrong. I like it, and I'm good at it, but I don't necessa
ily want to stay a front-desk manager for the rest of m
life."

"You've mentioned a promotion several times. Tell m
more."

"I didn't think you'd noticed when I mentioned it."

He put a hand to his heart. "I'm wounded."

"I apologize. I've misjudged you." Smiling, she considered the implications of his question. "Well, I'm not going to get it, so it hardly matters, but I had envisioned being the assistant manger of the hotel. I had visions of planning special events, costume balls and posh conventions, having some say in how the place is run." She shrugged. "I know it sounds silly, but I'd be good at it. And someday maybe manage the place completely."

"So hotels are where you want to be?"

"Not just any hotel. It has to be The Stanley, or I'd rather find another line of work." Leaning forward, she couldn't keep the enthusiasm from her voice. "I love that place. I always have, ever since I was a kid, and Nicki and I used to go down to her grandfather's stables on the grounds. Nicki would head straight for the horses, and I'd wander around the hotel, peeking in the rooms if the maids were cleaning them, riding up and down in that old brass elevator, pretending I was a grand lady in 1910, coming to stay at the hotel."

He found himself transfixed by the absorbed expression on her face. In the soft, romantic light, her eyes were the color of fine brandy, and every bit as intoxicating. "You've discovered your niche," he said softly. "That's wonderful."

"Yeah, I guess so." She gazed into his beautiful blue eyes, wishing she could tell him all that was in her heart. By way of transition, she murmured, "Sometimes it isn't enough, though. A person wants more."

"Like what?"

She lifted her bare shoulders in a noncommittal response.

"Like love, perhaps?" he suggested.

Pausing for several seconds, she kept her eyes on his
What she saw there encouraged her. "Like love," she whis
pered.

"Then I guess historians and front-desk managers have
something in common."

"Oh, Mason," she said in a rush, taking his hand and
squeezing hard, "I wanted to tell you, but I didn't know
how. I—"

The waiter appeared with their next course, and the two
of them smiled awkwardly and waited until he disappeared
before they resumed their conversation.

"To us," he said again.

She met his glass and his gaze with a great deal mor
confidence then the first time. "To us."

The food was marvelous, and they occupied themselve
with murmurs of appreciation for several minutes, steerin
clear of their previous subject by mutual consent. She had
after all, planned to wait until dessert. Why not let thing
take their natural course now, and deal then with the ser
ous, sticky stuff?

Suddenly Mason seemed to choke on a piece of vea
"Hayley," he said in a strangled sort of tone. "Carmelit
just walked in. And if I'm right . . . you're never going t
believe who she's with."

Hayley felt like hitting her forehead against the table i
frustration. Once again she'd been ready to confide in him
and once again, forces beyond her control had intervened
"Wouldn't be Mr. Peabody, by any chance, would it?" sh
asked acidly.

There was a thread of excitement in Mason's tone. "Th
way you described him to me, I'd say it's got to be. Look

Twisting in her seat, she glanced in the direction he'd i
dicated. "Oh, yeah. That's him." The genial expression, fu
whiskers and dancing eyes were hard to miss. The gree

corduroy outfit was gone, replaced by a more sedate navy-blue suit, but it was still unmistakably Harry. "But that's not Mrs. Carmichael with him, is it?"

His companion was a large, square woman, sturdily robed in a flowery dress with ruffles everywhere. She had bright, red-orange hair that couldn't possibly be real. As Hayley watched, Mr. Peabody pressed her hand warmly and twinkled at her, and the woman giggled girlishly.

"Good Lord." Hayley's hazel eyes widened with astonishment. "It *is* her."

"Carmelita, all gussied up and loaded for bear. Who'd have thought it?"

"Not me."

"Damn. They're leaving." He leaped to his feet and began to throw money onto the table.

"This was supposed to be my treat," she insisted.

"We haven't got time for arguments over the check. Didn't you hear me? They're leaving!"

"But Mason—"

He grabbed her hand and dragged her along behind him, deftly winding his way between the tables and making for the door.

"Why do we have to follow them?" Hayley protested. "I'd like to stay away from the man, thank you very much."

"Stay away from him? Hayley, he has my apple! This is it, I can feel it."

She had never seen Mason so agitated, except perhaps when he was in the middle of kissing her. *Don't think about that,* she commanded herself, trying hard to keep up with his long strides in her stiletto heels. *You're furious with the man. Forget the way he kisses!*

"Keys," he demanded when they reached her car.

Wordlessly she tossed them over.

She wasn't surprised when the Bug made coughing noises and spit a few times without starting. It never failed to falter when the going got tough.

"Damn." Mason groaned, frantically scanning the restaurant's small parking lot. And then, "That's it," as his gaze landed on a dynamic red convertible.

"Mason, you're not contemplating stealing—" But he was already jumping into the driver's seat and inching beneath the steering wheel. "Hot-wiring it? How in the world do you know how to hot-wire a car?" she cried, as the little M.G. roared to life.

"Basic electronics," he said matter-of-factly. "Hop in. I don't want to lose them."

Chapter Twelve

It was clear he was determined to go, with or without her. Knowing that her number was up and even her brother the cop would never be able to save her, she maneuvered her tight dress into the low-slung car. "At least I have a lawyer," she muttered, as wind blasted the hell out of her elegant coiffure and sent shivers from her teeth to her toes.

"Don't sweat it. We'll dump the car once we know where they're going, and no one will be the wiser."

"You have the most appalling lack of morals when you think your beloved apple is on the line."

His teeth gleamed white in the night as he gave her a rake's smile. "Necessity is the mother of criminal behavior."

She curled her fingers around the door handle and held on tight, attempting to ignore the amazing velocity of the car as its tires squealed over the curvy mountain road. "Necessity? What's necessary about driving like a bat out of hell in hot pursuit of two harmless old people?"

"Harmless?" He took his eyes off the road, sending her a shocked glance. "Hayley, this is it—the end of the road. If we get to Peabody before he gives it to Carmelita, there's still a chance I can go back to Omaha a hero. If I can get my hands on Atalanta's Apple—man, oh man, it's a dream come true.''

''What makes you think Peabody still has it?'' she asked archly. ''How do you know he hasn't already given it to someone else?''

''Don't be silly. Why would he be wining and dining Carmelita if he weren't negotiating terms?''

''Maybe he likes her.''

He laughed and swerved wickedly around a hairpin bend.

''Of course, if we end up at the bottom of a ravine, none of this will matter anyway,'' she moaned, closing her eyes so that she didn't have to see the black outline of trees and cliffs whipping past.

''Pessimist,'' he chided. ''Hang on. Enjoy the ride. How often do you go flying through the night on the trail of something like Atalanta's Golden Apple? It's once in a lifetime, baby.''

''Baby?'' she echoed, staring at him in disbelief. Good Lord. The man was starting to sound like a bad movie.

Some distance ahead of them, a pair of faint red taillights beckoned. ''That's them,'' Mason exulted. ''Has to be.''

''Hooray!'' The car in front of them slowed and turned onto a side road, and Hayley sat up straighter, getting her bearings. ''That's the back road to The Stanley,'' she whispered. ''They're going back to the hotel.''

Mason kept a respectable distance, following discreetly as the Mercedes in front of them stopped next to the side entrance. Harry got out to open Mrs. Carmichael's door. He kissed her sweetly on the hand, and she giggled her way into the hotel, spinning at the last moment and coquettishly blowing him a kiss.

''Puh-leez,'' Hayley commented.

But Mason was gearing up for the next leg of the journey, as Mr. Peabody got back behind the wheel and swung the Mercedes down the road and out of the hotel complex.

"This is very odd," Hayley said slowly. "We're headed straight for my house."

But old Harry had fooled her, she realized. Instead of taking the last turn to her house, he pulled his car to the side of the road, near a rocky path Hayley had climbed a few times when she was feeling adventurous. Again Mason held back, clicking off his lights and watching for their quarry's next move. Acting awfully spry for his years, Mr. Peabody hopped out of the car and began to climb the path.

"He's headed up into the mountains! What can he be doing?"

"I don't know," Mason said tersely. "But whatever he's doing, we're doing it, too."

She couldn't believe her ears. Outraged, she turned to him. "Mason, this has gone too far. We can't go up in the mountains without any supplies. We don't even have a flashlight! And look at how we're dressed. Do you expect me to take a hike in spike heels and a dress without sleeves?"

He took one look at her very bare dress and knew there was merit in what she said. "I'll have to go by myself, then."

"You can't go by yourself. I know the path—you don't. I know the mountains—you don't. You could get killed up there by yourself!"

"So what do you suggest?"

She took both his large hands between her own. If he was going, so was she, and there was only one way. "Look, my house is only half a mile from here. In the time it would take us to argue about this, we can go to my house and get what we need. Harry's not going anywhere," she added grimly. "That path doesn't go anywhere but up."

He nodded and gunned the motor. Her house it was.

Quickly, she raced up the stairs to the loft and started to peel off her clothes. "Don't stand there staring!" she shouted down into the living room at Mason. She yanked a denim jumpsuit on over the black lace *bustier* and tap pants she'd worn under the dress.

His eyes narrowed on the V of lingerie that was still visible in the front of her jumpsuit, where she was struggling with the last buttons. "What in God's name is that?"

"It's called lingerie, okay? Now will you get a move on? I thought you wanted to catch Harry."

He said nothing.

Meanwhile, Fluffy romped not far from Mason, barking and jumping and spinning, as if he thought he were in an Alpo commercial. "Mason, please—will you give the dog a treat or something? Oh—in the kitchen—get some food and a flashlight—it's in the broom closet—there's a backpack there, too. You can throw whatever you want in the backpack, okay?"

"Yeah, right," he muttered, shaking his head and shuffling into the kitchen. He shook a box of dog biscuits obligingly, and Fluffy gave up his crazy dance in the living room to go for the biscuits.

Struggling into a sweater, Hayley laced up her boots and grabbed a coat and cap out of the front closet. She threw a down jacket at Mason. "It was my father's," she explained. "He moved to Florida and doesn't need it anymore, so I stole it for snow shoveling."

It was a little small and some of the feathers flew out, but it was better than a suit jacket, and Mason squeezed himself into it.

In no time at all, they were parking the red convertible next to Harry's Mercedes and sprinting up the path behind him. Mason went first, lugging the backpack and wielding the flashlight, but it was scant help in the black, black night.

"Where are streetlights when you need them?" he inquired of no one in particular.

"No stars tonight, either, and the clouds are even hiding the moon." She took a deep breath. "I guess we're on our own."

The air began to feel thin, and still they climbed.

Hayley's head began to feel light, and her legs protested at the strain imposed by the incline. "No sign of him?" she asked.

Grimly he held out a bit of navy-blue cloth. "It was stuck on a bush. He must be ahead of us. But where is he going?"

"Got me." She shivered and pushed her hands into the pockets of her long, loose coat.

"Is it getting colder, or is it my imagination?" As if to answer the question, his breath puffed white in front of him.

And still they climbed. She was about to give up, let him call her a chicken, and suggest they turn back, when a wet spot suddenly appeared on her nose. She blinked; her eyelashes were wet, too.

"Mason," she said with dread, "I think it's snowing."

What had been an isolated drop quickly expanded into a blizzard of fat, fluffy flakes. It was beautiful, no question, but she was terrified down to her laced-up boots when she saw how swiftly the path was blanketed with heavy, wet snow.

"It's coming down pretty heavily." Even her voice was chilled. "Mason, we'll never find the trail back in this snow. We're going to have to find shelter, or we're going to freeze to death."

The cave they found was no more than an indentation in the rock, but there was space enough for two, and the entrance was shielded from the wind and snow by the boughs of a tall tree. The pine had kindly scattered its needles onto the floor of the cave, creating a more comfortable surface to sit on to wait out the storm.

Hayley took off her cap and shook out her hair. It was a dreadful mess from riding in the convertible, and now it was wet and cold, to boot. Running her fingers through it, she happened to glance at Mason, who sat stoically while her wet hair rained on him.

"I'm sorry," she said quickly.

"I don't mind. I feel like this is all my fault, since I was hell-bent to catch Mr. Peabody. I deserve a little extra cold water."

She edged around, trying not to bump him with her knees. "Don't worry—we'll be fine. The snow will melt as soon as the sun comes out."

His voice was light, but his eyes were serious. "What will we do until then?"

"I don't know. Sit? Talk?"

He gave her an acerbic smile. "Well, sitting is sort of a given, since it's not high enough in here to stand up."

She shivered and rubbed her arms through the damp duster coat. "Did you put matches in the backpack? Would it be possible to have a fire?"

"I brought matches, but a fire means smoke, and there's no ventilation in here. We'd asphyxiate."

"Then I guess a fire is out."

"Right. But there are candles." He smiled and set up a small, fat candle in a tin cup near the opening of their cave.

It cast a romantic glow in the tiny space, but Hayley felt very uncomfortable. "Well," she said, "I suppose we could eat something. What did you bring?"

"Miniature Snickers bars and some Mrs. Field's Cookies." He shrugged apologetically. "Plus there was a bottle of brandy in your backpack." He poured a stiff shot into the only tin cup left, now that he'd used one for the candle.

"For medicinal purposes," she told him. She took a long sip, then shuddered as the hot liquid snaked through her body. Softly, she offered, "The cookies are left over from that day in Boulder. Do you remember?"

Remember? Good Lord, he was haunted by the memories. As well as he knew his own name, he knew what she tasted like with melted chocolate chips from Mrs. Field's Cookies still clinging to her lips.

Swiftly, he pulled the cup of brandy from her hand and held it up to his lips. But the moment his lips touched the rim, the image of her full, moist mouth pressed against the same spot flooded his brain. Pushing away the tantalizing picture, he downed the remains of the brandy in one gulp and refilled the glass.

"Do you honestly think I could forget?" he muttered.

"Sorry," she returned sharply. She reached for the brandy and took a swig straight from the bottle, without bothering to retrieve the cup from him.

"Look, don't get mad. It just seems as if you always assume I won't remember things we did together, like I wasn't paying attention, like I run around in a fog all the time." He shook his head, sending a few droplets of his own her way. "I don't think that's fair."

"Oh, come on. You have to admit, you forget all about me when Olivia beckons, or when Angus knocks on the door, or Mr. Peabody shows up at our restaurant."

"Wrong," he said flatly. "I can pay attention to two things at once, that's all. And believe me, when you're around, I always know where you are and what you're doing. The only thing I have a problem with is figuring out what's going on—" he tapped her nose with the tip of a finger "—in that crazy head of yours. Do you believe me now?"

"I don't know." Her gaze wandered to the spot where the candle cast a dim, flickering light that danced over the pine boughs at the entrance to the cave.

"Why does it bother you so much that I pay attention to people like Carmelita and Angus? They're just colleagues."

"And what about Olivia?"

"What about Olivia? Are you telling me you're jealous?"

She gave him her best have-you-lost-your-mind stare. "Heavens, no."

"Yes, you are." He smiled slyly. "You're jealous of Olivia. Hayley, really. I've told you the only reason I tolerate her at all is because she's Scottie MacPherson's great-granddaughter. I don't want to find the apple and have her calmly take it away as Scottie's heir."

"What nonsense," she scoffed.

"That I only put up with her because of her connection to Scottie?"

"No, that you believe that junk. Olivia is a fake, Mason—a fourteen-carat fake. Her real name is Smith."

His eyes widened in disbelief. "Are you sure?"

"Pretty sure," she ventured. "I looked up her records at the hotel, and according to them, she's Olivia Smith from Milwaukee, Wisconsin. Plus Kate verified it—Scottie MacPherson died without heirs. I'm surprised you didn't run across that fact in your research."

"Well, I did see the stories about the search for an heir to Scottie's fortune," he said slowly. "But Olivia claimed her mother was farmed out to some distant relative and forgotten about, that nobody saw the stories. She had papers—copies of birth certificates right down the line from her great-grandmother to her father. I suppose they could've been forged. Especially when you consider that Olivia is so close to Angus, who is an expert on that kind of thing. Forging birth certificates would be child's play for Angus Potts." Suddenly he pounded the wall of the cave, hard. "Damn. I hate being fooled, especially by a dip like Olivia. She's been hounding me for months, and I was afraid to tell her to go jump off a cliff. I hate myself for being so gullible. I should have checked out her 'proof' more thoroughly."

Hayley patted his cheek sweetly. "You're an honest person, Mason—aside from a few side trips into burglary and auto theft—so you don't look for deception around every corner." *Like my corner, for example.* If he hated being fooled by Olivia, what was he going to do when he found about *her*?

"You know, Hayley, even granting that you are right about Olivia, you seem to be very sensitive on this attention issue. Why is that?"

"I don't think I'm any different from anyone else," she muttered in a decidedly defensive tone. "When a person, you know, feels a lot for someone else, they like to know that they're taken seriously, that they're important—more important than..."

"Than mythical golden apples," he supplied.

"Well, yes."

He pulled her around so that she had to look at him. "Hayley, you are more important to me than the apple. If you were Atalanta and I were Hippomenes, I would definitely throw my apples in your path to catch you."

She smiled uncertainly. "I wish I could believe you."

"Why can't you?"

"Why?" She glared at him. "Because I've lived my entire life in second place, okay?" she returned angrily. "I know what it feels like to come in second, and I hate it. In my family, my brother was the one who counted, every time.

My last boyfriend thought more of the Denver Broncos than he thought of me. I even graduated second in my high school class! Well, now I want to be first, do you hear me? *First,* for once in my life.''

"I get the idea," he said dryly.

"Look, I'm sorry. I didn't mean to blow up at you." Her voice grew low and husky. "But this is important to me."

"I understand."

Did he really? She pulled her gaze away, unable to look into those brilliant blue eyes without melting. Staring at her frozen feet, she ventured onto safer turf. "So, how about a cookie?"

They munched in silence, alternating bites of cookie with swallows of brandy. The snow flowed down the mountain, their bodies warmed toward each other from being in such close proximity, and the minutes ticked past, each one reminding them that they were all alone and empty hours stretched ahead of them.

She felt his solid, real presence beside her, warm and inviting, and her traitorous mind replayed images of him in provocative surroundings. As always, he smelled faintly of wild raspberries, and she remembered when he'd carried her from the dining room, out of harm's way, holding her securely pressed against his soft suede jacket. That was when she'd caught her first whiff of that strangely erotic scent. She wondered if she'd ever eat a raspberry again without thinking of Mason.

In her mind's eye she saw Mason in the candlelight glow of their dinner, lifting his glass to her. She remembered every detail, from the way his light brown hair fell over his brow to the way his eyes sparkled behind his glasses. And then there was Mason on the grounds of The Stanley, the time she'd thought he might kiss her, with snow glistening around them, with his long, clever fingers tangled in her hair. A small moan escaped her lips.

The easiest thing in the world would have been to give in, to share her body heat with him, to while away the hours in Mason's arms. But she wouldn't, she couldn't, make love with Mason when the apple still stood between them like a small, golden time bomb, waiting to go off. Sleeping with him, with the big lie hanging over her head, was impossible, and yet telling him under these circumstances was equally impossible. To know that his beloved apple was so close and yet so far away would probably kill him. "I can't," she whispered under her breath.

Mason didn't hear her. He'd been entertaining a few mental images of his own, with one picture front and center. It was Hayley in that damned black lace thing he'd glimpsed at the house, with creamy skin peeking out in all the right places, and erotic black lace skimming over the rest.

He groaned when he realized she was still wearing that garment. If he peeled off a few layers of denim and wool, he'd find Hayley, his Hayley, in that scrap of black lace.

"Hours till morning," she whispered frantically, gulping brandy. "What will we do?"

She wasn't sure she'd spoken aloud until he answered. "I have a few suggestions."

No comment.

They were so close in the confined space that he barely had to stretch forward to slip his fingers into her damp hair. "We ought to get you out of those wet clothes," he murmured. "You'll catch a cold."

"Mason, really." She tried to laugh, but it came out in a little squeak. "Not here. Not now."

His voice was deep and magnetic, lulling her into false feelings of security. "It's what's on both our minds," he said. He set the brandy bottle aside, next to the tin cup he'd been drinking from. His breath puffed warm and soft into her ear. "Our bodies know it, even if we don't say it aloud."

"Mason, I can't," she tried weakly. "It isn't right."

He brushed tiny kisses over her ear, unsnapped her coat and found her neck with his delicate caresses. "It feels right to me."

"No." Abruptly she pushed him away and tried to stand up, succeeding only in soundly cracking her head on the roof of the cave. Tears sprang to her eyes as she swore viciously and dropped back beside him, holding her head.

"Come on, sweetheart," he said soothingly, pulling her onto his lap and smoothing her hair over the injury. "Are you okay?"

"I'm fine," she mumbled. Her eyes were squeezed shut, but her fingers instinctively curled around the collar of his coat. He felt so good, and she was so cold, so cold inside. She leaned into the soft down of his jacket, she laid her cheek upon his shoulder, and she was lost.

His lips trailed from the top of her head to the curve of her cheek. He was very near her mouth, very near, yet tantalizingly remote. She tried to swallow, but her mouth was dry. She parted her lips; she needed air. She needed him.

And she knew she must speak now to end this damnable spell. She opened her eyes. "Wait," she managed to say. "There's something important you don't know. I have to tell you—"

His long, narrow fingers bracketed her face as he held her gaze captive. His eyes were so blue and so alive that she caught her breath. "If what you have to tell me is that you love me," he murmured, punctuating his words with the soft pressure of his lips. "I know that already."

"Well, yes, that's part of it, but—"

"I can tell by the way you look at me, by the light in your eyes, by the way you feel when I touch you." Two fingers traced a pattern on her cheek. "It's magic between us, and it has been since the very beginning, when I carried you in my arms. I can feel it, Hayley. You love me."

"Oh, my..." She felt a small stab of pain in her chest as she gave in to the emotion, the desire, the love spilling through her veins. "Yes, Mason, I do."

"And I love you, too," he whispered. "I want to make love to you because I feel so much, because we fit together so well. I've waited a long time to find you, and I know it's right. Don't say no, Hayley. Please don't say no."

"Yes," she breathed. "Yes."

He stripped off the down coat and laid it beneath them, then he held her close for a moment, wrapping her in his arms and telling her wordlessly what was in his heart.

She fingered the top button on his crisp, white shirt as his hard, strong arms surrounded and warmed her. Unbuttoning the shirt, she slipped her palms inside, gliding them over the smooth, hot surface of his chest.

"I knew you'd be smooth," she whispered.

His fingers brushed her cheek. "So are you."

After he peeled off her coat and sweater, he stilled his hands at the top of her jumpsuit. He waited for a long moment, sizzling her with the intensity of that blazing aquamarine gaze. "Are you sure?" he asked quietly.

Wetting her lips, she nodded.

In one swift movement, he ripped open the snaps down the front of her jumpsuit. She gasped, but there was no time for shock, no time to worry about the delicious ache throbbing deep inside her. Discarding clothing was difficult, however, with trembling hands, and finally Mason moved to help her; he slipped the tricky jumpsuit over her shoulders and down her suddenly overheated body.

He did it slowly, carefully, easing the stiff fabric a centimeter at a time, until she thought she might die if he didn't get it over with.

Finally she lay before him, on a bed of pine needles and down coat, clothed only in the strapless lace *bustier* and tap pants. His fingers traced the lacy edge, skimming the creamy skin ever so lightly.

"Whatever this is, I love it," he said with a catch in his voice.

Hayley tried to remember to breathe, but it wasn't easy. She wasn't sure she'd be able to remember her own name if he kept looking at her and touching her that way.

His fingertips exerted delicate pressure as they learned the ins and outs of her body, now grazing the high edge of the panties where they rode her thigh, now sketching a path from the curve of her breast to the valley where the *bustier* hooked.

He swooped down to taste her mouth, sweet and hot, then slid his hands to cup her breasts through the slick lace. It was exquisite torture.

"Please," she murmured, trying to tug him closer by clasping his shirt collar. "I need to touch you, too."

She helped him shrug out of the shirt, running her hands over his magnificent shoulders and down the long, lean length of his torso. He tossed his shirt away.

"I love your body," she said quietly, lying back and watching him as he discarded his trousers.

"Lady, it doesn't hold a candle to you."

As he watched, she became brazen. It wasn't like the person she'd always been, but she liked the knowledge of how it affected him as she released the tiny hooks on her *bustier* one by one.

"Oh, God . . ." He slipped in next to her on their make-shift bed, his voice husky in her ear. "And I thought I liked you in the lingerie. This is better."

His large hands held and cherished her, and she felt so warm, so right about being with him that happiness seemed to bubble inside her.

"Mason, I love you," she whispered, smiling next to his mouth. Their parallel smiles spun into a long, deep kiss, hungry, eager and moist.

Then she laughed deep in her throat and pulled him on top of her. Their legs tangled as they twisted together, aroused and exhilarated and on fire for each other.

Tilting back her head, she smiled up at him, and a soft groan escaped him. "You have the most beautiful smile. Like sunshine," he said hungrily. He wanted to feel that smile all the way down to his bones. Meeting her lips with his own, he kissed her as if there were no tomorrow.

As far as she was concerned, there wasn't. Tomorrow meant the riddle of the apple and Harry's deadline, and none of that existed anymore. For tonight, there was only the small, snug cave, the mingled scent of pine boughs and wild raspberry soap, the feel of his fingers on her skin, and Mason. Only Mason.

"Mason," she murmured. "Now. Please?"

Holding her fast, he slid her down the length of his body, joining them and slipping inside with a tender, sweet thrust that took her breath away.

She felt him deep inside her, moving so slowly, so perfectly, that she moaned his name in supplication. Dying for him, she clasped him to her with eager arms, pulling him in, needing him closer and faster.

All she could feel was Mason around her, within her. I was madness. It was marvelous.

Finally, blessedly, he began to move more rapidly, stoking the fire, burning away the last of her self-control. She cried his name again as they crested together.

Then, sated and sleepy, still tingling, she curled into the pillow of his shoulder and closed her eyes.

For tonight there was only Mason.

Chapter Thirteen

She awoke with a funny little smile on her face. Was she always that adorable when she slept, or was this just for his benefit? Mason wondered.

"Good morning, sunshine," he said softly, nuzzling her neck from the back. To keep her snug and toasty, he'd wrapped his body around her, since her coat provided little cover. It had worked very well, if the warm curve of her bottom sweetly pressed against him was any indication.

"Hi," she said sleepily, her smile widening as his tongue flicked over the curve of her ear. "Mason, aren't you tired yet?"

"It's morning," he whispered.

"Morning?" She opened an eye. "Oh, God, it's morning!" She sat up abruptly, clutching the old coat to her bare body and exposing Mason in the process. "Oh, I'm sorry," she blurted, blushing scarlet.

"After last night, you're embarrassed?" he asked with a grin.

"Last night? Oh, Mason—oh, no!"

Her eyes reflected something that looked like guilt to him.

"Is there a problem?" he asked slowly.

"Yes!"

He clenched his jaw, not appreciating what he was hearing, and Hayley tumbled forward to take his hand.

"No problem with you, Mason. Or it. What happened, I mean." She flushed again, a hotter shade of red. "It was wonderful. No, Mason, it's me."

Distracted, she covered herself with bits and pieces of clothing, dressing in a kind of random rush.

Quietly, firmly, he took her wrist. "Will you quit dithering and tell me what this is all about?"

"Me! The apple!" Those wide hazel eyes filled with tears. "Oh, Lord, Mason, I meant to tell you. I knew this would happen. I knew I'd fall for you and get you so far under my skin I'd never draw breath without thinking of you, and then I'd tell you and that would be that."

He shook his head, but it didn't help. "What are you trying to say?"

"I have it, Mason." Her voice slowed and became very sober. "I have the apple. I've had it all along."

"What?" he bellowed. His head was spinning, he couldn't breathe, and he felt as if someone had kicked him in the gut. "You?" he sputtered. "How long?"

She was finally awake enough to realize what she'd done. Mason, her dear, sweet Mason, so trusting that he even believed that twit Olivia, had just been dealt a severe blow. He began to advance toward her, quite naked and quite dangerous.

"Don't you think you ought to put your clothes on before we discuss this?" she asked.

"I'll put my clothes on when I damn well please," he growled. "Tell me, Hayley. When? When did you get it? From Peabody, I assume."

"Yes," she whispered, trying to back up half-clothed and on her knees. It wasn't easy. "Harry gave it to me, before Mrs. Carmichael went crazy with the umbrella. But I didn't know you wanted it then—not until that night at dinner, when Mrs. Carmichael let slip what you were all looking for. And by then..." She wiped moist hair off her brow and pleaded for understanding. "By then, two wishes had come true. Mason, it really is magic! I tried to tell you about it— I decided twice to give it to you—but Harry jumped in and told me I couldn't, both times."

"Hayley, you're out of your mind," he told her in a cold, dead tone.

"Look, we can go and get it right now—it's in my house." She took a deep breath and bravely met his icy eyes. "You can have it, Mason. You can have the apple of your eye."

"Right."

Methodically, rigidly, he threw on his clothes and swept the rest of their debris into the backpack. "Are you coming?" he asked, then he crawled out of their little cave and held back the tree branches so that she could exit, too.

"I still love you, Mason," she said sadly.

He closed his eyes for a moment. "Let's just get the apple, okay? We'll talk about this later."

She smiled wanly to herself. Suddenly she had a good use for her third wish. If she'd had the apple in her hot little grasp at that moment, she knew what she'd have wished for. *Mason, please forgive me.*

Setting a brisk pace, he hauled her down the mountain in no time. The red convertible they'd driven last night was still there, parked forlornly at the bottom of the trail, but Harry's Mercedes was gone. By unspoken mutual consent, they ignored the car and walked to Hayley's house. Somehow, last night's bravado and extravagance in "borrowing" the car seemed childish and pathetic in the bright light of day.

Hayley's steps were weary when she walked onto her crooked porch and pushed open the door. "That's funny. It's not locked. Didn't I lock it last night?"

Cautiously, she led him into the still house. "Fluffy? Fluffy?" But there was no greeting from the usually friendly dog. "I'm starting to get a weird feeling about this...."

She raced into the living room with Mason on her heels. "I left it on the coffee table last night, before we went out to dinner. I'm sure of it."

It wasn't there.

"Hayley, you didn't leave it on the coffee table."

"Yes, I did."

"No, you didn't." As she began to protest, he held up a hand. "I was here last night, remember? I was standing right next to the coffee table while you went upstairs and took off your clothes." A hot light flickered behind the ice in his eyes. "You do remember that?"

She swallowed. "Um, yes. I do."

"So where did you leave it?"

"I left it on the coffee table," she insisted. "I know— Fluffy took it once before. Maybe he was playing with it again. Start looking," she commanded frantically. "He could have hidden it anywhere."

Behind the sofa they found one worn tennis ball and half a chew bone. Under the coffee table there was a knotted, chewed-up sock and a squeaky toy shaped like a hamburger.

No apple.

Admitting defeat, Hayley turned to Mason with a drawn, white face. "I'm so sorry. I don't know where it could be!"

"It's okay," he told her softly. With a sigh he sank to the couch. "It just wasn't meant to be."

"Oh, no," she said roughly, hauling him up by the lapels. "I didn't get my third wish, and if one of the others stole it, I want it back."

"You know, you could be right. We were gone all night—the front door was open—any one of them could've taken it, if Peabody told them you had it," he concluded.

"Or even if they just got curious and went on a fishing expedition. I mean, I left it out in plain sight!"

"So?"

"So let's go to the hotel and get it back," she said firmly.

Mason's lips curved into the wicked, rake's smile he'd worn when he hot-wired the M.G. "You're on."

The only transportation available was bicycles, so they raced to the hotel, tossing aside the bikes outside the door and sprinting inside.

It didn't take long to locate their suspects. Mrs. Carmichael, wearing the odd, red-orange wig she'd had on last night, was pounding on the front desk and threatening more lawsuits. She was clearly not in possession of the apple.

Olivia and Angus were having a spat over near the Stanley Steamer. "Don't speak to me in that tone!" Olivia squealed, pulling back her arm and slapping him across the face for all she was worth.

Angus grabbed her hand. "Then marry me, damn it!" he yelled.

"Well..." She flicked a tiny tongue across her pouting lips. "Okay, then."

The people around them applauded, but Hayley couldn't tell if it was in honor of the proposal or the resounding slap Olivia had delivered. Whichever it was, those two were obviously too occupied with each other to have spent the night stealing apples.

"So who's got it?" Hayley demanded.

"Hayley?" A familiar voice called from the front door. "I just saw Fluffy—your Fluffy. You don't let him run around loose, do you?"

Hayley turned in time to see Nicki cruising into the hotel. "Fluffy? Here?"

"Well, out by the balloon races they're having down on the lawn. I went over to see how they were doing—it's great, you really ought to stop by—and I saw Fluffy. Having a great time, from the looks of things. There was a man playing with him."

"Wait a minute," Hayley interjected. "Balloon races? Here at The Stanley?"

"Yeah, down at the far end of the grounds. The Ides of March Classic, I think they're calling it."

"Ides of March?" Harry had told her to beware the Ides of March. "Good grief," she muttered. This was getting too bizarre for words.

"Is it okay for Fluffy to be running around like that?" Nicki asked with concern.

"Well, no, not really. He disappeared this morning."

"You'd better go get him," Nicki offered. "You don't think he was stolen, do you?"

Hayley didn't know what to do. "Mason? Should we go pick up the dog?"

"Do you know what I just realized?" Nicki interrupted. "Hayley, this is too wacky. You won't believe this, but the man playing with Fluffy—I think he was that little Santa Claus man of yours!"

"Harry!" Hayley and Mason exclaimed in chorus. "He's got the apple *and* the dog!"

They dashed off to the far end of the hotel grounds without even bothering to discuss it. Leaving behind arguments and anger, they were operating with a single purpose, a single mind. The site of the races was easy to spot. Several balloons were already inflated and wobbling high and colorful in the cool morning sky. Others sagged on the ground, partially filled, while brightly dressed balloonists scurried around, attending to last minute details.

Mason scanned the scene. "Do you see them?"

"Nope." She frowned. "Wait a second. I think I see—yes, that's Fluffy. I just saw his tail over by that pale blue balloon, the one with the clouds on the side. Do you see it? Sky Riders it says."

"I see the balloon, but I don't see Fluffy."

"He ran around behind it." She stuck two fingers in her mouth and emitted a shrill whistle. "Here, boy. Flu-u-uffy."

On cue, the dog came bounding their way.

"Oh, my God!" Mason's jaw dropped. "The dog has the apple. In his mouth."

"Fluffy—bring that here!"

But he made a wide arc, missing them completely, and raced off in the other direction.

"Fluffy, come back here!" they shouted, darting after him.

"Where did he go?" Mason demanded. "I lost him."

"That way," Hayley said, puffing. "The red balloon, the one that's—" she stopped dead in her tracks "—the one that's shaped like an apple."

As they watched, the dog leaped into the basket of the balloon, stood on his hind legs, and rested his paws on the edge. He seemed to be grinning at them, daring them to come after him. Behind him, what looked like a blowtorch fired hot air into the huge, red balloon. The balloon drifted slightly as it inflated, billowing into a full, round red apple; floppy little green leaves and a stem popped out of the top.

"I can't believe this," Hayley whispered. "It's shaped like an apple."

"It's from an orchard," Mason explained, pointing to the side of the apple, where Harry's Apple Orchard was gaily blazoned.

"Harry's?" Hayley echoed.

"There's no time to worry about it now." Grabbing her hand, Mason raced over to the oversize hot-air apple and jumped into the balloon gondola after the dog. Hayley had no choice but to follow. He swung her up and over the side, into the basket with him and the dog.

As all the frantic activity tipped the basket first to one side and then the other, Hayley grabbed the dog from the back. "Get the apple!" she shouted.

Mason knelt in front of Fluffy and wrenched the prize from the dog's jaws. "Got it!" he yelled jubilantly, swaying with the motion of the balloon.

As they beamed at each other in triumph, Fluffy wriggled free, lunged over the side and out of the balloon. The sudden loss of his weight sent the apple balloon soaring higher.

Hayley got to her feet and peered over the edge. "Mason! We took off!"

Fluffy, the traitor, stood happily on the ground, thumping his tail against a cheerful little cherub with twinkling eyes and a full, white beard.

"Harry!" Hayley cried. "How could you?"

"I told you to beware the Ides of March!" he shouted. "You'll be all right. You have each other, and you have a wish left!" He grinned and waved.

The balloon bobbed and swayed, wafting higher and higher, until Harry and Fluffy were only miniature figures on the ground.

Hayley sank to the bottom of the basket. "I can't look."

Mason pulled her into the circle of his arms. "You're going to have to look sometime. We have to steer this thing sooner or later."

"I don't suppose you're a hot-air balloon pilot in your spare time?"

He raised an eyebrow. His cynical expression provided his answer.

Meanwhile, the balloon sailed along, carefree and smooth, drifting in the breeze. The view was spectacular, but she found it hard to appreciate. All things considered, she'd rather have been on the ground.

"At least we have the apple." Hayley held it up for him to look at.

"Atalanta's Apple," he said reverently, turning it this way and that so that it caught the light. "I never really thought I'd see it or hold it. It is beautiful, isn't it?"

She nodded, sparing it a glance before she stared back over the side of the balloon. The treetops seemed to be getting farther away. She looked up. They were heading straight for the mountains. The balloon was going to be smashed, and they were going to die.

"Mason, I think you'd better give me back the apple."

"Why?"

"I have to make my third wish," she said calmly. "I've tried to be careful with this one, but the time is here."

"Hayley..." His eyes were kind. "There are no magic wishes. It's a little gold apple. It's pretty and it has historical significance, but it's not magical."

"Mason, please," she pleaded. "I'm not sure we have time to argue."

Reluctantly he handed her the apple and she sighed with relief. Holding it again, she felt strong and more sure of her course than ever.

She smiled ruefully at the man she loved. "I've thought about wishing that we would live happily ever after, or that you'd love me forever, or a million other variations on the theme."

"Oh, Hayley." He ruffled her hair. "We don't need that kind of nonsense."

"I agree." Her smile widened, and it warmed him with its bright glow, as it had from the first moment he saw her. "You know, Mason, I think that's the moral of this story. When it comes to love, I think we have to trust ourselves. I know in my heart," she told him, her smile never wavering, "that we'll be fine, with or without wishes." She swallowed, and the image of her twinkly little friend filled her mind. "I really think this is what Harry would want me to do." After one last deep breath, she closed her eyes and leaned back against the rough surface of the basket.

"I wish we could get down safely," she said loudly, before she had a chance to change her mind. But still the wind carried them nearer to the mountains, and still danger loomed large on the horizon.

"Why isn't it working?" she cried.

Behind her, Mason started playing with the cords and levers located near the torch that had fired the balloon. They dipped, caught an updraft, swung violently down, and then bobbed along at their previous pace.

"I can't seem to get the hang of it," he admitted. "I knew I'd regret not going into physics."

"Come on, Mason." She slid onto the floor, tugging his hand until he sat down, too. "If we aren't going to make it, there are some things I want to say first."

"Me first." He touched one finger to the curve of her cheek, above the corner of her mouth. "I love your smile, Hayley. You have the most beautiful smile I've ever seen. I think I've loved you from the first time I saw you smile."

She felt more like crying than smiling. "That's the sweetest thing anyone's ever said to me," she answered quietly. Her eyes were wide and luminous, very sincere. "And I think I've loved you from the moment I saw you in your Indiana Jones hat."

Then he smiled, and she couldn't help reflecting that bright, mischievous grin. But she sobered when she considered the rest of their story. "Mason, I'm really sorry I didn't give you the apple right from the beginning. I hope you can forgive me."

"Hey, I got to hold it, didn't I? How many men can say that?" He smiled and hugged her. "I think I only started this caper and put on my Indiana Jones hat to try to give myself an adventure. Well, ever since I met you, I've had the adventure of a lifetime. How can I regret that?"

"No regrets?"

His smile widened. "Not a one."

"But if I'd told you at the beginning—"

"I'd have run back to Omaha and stuck the apple in my museum." He stared up, into the airy center of the red balloon. Lightly, he added, "And I'd have missed the chance to know you. You're a once-in-a-lifetime find, do you know that? To meet you, I'd have given anything."

"Even Atalanta's Apple?"

"Even that." He pulled her onto his lap. "I told you, like Hippomenes, I'd throw the apple in your path." Winding his arms around her, he squeezed her warmly. "And then I'd catch you for good."

"Then you've forgiven me?"

The aquamarine eyes she found so compelling glowed soft and sweet. "I love you. Of course I've forgiven you."

She mouthed her response. "I love you, too, Mason."

One side of his mouth lifted in a mischievous smile. "Of course, if we survive this, I may still get the apple for my museum. I seem to be on friendly terms with the owner."

She shook her head sadly. "Oh, no, Mason, I took my third wish. Harry will take it back. I'm sure of that."

Mason sighed. "I don't suppose anything I say will convince you that Harry is not some wizard, and he's not going to appear magically and snatch it back?"

"No," she said softly. "I know better."

They settled into the bottom of the gondola, leaving their fate to the whims of the wind. Whichever way the breeze carried them, they were content to go. As she lay there, snuggled next to Mason, Hayley felt curiously safe and not at all scared.

"I wished for it," she whispered. "We'll be fine."

For a long time they dangled in the sky, drifting along on the wind, when Mason suddenly stood up.

"We're dropping. I thought I felt it."

Hayley joined him at the edge of the basket. "Aren't we falling kind of fast?"

But there was no time to worry; the ground was coming up to greet them perilously soon. She began to rethink her desire to be back on land.

"Brace yourself!" he shouted, and they grabbed the sides on opposite ends of the gondola, facing each other and smiling with false bravado.

Bump. They hit the ground.

The balloon sagged and fell to one side, rocking the gondola almost parallel to the ground. Mason lost his grip and hurtled in Hayley's direction.

Whoosh. A gust of air caught the balloon and heaved it the other way, twisting the basket one hundred eighty degrees and toppling Hayley on top of Mason.

She clutched on to him and he held her securely. Finally the balloon breathed its last and lay on one side. Crawling out from under it, they looked at each other for a long moment.

"We're alive!" she shouted, throwing herself at him and kissing him with relief.

"You're alive!" people shouted from all around them.

As they glanced up in amazement, they saw Nicki and Kate—even Olivia, draped all over Angus, with Mrs. Carmichael trailing behind.

"We followed the balloon," Nicki told them, running up for a quick hug. "We thought you were goners when you seemed to be headed straight for the mountains. Boy, are you lucky you caught that last gust of wind, or you'd be in pieces on Longs Peak!"

More cars pulled up near the grassy knoll where they'd landed. There were photographers and well-wishers; someone had even brought Fluffy, who rushed up and anxiously licked his mistress.

But Hayley had other things on her mind. Grasping the apple securely in the palm of her hand, she scanned the faces in the crowd. "Where is he?" she whispered to Mason. "I know he'll come back for the apple."

As she spoke, a familiar "Psst" sounded behind her.

Leaving Mason safe with Nicki and Kate, she slipped back and surreptitiously wound her way to the edge of the crowd. From behind a tree, Harry peered out and gestured to her, beaming the whole time.

Wordlessly she held out her hand and offered him the apple.

He took her other hand and patted it gently, but made no move to take the apple. "You did well," he told her softly. "Very well. You will always hold a special place in the long history of Atalanta's Apple, my dear."

"Thank you, Harry." Still clasping the apple, she bent to place a small kiss upon his round cheek. His eyes seemed a little misty as she straightened and regarded him for a moment. "I have to give it up now, don't I?"

"Yes, my dear, I'm afraid so."

"I don't know why you picked me, but . . ." She paused, feeling tears well up in her own eyes. "Thank you, Harry. Thank you for choosing me. I'll always remember the apple and you, Harry, and I'll always be proud that you chose me."

"My dear Miss Austin, I am the one who should be proud. I chose so well this time." His merry little smile touched her with its sparkle.

"Would you like to meet Mason?" she asked suddenly. "I'm sure he'd love to meet you."

"Oh, no." He shook his head sadly. "That wouldn't be proper, I'm afraid. There isn't time, really."

She nodded. "I understand. I guess."

"Miss Austin?" he asked gently. "I think you'd better return it now." He held out his hand.

Clutching the apple, she reached out very slowly, bringing it closer to Harry. She couldn't believe she was holding the apple for the last time. It still felt so vibrant, so alive, so warm, as if it belonged to her.

But she knew the time had come. Taking a deep breath, she placed the tiny golden treasure in the palm of his hand. "It is beautiful," she whispered.

"It is," he echoed.

"Take good care of it, Harry."

"I will," he promised.

Then he backed away from her, as if he meant to disappear into the cover of the trees.

"Harry?" she called out. "Will you tell me one thing before you go?"

"If I can," he said carefully.

"It's Mason. . . . Is he . . . ? Does he . . . ?"

"Does he love you only because of the apple and because you wished for him?" Harry smiled. "Heavens, no, my child. He loves you because you are the right woman for him, and he was the right man for you. I simply expedited the process."

She nodded. He had almost reached the trees now. "Harry? Will you come and visit me sometime?"

"No," he said softly, indistinctly. "I'm afraid that's not permitted."

"I'll miss you," she whispered, but now she was only talking to the wind. Swallowing around a lump in her throat, she rejoined the impromptu party that had sprung up at the scene of their miraculous landing.

More spectators had arrived while she was talking to Harry, including, of all people, the manager of The Stanley Hotel.

"Are you all right?" he asked her anxiously. "We wouldn't want our prime candidate for assistant manager getting injured."

"Prime candidate?" she exclaimed, astonished. "Me?"

"A Mr. Peabody came into the hotel to explain that the unfortunate situation the other day wasn't your fault. Plus the Carmichael woman has dropped her suit against the hotel, apparently because your attorney convinced her attorney there was nothing to it." The manager beamed at her. "We reward that kind of initiative, young lady. Although we have to look at all the candidates who've applied, I think there's a very good chance you'll be looking at a new job and a new title in about a month."

"Mason, did you hear?"

Nodding, he swept her into his arms and began to carry her along. "I told you so," he crowed.

She cast one last look over his shoulder at the apple balloon they'd ridden in, then firmly turned her gaze toward the future. "It's going to be fabulous," she said suddenly. "I'm going to get that promotion, I know it. Then all we have to do is start your museum here in Estes Park, and this show is on the road.''

"Sounds great to me.'' He bent and kissed her, and it was a long moment before she spoke again.

"Who needs magic wishes?'' she asked of no one in particular. "My life is going to do just fine all by itself.''

Epilogue

One more chapter in the apple's history was now complete.

Harry smiled. Soon, too soon, he would have to part with his beautiful toy again. But not quite yet.

First he could savor the satisfaction of having chosen the right person this time. Yes, this time, he thought fondly, it had all worked out so well. He weighed the smooth lump of gold in the palm of his hand, turning it, fascinated as always by the play of light over its gleaming, radiant surface.

The apple was everything and nothing. Only a lump of gold, after all.

But in the right hands...

And this time he had found the right hands. Triumph filled his heart as he gazed down at his little golden beauty. All the desire, all the joy that the apple promised had this time become reality.

He held the golden apple, letting it warm his hand with its soft glow. He could almost feel the life, the pulse, of each of the thousands of years of its existence.

If he concentrated, he could see again the parade of faces in its history, each lovely in her own way... from Atalanta, the Athenian maiden who ran more swiftly than any man, to Hayley Austin, the slightly eccentric front-desk manager whose heart was as golden and pure as the apple itself.

Who would be next?

Harry's smile was bittersweet. Each recipient was touched by the golden apple, but not everyone was as lucky or as clever as Ms. Austin. In the end, only a few of the apple's ladies could see through its obvious temptations to find the magic hiding inside. Now that Hayley's story had turned out so well, what were the chances that the next lady would be equally fortunate?

He sighed. It was always difficult to find the right person. She had to be beautiful inside, and she had to believe in dreams and wishes. There weren't many left like that anymore.

But of course there was hope. There was always hope. *Chin up, old man. You found Hayley, didn't you?*

Next time, Harry mused happily, he would choose just as wisely.

Next time, the apple would again bring wonderful wishes, great magic, incredible happiness. Next time...

Harry laughed out loud and rubbed his hands together.

Next time... He couldn't wait.

ABOUT THE AUTHOR

After deciding what to do with her life, Julie Kistler graduated Phi Beta Kappa from college, got a law degree, married her childhood sweetheart and began writing fiction. She and her husband live near Champaign, Illinois, with a cat named Thisbe.

Books by Julie Kistler

HARLEQUIN AMERICAN ROMANCE

158–THE VAN RENN LEGACY
207–CHRISTMAS IN JULY
236–WILDFLOWER
266–ALWAYS A BRIDESMAID

Don't miss any of our special offers. Write to us at the following address for information on our newest releases.

Harlequin Reader Service
901 Fuhrmann Blvd., P.O. Box 1397, Buffalo, NY 14240
Canadian address: P.O. Box 603,
Fort Erie, Ont. L2A 5X3

H A R L E Q U I N
American Romance®

COMING NEXT MONTH

#333 SIGHT UNSEEN by Kathy Clark

It wasn't a whimsical flight of fancy that stable owner Nicki Chandler reported to detective Jake Kelly. Nicki had been visited by a series of waking dreams—dreams she was convinced mirrored a real-life tragedy. Jake never expected that Nicki's dreams held danger—and a direct challenge to a new and fragile love.

Don't miss the second book in the ROCKY MOUNTAIN MAGIC series.

#334 MEANT TO BE by Cathy Gillen Thacker

He was a man with everything—everything but a family. Tom Harrigan, the eldest son in the prominent Harrigan clan, had always won his heart's desire. But now, the surrogate mother of his baby son threatened to destroy his dreams. Cynthia Whittiker, the attractive court-appointed guardian, showed him that love was never a game of lose or win.

#335 NIGHTSHADE by Ginger Chambers

Christian Townsend was rich, handsome, self-assured and smart, and museum employee Sonya Douglas didn't know how she was going to manage him. When Christian probed the unsolved theft of priceless artifacts, he brought the museum close to scandal. But when Sonya finally succeeded in dividing his interest—which then focused on her—the situation got totally out of control.

#336 TALL COTTON by Lori Copeland

Kelly Smith had always planned to follow in her father's footsteps on the horse-racing circuit, but now it seemed those footsteps led to betrayal. Could she prove her father had been innocent of the charges against him? She'd been forced to deceive Tanner McCrey, the man behind the accusations, to find out whether he was ally or enemy. Now would she ever be able to win his love?

THE STANLEY HOTEL— A HISTORY

Upon moving to Colorado, F. O. Stanley fell in love with Estes Park, a town nestled in an alpine mountain bowl at 7,500 feet, the Colorado Rockies towering around it.

With an initial investment of $500,000, Stanley designed and began construction of The Stanley Hotel in 1906. Materials and supplies were transported 22 miles by horse teams on roads constructed solely for this purpose. The grand opening took place in 1909 and guests were transported to The Stanley Hotel in steam-powered, 12-passenger "mountain wagons" that were also designed and built by Stanley.

On May 26, 1977, The Stanley Hotel was entered in the National Register of Historic Places and is still considered by many as one of the significant factors contributing to the growth of Colorado as a tourist destination.

We hope you enjoy visiting The Stanley Hotel in our "Rocky Mountain Magic" series in American Romance.

RMH-1